IN A HEARTBEAT

IN A HEARTBEAT

Elizabeth Adler

Hodder & Stoughton

First published in Great Britain in 2000 by Hodder and Stoughton
A division of Hodder Headline

10 9 8 7 6 5 4 3 2 1

British Library Cataloging in Publication Data

Adler, Elizabeth (Elizabeth A.)
In a heartbeat
I. Title
823.9'14 [F]

ISBN 0 340 74838 9

Typeset by Palimpsest Book Production Limited,
Polmont, Stirlingshire
Printed and bound in Great Britain by
Mackays of Chatham plc, Chatham, Kent

Hodder and Stoughton
A division of Hodder Headline
338 Euston Road
London NW1 3BH

Chapter One

It was a beautiful flight. A blue-gray dusk had fallen over Manhattan. Lights twinkled bright as the new stars, delineating streets that, for him, were paved with gold, and traffic that, for everyone else, came straight from hell. The little single-piston-engine Cessna Skylane 182 responded so fluidly to his touch he almost felt he had sprouted wings. Forget jets, he thought as he began his swooping descent through Manhattan's sparkling towers into La Guardia. This was what flying was all about. The freedom of it, escaping for a couple of hours from the mundane world, pretending, like a little kid, that you could really fly.

He hadn't expected to be en route to New York tonight, but the phone call had been urgent. He was in negotiations for an important Manhattan property and somebody was determined to outbid him. *Who* exactly, was what he was about to find out. Tonight.

He grinned as he touched the tiny plane down, bumped lightly once or twice then taxied smoothly toward the hangar. He felt about his customized silver plane the way some people felt about a racehorse. After a flight, he almost wanted to rub it down, throw a blanket over it, feed it some fresh hay and a carrot . . .

He was laughing at himself as he brought the aircraft to a stop, unbuckled and climbed out. He patted the fuselage affectionately, then remembered he had left his briefcase inside. He was about to climb back in when he heard his name called. That would be Jerry, the mechanic. He was expecting him, and he was the one who would curry-comb the Cessna, check out its innards, make sure it was in tiptop shape for the flight back to Charleston tomorrow. When he had taken care of this business.

'Mr Vincent?'

'Yeah?' He was smiling as he swung round.

He stared right into the barrel of a Sigma automatic.

And then all the world went red.

Chapter Two

'He's not going to make it.'

Ed Vincent heard those words, clear as a bell, but it was several seconds before he realized it was him they were talking about.

The gurney bounced agonizingly as they rolled him out of the Medevac helicopter. He heard the whoosh of automatic doors opening as they raced him into Emergency; heard the Medevac nurse calling out the circumstances of his shooting and his injuries and condition; heard the shouted commands. *'Does he have a femoral pulse? Heart rate's down to thirty-six — he's crashing . . .'* He felt the clothes being cut off him. Then he was lying naked, like a just-landed fish, under a hot glare of lights with what felt like the eyes of the world on him.

'A small thing but mine own,' he thought, grinning mentally because he was unable to work the necessary facial muscles. His face under the oxygen mask felt frozen, his arms and legs numb, his body did not exist. *Until someone started to dig a hole in his side with a sword.* He let out a roar of pain then, but it must have been only a whimper because his throat refused to move too.

'We're just intubating you, putting a tube in your lungs, got to drain the blood quickly,' a soothing female voice said, close to his ear.

Well what the fuck happened to anesthetic, he wanted to shout back. But of course, he could say nothing.

'What's your name?' someone else yelled at him. *'Open your eyes, look at me . . .'*

Weren't his eyes open? He could see faces peering down at him under a halo of light, feel hands on him, hear them speak. He just could not answer.

'Blood pressure's gone, we're losing him . . .'

The gel they smeared on his chest was cold. He thought someone should tell them about that, tell them to warm it up a little so it's not such a shock to the system. The next thing he knew his heart was jumping out of his chest as the cardiac shock jolted his body upwards in an arc. Again. And again.

'What's the reading?' someone demanded.

Why bother, he thought wearily. I'm already waiting to see that light at the end of the tunnel, the light that welcomes the dead.

He was so tired. He knew he was going. He was on his way. He felt his body jolt one more time, but the voices were dimmer now. He gave a mental shrug. He'd had a good life, he guessed. As good as it gets. At least in the latter years. He couldn't grumble. He had no wife, no kids, no family. Not much to live for, really. Except maybe another dinner at the little Italian place he favored. Or one last weekend at the old beach house, out on the promontory, alone with the elements, taking out the boat he had painstakingly renovated over the years.

He loved that place in any weather – the silent, rolling spring fogs; the hot sizzle of August; the languid late-summer nights; the gray, rain-lashed storms of winter. He'd always thought he had found paradise. Until now, when he was about to discover the real thing . . .

'Try again . . .' a stern voice commanded the storm troops, and again the cardiac shock ricocheted through his body.

Just give it up, guys, why don't you, he wanted to say. It's just too hard to make the effort to live now . . . This is easy, sliding into the tunnel, waiting to see the light . . . Maybe to see God's face, finally, the way the preacher always used to tell us we would, way back when we were kids in that little cedar-plank Baptist chapel in the foothills of the East Tennessee Mountains . . .

'*There's no pulse,*' someone yelled.

Of course there isn't, I'm dying. He relaxed into it. There was nothing to live for. No one.

He felt a piercing pain as they injected a stimulant directly into his heart. He wanted to scream.

'*One more time,*' the command came and his body jumped again.

Zelda. The name zapped through his brain along with the cardiac shock. *What had happened to Zelda? Where was she? They had killed him. Now they would be after her.*

'There's a pulse.' The nurse's voice was triumphant as they all gazed at the monitor with the little green peaks and valleys that showed his heart was beating again.

With a monumental effort, Ed opened his eyes. 'I've got to get out of here,' he said in a throaty whisper.

Chapter Three

Homicide Detective Marco Camelia stood to one side in the emergency room, watching the battle between life and death. So far as he could see, death was winning. And that would make his job of finding the perpetrators of the crime a hell of a lot more difficult. Now if only Ed Vincent would come out of it, wake up and tell them who did it, he would have it made.

Camelia was forty-six years old, a lean, wiry Sicilian, of medium height, with thick dark hair and brown eyes that looked almost black when he was mad, which was a good part of the time. He was attractive in an offbeat kind of way; clean-shaven but with a perpetually blue-stubbled chin, and he always wore the same immaculate 'uniform'; a dark suit, white shirt and silver-gray tie.

Camelia had joined the force at the age of twenty after dropping out of Queens College and marrying his high-school sweetheart, Claudia Romanos, a Puerto Rican beauty who saw him through the distorted eyes of love as a kind of Arnie Schwarzenegger. She adored him. As did his four kids, two boys and two girls, who spoke Spanish as well as Italian and straight-ahead American. His own little United Nations, he called them.

Despite the fact that he was a family man, Marco Camelia had a reputation and he knew it. Tough cop; a fighter; a trouble-shooter. He'd been suspended and investigated a couple of times, both killings in the line of duty, and just before the felons could kill him; but both times he had been proven right. He was just a dogged cop is all, he left no stone – or bullet – unturned, and no killer was ever gonna get away from him. So far, none had.

Camelia felt sorry for Ed Vincent. And he admired him. He was a regular guy, a rich man who did good things with his money. He helped many charities, including Pediatric Aids. He supported special boarding schools for the underprivileged and rehab camps for delinquents, which was quite something, since many of the kids were crack addicts and gang members who wanted anything but to be rehabilitated. But those who made it through would be eternally grateful that Ed Vincent had cared. He was also a strong supporter of the police force and law and order, and that counted for a lot with the guys of the NYPD.

Forty-four-year-old Vincent was a bit of a mystery man, though. Despite his success, his private life was just that. What was known about him was that he was a Southerner, from Charleston, an heir to a fortune, the media said. He had parlayed his fortune in real-estate development, erecting the two magnificent Vincent Towers in Manhattan. Ed Vincent was not short of brains, nor savvy. He knew how to make a buck and he knew how to make a deal, but he was still spoken of as a gentleman. And there were few enough of those around in business these days.

As a property developer, Vincent had no equal for his flashy public style nor for his personal reticence. His business life was public. His private life was just that. He never gave personal interviews, never talked about his past, never invited a member of the media into his penthouse home in the Vincent Towers on Fifth. And they said that no one, not even his friends, had ever been invited to his private retreat, the beach house north of Charleston in South Carolina.

Which was where Ed had just flown from, piloting his own Cessna into La Guardia, when he had been shot.

'Four bullet wounds to the chest,' the resident intern called out, lifting Ed's torso searching for exit wounds. 'Looks like one nicked the left pulmonary artery, that's why the internal bleeding and the collapsed lung. They missed the liver, but there's another wound just above the heart. Got to get him to the OR right away. Open him up and find out what's happening.'

Camelia thought gloomily it did not sound good. In fact, the only good thing to happen to Vincent had been the immediate accessibility of the Medevac helicopter that had brought the victim, fast, to Manhattan's finest hospital. If Vincent could be saved, then timing and good medical care were on his side. Camelia doubted it. The guy was a goner.

They were running a tube into him. No time for anesthetic, just sliced him neatly open and stuck it in there. Camelia's own heart flipped sickeningly as he watched. Vincent looked like death, and God knows Camelia had seen enough of that to know how it looked.

Then, goddammit if the tough bastard didn't lift his head and speak. *I've got to get out of here.* That's what he said.

Camelia stepped forward, anxious to question him, but was immediately pushed aside by the nurse. 'Get out of the way,' she yelled. 'What's the matter, can't you guys wait?'

'Sorry, sorry.' He put up his hands, backing away as they rolled Vincent on the gurney to the OR. Somehow, looking at the guy, he had a feeling this had been his last chance. No way was Ed Vincent gonna walk out of here. He was never gonna be able to tell him who shot him as he climbed from his Cessna outside the hangar at La Guardia airport. Nor would he be able to tell him why. It was up to Camelia to find out.

Chapter Four

Dr Art Jacobs, the eminent cardiologist, hurried into the emergency room, summoned from a Broadway opening-night party by the Chief Resident, who had worked with him and knew him to be a good friend of the patient.

In an impeccably cut tuxedo, Art Jacobs was as out of place in the seething emergency room, with its bloody, mutilated bodies and hordes of wailing, terrified relatives, as an orchid in a cow pasture. Fifty-six years old, tall, balding and dapper, he wore what was left of his silver hair long over his collar to remind himself that he was not totally hairless yet.

He looked down at his friend as the Chief Resident filled him in on the seriousness of his condition.

He adjusted his glasses, thinking how terrible it was to see a big man like Ed Vincent, rugged, larger than life, brought down to this pale spectre on an emergency-room gurney. 'Has he been alert at all since he got here?'

'For a couple of seconds. Said he had to get out of here,' the resident told him with a wry grin.

'Can't say I blame him. Who's operating?'

'We got lucky, Frank Orenbach was on the premises.'

Jacobs nodded. He knew Orenbach, knew he was a good and capable surgeon.

'I'll assist,' he said, walking toward the scrub room. 'It's all I can do for you, Ed,' he said. 'As well as pray,' he added grimly.

Art Jacobs had known Ed for fifteen years, and considered himself a good friend. Ed sent Art's wife flowers on her birthday. They dined together once a month at the old-fashioned little Italian place in Greenwich Village that Ed liked. He had met Ed's girlfriends, as well as many of his numerous business acquaintances. But he had never once been invited to Ed's home atop the Vincent Towers on Fifth Avenue.

Ed was funny that way, and Art accepted it. The man guarded his privacy like the Holy Grail, and in these days of public muck-raking and exposés by the tabloid media, he did not blame him. And, as far as he knew, no one – not even a woman – had ever visited Ed's personal nirvana, the beach house. While other rich men socialized in summer mansions in the Hamptons, Ed Vincent took himself off for long weekends of solitude, fishing from his old forty-foot Europa, or painting his deck, or just hanging out with the gulls and the seals. He liked it that way, and Art admired him for his freedom and independence.

He only wished he could do more to help him now.

Chapter Five

Detective Camelia was getting exactly nowhere. There were no witnesses to the shooting. Only the mechanic who was to take care of the Cessna had heard the shots and come running from the hangar. He said he thought he saw a pickup pulling away but was so panicked he could not even recall the color and make, let alone the number.

'What d'ya want me to tell ya,' he yelled. 'Ed Vincent's lying on the floor, bleeding all over the place and I'm supposed to be writing down license numbers? I was on the phone to medical emergency, you asshole.'

Camelia raised his eyebrows, and the mechanic remembered who he was talking to and growled an apology. 'Y'now how it is,' he gave a little shrug. 'I'm upset. I worked for the guy. I liked him. It's tough shit that this has happened to him.'

'You're right. And you did the right thing,' Camelia calmed him down, hoping he might recall something later. Often witnesses remembered more than they thought, subliminally. Something might just pop into his mind. That it was a white Chevy or a Dodge Ram, for instance. And that the guy driving it was Caucasian, or black, or Hispanic. Anything was possible. He could only hope.

The hangar and the area outside, where the cement was liberally stained with Ed Vincent's blood, had been cordoned off with yellow crime-scene tape. Camelia didn't know how a man could lose that much blood and still live, even a big guy like Vincent. He guessed it was a question of mind over matter at that point. Strength of will over strength of the body. Give the man credit: he would never have thought he'd still be in the land of the living, even though it was only just.

Detectives were still combing the area, and forensics were doing their stuff, searching for hairs, for fibers and powder burns, for greasy tire marks, and possible gasoline leaks from the pickup's engine. Tiny pieces of nothing that could amount to everything in the final scientific puzzle they would compile.

Watching them, Camelia sometimes wished he had chosen that field. He had graduated from police college. He could have gone on from there, but he'd had a wife and two kids by then and besides, he enjoyed the action, the camaraderie of the precinct house. He even enjoyed the ribbing he got over his name – 'Hey, Camille' – they would shout to him, laughing as the wiry little Sicilian gave them an angry, black-eyed glare. It was his life. He liked it. He felt a part of it in a way the scientists with their solitary pursuits were not.

He had worked his way up through the ranks after years driving a patrol car in the Bronx. Those were really the hard times, he thought. Nothing could ever equal those rough, tough days. He crossed himself thankfully. Like Ed Vincent, he was lucky to be alive, and he knew it.

From the patrol car, he had done time on the bomb squad, then vice, and drugs, then finally homicide. He had seen it all. Been there, done that. And he never dreamed about it at night. No sir, he kept his work life in one compartment and his home life in another. When he got home late, Claudia would already be sleeping. She would curl herself, spoon-like, around him, and he never thought about another thing, except the way she felt, and the way she smelled so sweetly of Arpège, his favorite perfume. He was a lucky man. Luckier, he knew now, than the rich guy on the operating table.

Detective Jonas Machado drew a chalk circle on the cement around a shell casing, and the crime-scene photographer took pictures of it, showing its measurements and location. Machado picked up the brass with tweezers and dropped it into the ziplock. 'That's three,' he said to Camelia. 'We're missing one.'

'Looks like one went through the fuselage.' Camelia peered into the customized silver Cessna, taking a minute to admire the taupe leather seats. He thought the interior of the little aircraft looked like an expensive sport utility vehicle. 'They probably missed him with that shot,' he said. So there should be one slug inside the aircraft, plus at least one other. 'Keep on looking, Machado. We need it.'

He sighed, watching the ongoing search. All they had so far were three .40mm bullet casings and the information that a pickup had been observed departing the scene of the crime. Not one of his better nights in police work. This one was going to be a toughie. And with an important man like Vincent, all hell would break loose once the media found out. Meanwhile, there was a blanket of silence until the next of kin could be found and informed. Trouble was, so far they had failed to turn up any next of kin. Sooner or later they would have to tell the press. That was, of course, if the nosy bastards didn't find out first.

Chapter Six

Vincent Towers Fifth was an imposing building clad in pale unpolished travertine, soaring fifty floors above Fifth Avenue, with a fabulous view of the park. The smartly dressed door-man had a look of alarm when the squad cars drew up outside. Police were definitely not a part of the curriculum at Vincent Towers.

The concierge came hurrying, anxious to remove whatever trouble there might be from the pristine lobby of his building. But the expression on his face altered when Camelia showed him the search warrant, told him there had been an accident and that Mr Vincent was in hospital.

The elevator walls were paneled in pale wood and a beveled mirror reflected back their silent images as they soared smoothly upward. Then the door slid back silently and they were in the foyer of the penthouse.

The concierge hovered near Camelia, watching his every move as he sauntered through the rooms, eyeing the sparse decor, the simple bedroom, the stark bathroom. He thought it surely looked like a bachelor pad to him, though 'pad' was hardly the right word. This place could have been inhabited by a monk.

The concierge was breathing down his neck again and Camelia sighed as he said, 'It's okay, sir, you can leave now.

I'm not gonna steal the silver.' If there were any silver to steal, he thought, still surprised by how austerely Vincent lived. And him such a rich guy. Maybe money didn't mean everything after all.

The elevator pinged again and Camelia's cohorts arrived, men in blue looking tough and businesslike. Forensics was there too. And, of course, the photographer.

'Nothin''s been touched,' he told them. 'Take your pictures before we start turning the place over. And I want every print in the place. Okay?'

He waited while the police photographer did his stuff, then he set to work, starting in the bedroom.

The bed was made up – with fresh sheets – Camelia checked just to make sure. There wasn't a speck of dust in the room, nor much comfort either, he thought, remembering his own cosy master bedroom. Kind of a love nest, Claudia had made it, in deep red Paisley with muted lighting and soft rugs. None of that here. Ed Vincent obviously didn't like fuss.

The bathroom was tiled in stark white and the shower doors were clear sheets of thick glass, not a scrap of gold in sight. Luxury reduced to minimalism. Not his style, but who could tell with rich folks? Whoever it was had said they were different from us, had got it right.

No waterdrops on the shower doors, no toothpaste uncapped, no mess in the sink. A pile of plain white towels awaited the master, as did a single clear lucite toothmug and a fresh bar of some fragrance-free white soap on the matching holder. Looking for clues to a killing in here was like searching for a snowball in a glacier.

Camelia dialed the concierge on the in-house phone. 'Who cleans Mr Vincent's apartment?' he asked.

'It's the building cleaning service, sir. They come every day.'

'So they were here this morning?'

'No sir, not yet. They were here yesterday, though.'

'Thanks. One of my men will be down shortly, you'll give him the name of the cleaning service, and he'll want to speak to the person in charge of Mr Vincent's apartment.'

'Yes, sir.' The concierge was all business now. Camelia guessed he was nervous about men in blue littering his posh lobby. Well, tough. This was more serious than a few rich folks with upset feelings. Ed Vincent was almost a dead man.

He opened the drawers, sifted through the few personal things in there ... the kind of things any man kept in his bathroom ... electric razor, spare toothbrushes, condoms ... Camelia speculated whether the spare toothbrushes were for his female overnight guests – and he was glad that Ed practiced safe sex.

He went through the drawers in the enormous walk-in closet that would have easily accommodated one of his kids' bedrooms. He hated going through a man's things, hated prying into his life, but this was his job. And he was nothing if not thorough. But this time thoroughness got him exactly nowhere.

The print man told him there were very few prints because the place had been thoroughly cleaned, and the uniforms found nothing of significance, though they went through every pocket of every garment, as well as every cupboard and drawer. It beat Camelia how the man could live without a trace of clutter. There was nothing in the refrigerator, not even the rich-bachelor token bottle of champagne. He just didn't get it. If it were not for the clothes in the closet, he could swear nobody lived here.

Sighing, he called it a wrap. 'Thanks, guys,' he said, as they departed in the soundless elevator. Then he walked back into the closet and studied the small safe set into the wall. It would need a locksmith as well as a warrant, and he got on his cellphone to try to organize both.

He was thinking of his own small, immaculate home in Queens. Kinda lived-in, a touch worn after four kids. But it was a real home. This was merely a shelter from the storm. A cave.

After that, he called Claudia just to say hi and ask what

she was up to. Not that he was controlling or anything; he just liked to know where his family was. Claudia believed it was a spin-off from his job. The Permanent Detective, she called him, with that nice silky laugh of hers.

She would hate this place, he thought as he waited for the elevator. Give her the creeps. It was less like a home than any hotel room, and he wondered again about Ed Vincent, the man. Who he was. And what he was.

Chapter Seven

There *was* a place between life and death, Ed knew it now. It was called *Limbo,* and it was the most frustrating place to be, half-way between earth and heaven. It felt more like hell, with all the worries and problems of life and none of the ease and relaxation of death. *How dare they do this to him.*

He thrashed wildly in the narrow hospital bed, and the watchful ICU nurse hurried to his side. Her patient was just three hours out of OR. His status was critical. She checked the ventilator that kept him breathing, checked the drains in his chest, and the tubes feeding fluids into a vein. She watched the monitor for a minute, then looked again at her patient. He was still now, though his breathing sounded as labored and raucous as a tractor engine.

He was big, six-four, broad-shouldered, rugged, but right now he looked way different from the great, handsome bear of a man she had seen on TV, at the opening of one of his new Vincent Towers buildings in Manhattan.

She looked at her watch. It was midnight, and the doctor on duty would be doing his rounds soon. Plus, no doubt Mr Vincent's own medico, Art Jacobs, would also make an appearance.

She checked her other intensive care patient, a woman just out of the OR after an emergency quadruple bypass following a heart attack earlier that evening. Each nurse in ICU had two patients under her care. This second one had gotten a break. She would live. Her first patient, Mr Vincent, might not be so lucky.

There was nothing else she could do for either of them right now. She walked back to the sectioned-off area at the end of the ward where another wall of monitors displayed each patient's current state, took a Diet Coke out of the refrigerator and sank thankfully into a chair. It was going to be a long night.

Which was just what Ed Vincent was thinking. In fact, he was thinking this might be the longest night of his life. Perhaps, like a drowning man, his life should be passing before his eyes. Isn't that what was supposed to happen when you were dying? God, it was ironic how all the old sayings and myths just flew into his brain, when the truth was nobody really knew what happened, because nobody who had died had ever lived to tell the tale.

Zelda, he thought, agonized. *Ah, Zelda, you crazy, pixie-faced golden girl.*

He'd never met anyone like her. Extrovert, ditzy, outspoken. With Zelda every entrance was An Entrance. Every meal A Feast. Every meeting A Rendezvous. She had the happy knack of making An Event out of the most ordinary occasion. He figured even brushing her teeth must be a scene from a movie.

'Where's the real you?' he'd asked her, bewildered and laughing.

'I wish I knew,' she'd replied serenely. 'I'm out there somewhere.'

She certainly was.

She had popped into his life 'out of the blue,' you might say. He'd thought she was nuts, then. Still did in a way, but it was her nuttiness that he loved. He loved her seven-year-old daughter, Riley. He even liked that ratty little terrier dog of hers that bit his ankles every time it saw him.

Zelda was unique. Though of course 'Zelda' was not her real name. Only *he* called her that, because of her Georgia-peach accent, and her Southern charm. 'You're straight out of Fitzgerald,' he had laughed. 'They should have called you Zelda.'

She had laughed with him, and from then on it had become his name for her. Only she knew that name. Only he knew who it meant. And she called him 'honey.' He had been surprised, when at their first meeting she addressed him as, *Mr Vincent, honey.* Until she'd apologized and told him not to mind her, she was from the South and called everybody honey, that's just the way she was.

Oh, what he would give to hear her call him 'honey' one more time. Even 'hon' would do.

She lived at 139 Ascot Street, Santa Monica, California, an old craftsman-style Victorian cottage on a leafy side street, a place so small that, when he first saw it, it had reminded him of his own birthplace, the two-room cabin in the foothills of the Great Smokies.

'Hi, Zel,' he would call her on the phone from New York. 'How's my girl today?'

'Busy,' she might snap. 'It's suppertime here, and I'm just giving Riley her grits.'

He laughed, imagining her with the phone tucked into her shoulder as she juggled pots and pans on the stove. Of course, she wasn't fixing grits. And a cook Zelda was not. Nevertheless, she insisted on giving Riley a home-cooked meal, including fresh vegetables, every night.

And she kept Sundays free only for Riley. Even he had not been included. Riley's day was Riley's, to do whatever she wanted. Which usually meant homemade buttermilk pancakes for breakfast while still in their pj's, then rollerblading on Venice boardwalk, afterward catching a bite of lunch and maybe a movie. Then supper somewhere later, to which he had been privileged to be invited several times by Riley herself.

What a kid that was. Had he ever been lucky enough to have one of his own, he would have wanted her to be like Riley, with her mop of copper-red curls, her big brown eyes just like her mom's, and that engaging gap-toothed smile. He'd even mentioned to her that it might be a mistake to grow new teeth, it was so cute just the way it was.

'Thanks a lot,' she had replied, whistling slightly through the gap as she spoke, 'but I don't think I'd be a very good kisser without my front teeth.'

'*Kissing? What* kissing?' Zelda had been so outraged at the idea, Ed and Riley had laughed at her.

Good times, he thought. Those were such *good* times. What a pity he hadn't noted them down then, said, *Listen buddy, make the most of this day. This may be all there is.*

He shifted restlessly in the narrow bed, heard the nurse's soft rubber-soled footsteps, felt her cool fingers on his wrist as she took his pulse. He heard her say, 'Good evening, Dr Jacobs.' Then heard his friend and doctor reply, 'How's our patient, Nurse?'

'Much the same, sir. Though he has been a little restless.'

'How're you doin', Ed?'

Art Jacobs bent over him. Ed could smell his cologne, guessed he'd been out to dinner and was wearing his usual smart Italian suit. Art was a fashion plate in the medical world, had all the nurses running after him, which was how he'd met his wife. A good guy. One of the best, and a dedicated medico. He wanted so bad to see him, tell him hi, one last time . . .

No. It couldn't be the last time. He had to get out of here. Zelda was in danger, they would kill her too – and Riley. He had to find Zelda. Protect them . . .

Dr Art Jacobs straightened up. He patted his old friend's arm. 'Doing good, old buddy,' he said. 'It's all you can expect with wounds like yours.' He took a step back, startled, as Ed's eyes flew open. They stared maniacally into his.

Dr Jacobs leaned over him again. 'What is it, Ed? I can tell you need to say something. Look, if I put pressure here, on the tube in your throat, you can speak. Try to tell me, buddy. Tell us who did this to you.?

'Zelda.' Ed's voice was a throaty gurgle.

'Zelda did it? Zelda who?' Art kept his finger on the tracheotomy tube, but it was no good.

Ed groaned in frustration and despair as he felt himself retreating again. *Oh God, not the tunnel. Not now. It was almost funny ... when he wanted to leave this world, he couldn't. When he didn't want to — it seemed they came looking for him. Damn it, he wasn't going down that tunnel now, though he could see that light shining ...*

'Quick, he needs a shot of dubotamine.' Dr Jacobs was all business as he injected the stimulant directly into Ed's heart. 'Jesus, Ed,' he muttered, 'I'm not gonna lose you now, not after all this.' But he knew it was touch and go.

Chapter Eight

'How's he doing, doc?' Brotski, the young duty cop outside the ICU prowled, big-footed and out of place in his uniform and weapons, down the silent antiseptic-smelling corridor. He was there in the hope that Ed Vincent would come out of his coma before he died and tell them who had shot him. 'Any chance of him waking up?'

Jacobs buttoned his Armani jacket. He straightened his tie, wondering what to tell him. After all, Ed was in some other world; the name he had mentioned could be meaningless. But he had to do his duty. 'Mr Vincent opened his eyes for a minute, seemed like he wanted to say something.' He paused, remembering Ed's crazy, urgent stare. 'I asked him who did it.'

'Jeez. What'd he say?'

'*Zelda*. That's all he said. *Zelda.*'

Art surely hoped he was doing the right thing, but that was what Ed had wanted to tell him. Anyhow, now the deed was done. If this woman, Zelda, had shot him, the cops would find her, and Ed would at least be vindicated.

As he walked away, thinking this might be the last time he saw his friend alive, the cop was already on the phone to Homicide Detective Marco Camelia. The wheels of justice were already in motion.

✻　　✻　　✻

Camelia was at the hospital in minutes. And so was the media, who in true hack fashion had gotten wind of Ed's identity and were all over the place. Tabloid reporters camped outside and attempted to sneak in, and TV units filmed the blank hospital façade, as though it were of importance. Ed's shooting was now hot news.

Officer Brotski was waiting for him, self-important with the news.

'Mr Vincent has not woken up since he said that name, sir. *Zelda*.'

Camelia gave a disappointed grunt.

'Dr Jacobs asked him specifically who did it. His answer was . . .'

'*I know, I know, Zelda*.' Camelia thought wearily that youth and enthusiasm could be trying on a man's patience.

Zelda. Zelda had done it. She had shot him. That's what Vincent had told his friend Dr Jacobs. But when he'd spoken to Doc Jacobs on the phone, he had told him he didn't know any 'Zelda.' Besides, he'd added, Vincent could have been hallucinating, they shouldn't take it too seriously. He was comatose, his brain out of synch, travelling off in some dreamworld, who knew where.

Still, *Zelda* was the only name to come out of his mouth. The only thing Camelia had to go on.

The following morning, he climbed into the police car and headed downtown to Ed's office where he had an appointment with Rick Estevez, Ed's assistant, and, he assumed, right-hand man.

Vincent Towers Madison speared skyward, a sheet of glass and rough-faced limestone reminiscent of LA's Getty Museum, only without the sylvan setting. Arcades of bamboo and indoor plantings softened the echoing, streamlined triple-height atrium, arranged in serried geometric rows that, though he wasn't one of your 'modernists,' Camelia found extremely pleasing. Surprisingly unbusy people lounged at small steel tables, sipping *caffè latte* under green umbrellas, just as though they were in a park, and shoppers wandered in and out of the smart boutiques.

Whatever else, Vincent had good taste, Camelia thought as he was whisked soundlessly upward to the fiftieth floor and decanted, with not so much as a bump, into the reception area of Ed Vincent's palatial offices.

The receptionist was a stunner, a sleek, elegant blonde with deep blue eyes that looked as though they had been shedding tears not too long ago. Could she have been crying for Ed? he wondered, surprised at such loyalty. Nah, more likely it was her boyfriend acting up.

She sniffed back a tear as she greeted him, said he was expected and offered him a cup of coffee which he refused.

'You're upset,' Camelia said, stating the obvious.

'Yes, sir. We all are.' She mopped the tears hastily. 'Mr Vincent is not only a good boss, he's a good man. I'll bet there's not one person in this office whose life history he doesn't know, and most of whom he's helped out in some way. You don't find that too often – not in New York,' she added as she walked him down a corridor and flung open the big double doors at the end.

Rick Estevez was Hispanic, probably Cuban, Camelia guessed. Medium height, stockily built, smartly dressed in a gray suit; a shock of thick silver hair, a permanent tan and intense dark eyes that, Camelia knew, took him in at a glance. No wonder he was Vincent's right-hand man – Mr Estevez was one sharp cookie. Not only that, he was sitting in what Camelia knew must be Ed Vincent's green leather swivel chair, behind the slab of steel that was Ed Vincent's desk.

Interesting, Camelia thought as he shook hands and took the seat opposite, watching as Estevez settled himself back in the green leather. He looked mighty comfortable there. For a man in the boss's seat. *And* the boss wasn't even dead yet. Mmm, Camelia thought again, I wonder . . .

'Bring coffee, Lauren, if you please,' Estevez said, and the receptionist nodded, yes sir.

'An efficient young woman.' Estevez fixed his full attention on Camelia. 'But then, if she were not, she would not be working for Ed Vincent.'

'He's a stickler for efficiency, is he?' Camelia searched his pocket for the Winstons, then remembered where he was. He folded his hands in front of him, watching Estevez watching him.

'You might say he's an efficiency nut.' Estevez smiled showing, Camelia noted, perfect white teeth. 'And I guess you might say that's how he got where he is today.' He sighed. 'And where we hope he will still be tomorrow and forever after amen. This has been a terrible shock to us all, Detective,' he added, leaning earnestly forward, clasped hands on the steel desk, dark eyes locked onto Camelia's.

'I can imagine.'

Lauren returned with a tray containing a steel coffee flask and two sensible white mugs. They waited while she poured and Camelia helped himself to three sugars and no milk, thanks. Estevez took it black.

Lauren departed and Camelia began with a strong left hook. 'You must know who did this, Mr Estevez. After all, you are the one closest to Mr Vincent.'

If the blow hit a tender spot, Estevez didn't show it and Camelia thought he was either a very good player or an innocent man. Meanwhile, he was as much under suspicion as the unknown Zelda. Business was business, and greed and envy were strong motivations for murder. Especially when the stakes were this high.

'I admit I know Ed as well, maybe better, than anyone here.' Estevez took a sip of the hot black coffee, pulling a slight face as he did so. 'Ahh, when will they learn to make a decent cup,' he sighed. Then he looked Camelia in the eye again. 'But you're wrong if you think I was ever his confidant. We never socialized. I've never had dinner with the man, unless it was business, and I've never visited his home.'

'Homes,' Camelia corrected. 'I understand there is also a beach house near Charleston.' He also took a sip of the coffee. He thought it was pretty good, but then anything with that much sugar would taste good.

'Homes,' Estevez agreed. 'And no, I've visited neither one.'

'But on a business level, you know everything there is to know.'

Estevez nodded. 'Within reason. That is, I know as much as any boss wants to tell his assistant.'

Camelia nodded, too; he understood that. A man like Ed Vincent would never trust anyone with the whole of his life story, his life's work, his business deals. He would always keep something back, hold onto the secrets until he had negotiated his way through the deal.

'Happiness for Ed was a successful deal,' Estevez said. 'A new Vincent Tower was — literally — the height of his dreams. And the next one was to be the super-tower. He had the architect all lined up, knew exactly what he wanted ... his dream was about to become reality. Until somebody threw a spanner in the works.'

Camelia sat up. 'What works?

'This is in confidence, you understand.' Estevez glanced round the sun-filled office as though it contained hidden spies. 'Ed was involved in a big property deal that was going sour. He had put in a bid for airspace above a Fifth Avenue store. He had been assured that it would be accepted and that there was a deal. Then, a couple of days ago, some anonymous bidder claimed prior rights, saying he had bid higher and earlier. The deal was in jeopardy, and as you can imagine, Ed was pissed off. Especially since he did not know the identity of the other party.'

'He didn't know who was bidding against him?'

'He believed it must be an overseas entrepreneur, Hong Kong, or Saudi, perhaps. Anyhow,' he shrugged his elegant gray-jacketed shoulders, 'the lawyers for the other side claim they don't know the true identity of the buyer. But the fact is there was a definite offer on the table before ours. Or at least, that's the way they are telling it.'

'You mean you think the sellers are lying?'

Estevez thought about it. 'No, I don't think they are lying about the anonymous buyer. They don't know who he is. But I think somebody is lying about that offer being on the table before ours.'

Camelia refilled his cup. 'So you believe the shooter might be a business rival?'

'He might.' Estevez was back in his usual position, hands folded on the steel desk, eyes fixed unwaveringly on Camelia. For a second Camelia wondered uncomfortably who was doing the interviewing here, then he pulled himself together and out of the blue said, 'So who's Zelda?'

Estevez's heavy black eyebrows lifted in surprise. 'Zelda? I've no idea.'

'You don't know if she was a friend of Mr Vincent's?'

'I've never heard that name before. But wait a minute,' he held up his hand. 'Let's check it out in Ed's book.'

He removed a thick address book covered in green leather from the single central drawer in the steel slab, and flicked through to the Zs.

'Zelda, Zelda, Zelda . . . mmmm, no, nothing here. Of course it could be listed under the last name. But that would mean going through the entire book.'

Camelia held out his hand. 'I'll take charge of the book, sir.'

'Well . . .' Estevez was hesitant.

'We are trying to find out who attempted to kill Mr Vincent,' Camelia said curtly. He glanced at his watch. 'In fact, who might already have killed him. He wasn't looking too good last time I saw him.'

'Jesus,' Estevez shoved the address book hastily across the desk. 'Jesus, man, don't say that.' For a minute his slick façade seemed to crack and Camelia caught a flicker of what appeared to be genuine pain in his dark eyes.

'Ed Vincent's a good guy,' Estevez said, and this time there was a definite tremor in his voice. 'He took me, a Cuban refugee, an immigrant, off the streets of Miami. I didn't have a dime in my pocket, but we happened to be sitting next to each other on a bench, looking out at the ocean. He bought me a cup of coffee and I told him my life story, how my father was a cigar manufacturer, that I had been well educated, gone to business college. How I stayed all those long, weary, impoverished years in Cuba because my family refused to move. Even after they took away his business, my father hung on, he insisted that one day they would give it back. He believed in God and honor, and he refused to recognize that there was no honor among thieves.

'The day came when I knew I would have to leave. I had a wife by then, and two kids. I had to make a living, offer them something better.'

His dark gaze met Camelia's. 'Do you know what it is to leave your elderly parents behind, knowing you will never see them again?' A frown furrowed his brow and he shook his head. 'The pain is indescribable, the guilt overwhelming. But I looked into the eyes of my sons, and my father saw that. "Life belongs to the young, Ricardo," he told me. "Go in peace."'

'We left on one of those terrible boats, not knowing whether we would make it across that treacherous strip of ocean. But we did, and America, God bless her, took us in. But work was not plentiful for a Cuban immigrant, and I was in despair when I met Ed on that park bench.

'We sat in that coffee shop for a long time, while I told him my story. But you know what, Detective? Ed never told me his story. Not one word about his past. Only about what he was doing, his ambitions. He offered me a job, found me an apartment in New York, paid for clothing and plane fares. And ultimately, he put my boys through college.

'So you see, Detective Camelia, though I know you have been thinking maybe I was the shooter, you are definitely barking up the wrong tree. I love Ed Vincent. I wish it had been I who was shot, and not him.'

Estevez opened his arms, spread his broad shoulders wide. 'Everything I am, everything I and my family have, is because of this man.'

Camelia shuffled uncomfortably in his seat; he hadn't expected quite such a soul-baring experience, but he was glad Estevez had come clean. There was no doubt that every word he said was true and he respected him for his openness.

'Then can you tell me of anything else unusual that might have happened recently, besides the deal going sour and the anonymous bidder?' He threw out the question, not knowing what to expect, and waited patiently while Estevez thought about it.

'There's just one thing I noticed when I was going through the records recently. About a month ago, Ed transferred a large amount of the company's stock to a Melba Eloise Merrydew. It was a shock to me, especially since I had never heard of the woman.' He shrugged. 'But then again, I know very little about Ed's private life.'

'How much stock?'

'As you know, Vincent Property Developers is a privately owned company. The stock division is like this: seventy percent is owned by Ed, twenty percent is mine. And the remaining ten percent is divided among the employees. Ed figured he wasn't only buying loyalty that way, but that everyone was getting a fair share.' He smiled, showing those perfect white teeth. 'That's just the way Ed was, Detective.'

'The way he still is, I hope,' Camelia said. 'And exactly how much did he transfer to Melba Merrydew?'

'Thirty percent.'

Camelia stared at him, stunned. Then he got to his feet, thanked Estevez, said that he might need to talk to him again and said goodbye.

He left with the thick green address book, which he knew would keep him up all night, and a bunch of information that would probably lead nowhere and was of no help to him. And of no use at all to poor Ed Vincent.

Chapter Nine

At seven the following evening, Ed Vincent was still alive. He was in a private room, wired up to the bank of monitors with tubes leading into his body. Only now there was an additional one. A shunt had been inserted into his head, draining excess fluid from his brain. His heartbeat ticked slowly on the monitor, pumped by the machine, and his pulse fluttered, weak as a sparrow's. He was not in good shape.

Detective Camelia paced the long, empty, highly polished corridor outside Ed's room. Twenty paces one way, twenty the other, hands clasped behind his back, head bowed, like royalty at a funeral.

Ed was not expected to last the night, but Camelia wanted to be there in case he came round again. He wanted a chance to check that name Zelda with him. Sounded like a crime of passion to him, a 'woman-scorned' scenario.

Last night he'd gone through every name in that darned green leather book and there was no mention of her. And no mention either of a Melba Eloise Merrydew. Strange that Zelda's number wasn't in Ed's book, though. And nor was Melba's. That's where a man usually kept the names of his lady friends.

Camelia stroked his bristly chin, peering out into the gathering dusk. Could the mysterious foreign bidder have wanted to eliminate his rival? This was big international business. Billions of dollars were at stake. You never knew. But so far, all efforts to trace the identity of the mysterious bidder had drawn a blank. There was a curtain of obfuscation between the US and certain foreign countries in the Far and Middle East, as well as in Latin America, that was impenetrable. He sighed again. Life was not easy. Not for a detective. And certainly not for the poor bastard lying in the hospital bed.

Ed could hear his own heart beating. It sounded so slow he found himself waiting for the next leaden thunk, wondering if it was going to make it. Drugged with morphine against the pain, he felt a kind of false peacefulness, hardly aware of his physical self except for that slow-thunking heart.

He drifted between a state of conscious thought and periods of time when there was simply blackness; a dark, warm feeling, like the blood being pumped through his body by that machine. And then there was another layer, under that blackness, a hidden part that never surfaced in his day-to-day life. Hadn't for years ... not since he was a boy and had buried those memories ...

He was thinking of the past now, though unwillingly, wondering if this was what it meant to have your life flash before your eyes in the final seconds.

Oh, God, he thought, I don't want to remember this, I've buried it all in the past ... I want to be back in the Cessna, my sturdy little winged horse, flying back to Zelda again ... Oh, God, Zelda, why, why ... why?

Camelia took another sip of bitter coffee from a paper cup. Feeling that familiar acid twinge in his stomach, he tossed the cup into the trashcan. He wondered how many such drinks he had consumed in twenty-six years of being a cop. Should he ever have the misfortune to end up on a marble mortuary slab, when the ME cut open his stomach it would look like a rusty old iron tub, brown and pitted and scarred with acid. Jeez, he should give up the stuff right now. And he would have, if only he didn't enjoy it so much.

The uniform sitting outside the ICU was trying hard to stay awake. He was all of twenty years, and right now his head kept dropping onto his chest. Camelia grinned. He didn't blame him. Hospital duty was a boring detail.

He took out an Interdent and probed his gums. Dammit, he would have to make time to get to the dentist soon. His gums were sore as hell. The door opened and an ICU nurse emerged. The uniform was on his feet, alert in an instant.

Camelia had just found a sore spot with the Interdent. 'How's he doin', Nurse?' he mumbled.

She threw him a withering glance and he hastily removed the toothpick.

'Mr Vincent is still in a coma, Detective. There's no communication with him. Right now, he's being kept alive by machines. We can only hope for an improvement.'

Camelia nodded. 'Thanks, Nurse.' He might as well go home.

'Hey, Brotski,' he said to the uniform, 'take a break. Get a cup of coffee and a donut. Wake yourself up a bit. I'll stay here till you get back.'

The young officer's face brightened. 'Thanks sir, Detective Camelia. I appreciate that. It's kinda slow out here, puts a guy to sleep.'

Camelia watched him striding away. His uniform seemed too big for his skinny frame, and his pale orange hair had an unruly cowlick. He looked very young. He sighed. They weren't making cops the way they used to when he was a rookie. Then everyone had been over six feet, big and burly. Except himself, of course.

He took Brotski's seat outside the ICU. Arms folded, head tilted back, he stared at the ceiling, thinking about Ed Vincent. He wondered why he was such a reclusive kind of guy in his personal life. And why he never talked about his past. Did he have something to hide?

Down the hall, the elevator pinged and the doors slid open. Camelia turned to look. A woman was hurrying down the long, shiny corridor, half walking, half running. She was tall, slender, awkward as a teenager in her high heels. Short-cropped golden-blonde hair, huge, anxious brown eyes, long, suntanned legs and a very short skirt. Definitely not New York. He stood as she approached.

'Is this the ICU? Where Ed Vincent is?' She hitched the strap of her bag onto her shoulder and tugged at her short skirt. She was breathing heavily and looked tired and disheveled.

'Why do you want to know that, miss?'

'Are you the doctor?' She clutched his arm, gazing beseechingly at him. 'Oh, thank God, I need to talk to you. Just tell me Ed's going to be all right. Tell me he's going to live, Doctor. *Please*.'

Camelia glanced at her left hand. He saw no wedding ring. In fact she wore no jewellery at all, and her clothing was simple and inexpensive. 'I'm not the doctor.'

Her knees buckled and she almost fell. He helped her onto the chair, where she slumped, head bowed.

Thinking she was about to faint he hurried to get her some water from the machine. She must be a relative, he thought, offering her the paper cup. Or a devoted employee. She was certainly concerned. 'And who exactly are you, miss . . . ?'

She lifted her long golden lashes and looked at him with those big, soft amber-brown eyes.

'I'm Zelda,' she said.

Chapter Ten

Camelia hid his stunned smile with a little cough. He introduced himself. 'Homicide Detective Marco Camelia.'

She stared at him. *'Homicide?* Ed's not *dead,* is he? Oh, *please.'* She jumped to her feet, ran past him and pushed open the door to the ICU.

The nurse's head swiveled as she passed her, then she too was on her feet. 'Hey, wait one minute ...' she began angrily. But Zelda was already at the bedside.

Ed's face looked like a stranger's, coldly pale and without his usual beard. His eyes were closed, and for a big man, he looked horribly fragile.

Mortal, Zelda thought, slipping to her knees and taking his hand carefully in both hers. Her heart was a leaden lump in her chest. It had slowed so she could hardly breathe. *Those could have been her blips on that screen — plummeting lower and lower. She was dying with him ...*

'Young woman, you have to get out of here,' the nurse hissed in a furious whisper, grabbing her arm. She didn't seem to hear, she just stared at the patient.

'"I told you so," would be appropriate, you great oaf,' Zelda said, sniffing back the tears. 'Damn it, Ed Vincent, maybe next time you'll listen to me.'

Marco Camelia indicated to the nurse to leave her alone.

'I'm in charge here, Detective,' the nurse whispered angrily. 'You are disturbing my patient. He's in an extremely critical condition, he needs to be kept quiet.' She glanced anxiously at the monitors as the minimal peaks and valleys changed suddenly to irregular zigs and zags. 'Just look what she's doing to him.' She ran to summon the doctor.

Camelia was looking. The agitation was there for all to see. Ed Vincent was reacting to the presence of his killer. *Would-be* killer, he reminded himself. They did not have a body. Yet.

'Zelda.' Camelia's hand was firm on her shoulder and she turned to look at him. Her face was pale, bruised-looking, and her eyes had the dilated pupils of a person in shock. He said, 'We have to let him rest now.'

Her eyes followed Camelia's to the jumping pattern on the monitor. She scrambled clumsily to her feet and stood for a moment, looking at the man lying motionless in the bed. Then she bent and gently kissed his cheek.

Soft as a feather, Camelia noted, just as the duty doctor swung through the door, summoned hastily by the nurse.

'What the hell is going on in here?' He spoke in a low voice, but his anger was clear. 'Who are you? No, don't tell me, just get out.'

Camelia hurried Zelda from the room, urging her out even as she turned for one last look at Ed Vincent.

It occurred to him that if Zelda were really 'a woman scorned', she certainly seemed to care about Vincent. Cared enough to kill him rather than lose him, he guessed. That was the way of the world. They should run an ad campaign like they did for drugs – *Domestic Violence Kills*. Much good it would do, he thought wearily.

Zelda dropped onto the chair outside the door as though her legs were no longer able to support her. 'Why?' she demanded, staring blankly down the empty corridor. '*Why* would they want to kill him?'

Camelia made a mental note of the phrase '*they* want to kill him.' 'That's exactly what we would like to know. And that's why I'm taking you in for questioning.'

She looked up at him, uncomprehending.

The elevator stopped on their floor and the uniformed officer strode toward them.

'Brotski, I'd like you to read Miss Zelda her rights.'

'*Sir?*' Brotski's face was a picture; he'd only been gone fifteen minutes and 'Camille' was already reading rights to a strange woman outside the ICU. He'd missed it all.

'Mirandize her,' Camelia ordered, frowning.

'Yes, sir.' The woman stared astounded at Brotski as he warned her that she had the right to remain silent and was entitled to legal counsel.

'What's happening? What does he mean?' She looked back at Camelia, puzzled.

'We are taking you in for questioning in the attempted homicide of Mr Edward Vincent.' Camelia was all business. He had his perpetrator now, he felt sure of it. Vincent had named her, and now he had her.

'*Are you out of your mind?*'

Sparks flew from her big brown eyes as she stood up. She towered over his five-eight and Camelia figured, uncomfortably, she must be well over six foot in those heels.

'I only just got here, I flew in from LA,' she yelled, 'I didn't even know Ed had been shot until I saw it on TV ... Jesus.' Her voice wobbled as the realization hit her. 'You can't think *I* did it.'

'We just want to question you, Miss Zelda.' Camelia was calm, matter-of-fact. 'Maybe the first thing you can tell us is your full name.'

Her eyes swiveled between the ICU door and the long corridor. Figuring she might make a run for it, Brotski stepped between her and the elevator.

'Melba Eloise Merrydew,' she said finally in a voice like a sigh, and Brotski could almost see 'Camille's' heart hit his boots as he registered the fact that he might have the wrong woman after all.

But Camelia was remembering that huge transfer of shares. 'I thought you said your name was Zelda?' he snapped.

Tears filled her eyes again, and she let them run, unmopped, down her face. 'It's Ed's name for me. It's what he called me.'

'Sort of a pet name,' Brotski added helpfully, then shut his mouth firmly at Camelia's glare.

Camelia knew he had the right woman, he was sure of it. The motive was there somewhere – if only he could figure it out. He remembered that huge transfer of shares. Money had to be at the bottom of it. Money and sex – that's usually what it turned out to be, and this was no different.

'Miss Merrydew, why don't you just come along with me and we'll talk about this? You understand, I'm not accusing you of anything. We just need to have you fill us in on a few details of Mr Vincent's private life.'

'Do I need a lawyer?'

She wasn't as dumb as Brotski had thought.

'If you wish one to be present, certainly.'

'But I *want* to help you. I'll do everything I can. I've nothing to hide …' She threw an imploring glance at the closed ICU door. 'Just let me see him one more time, say goodbye …'

Her voice broke, and for a split second Camelia's implacable surface cracked. She looked so distraught, so vulnerable, he wondered how he could suspect her of such a heinous crime. But he knew from experience that the guilty could be as charming and persuasive as the innocent, and much more cunning.

'I'm afraid the doctor won't allow that, Miss Merrydew. Maybe later …'

He took her by the elbow, guided her to the elevator, but she swung round suddenly. 'Goodbye, Ed,' she yelled, loud enough to wake the dead. 'Goodbye, honey. I'll be back. Wait for me.'

Inside the ICU, the duty doctor and the nurse both

witnessed the slight lift at the corners of Ed Vincent's mouth as her final words reverberated through the room. The zigs and zags on the monitor were big as pyramids, jolting rapidly across the screen.

'You might almost have thought that was a smile,' the doctor said, awed.

He checked the patient's vital signs, lifted his eyelids, searched with a tiny light into his pupils. Everything was still the same. Ed Vincent was still in a coma. The facial twitch had been a mere coincidence.

You found me, Zelda. You got here in time. Don't go away, baby, he wanted to yell after her. *I might not last until you get back again . . . Stay, Zelda. Please stay. Talk to me about what you've been doing, tell me about Riley and the dog, about Moving On . . . Tell me again how we first met . . .*

Chapter Eleven

Dr Art Jacobs was at a charity dinner at the Waldorf in aid of Cardiac Awareness. He knew Alberto Ricci to say hello to; they were passing acquaintances at these charity events. Their wives had served on some of the same committees — that sort of thing. But tonight when Ricci came over to him, and said, 'How are you, Art?' Art was surprised.

'Good, Alberto. Everything okay with you?' Usually when people sought him out at parties it was because they wanted a bit of free medical advice.

'Fit as a fiddle, thanks, Art. I see you have an important patient now. Ed Vincent?'

'Yeah. Poor Ed. He's a good friend of mine.'

'Is he doing okay?'

Jacobs shrugged. 'He's holding on. For now.'

'Any chance he'll recover?'

'There's always a chance. I doubt it, though, he's a very sick man. Still,' he shrugged again, 'Ed's held on for two days now, he's a tough bastard. You never can tell.'

'Well, let's hope,' Ricci said, as he nodded goodbye.

And just what was all that about? Art wondered. Why would Alberto Ricci want to know how Ed was doing? As far as he knew, the two had never met. He shrugged one more time. Probably just idle curiosity. The shooting had made the headlines. Now Ricci could tell his friends he'd heard it straight from the horse's mouth. Ed Vincent had a chance. But not much.

Chapter Twelve

'I'll tell you how it all began.'

Melba was in a small, windowless cubicle in the precinct house in midtown Manhattan. She was sitting upright in an uncomfortable wooden chair, knees crossed, showing a lot of leg and looking alert now, though still disturbed. Camelia thought she was oddly beautiful. There was just something about the slant of the copper-colored eyes, the graceful length of her neck, the sweetness of her full mouth.

At least she wasn't crying, he thought, handing her a cup of coffee. He took a pack of Winstons from his jacket, shook one out, offered it to her.

She shook her head, 'No thank you.'

He watched silently while she sipped the coffee. He didn't trust her an inch. Thirty percent was a lot of shares. He wondered exactly *what* Ed Vincent had left her in his will.

Waiting, Melba thought. *He's waiting for me to tell him that I did it. He thinks he has me.* For a second she wished she smoked; it would have given her something to do with her hands. Then she told herself to stop being nervous of this man, who anyhow looked like Al Pacino in a cop role.

She looked at him, really looked at him, for the first time. He was handsome in a tough sort of way: sleek black hair; broad, lined forehead; dark eyes under heavy black brows; a firm, blue-stubbled chin. In good shape, too; a hard, muscular body. A tough cop.

For a minute she felt the unreality of the situation, as though she were playing a part in a movie. And then reality hit her like a punch in the stomach. She looked the detective in the eye, reminded herself he was there to help Ed. He *needed* her.

'I told Ed someone wanted to kill him.' She set the styrofoam cup unsteadily on the scarred wooden desk. 'I told him so.'

'Oh? And when exactly did you tell him this, Zelda?'

She glanced sharply at him and Camelia knew he had made a mistake. 'Zelda' was Ed Vincent's private name for her.

'I told him three months ago,' she said, coldly. 'The first time I met him.'

Camelia loosened his silver tie, letting that one sink in. Only three months – and he'd given her thirty percent of those shares ... she must really have something. He took a drag on the cigarette his wife had forbidden him to smoke, then stubbed it out in the glass ashtray as Zelda-Melba waved the smoke away.

'Excuse me, I didn't realize the smoke would bother you.'

'You should know better, Detective Camelia,' she said, disapprovingly. 'Smoking kills.'

So do bullets from a .40mm semi-automatic, he thought, but said nothing.

They sipped their coffee in silence.

'Perhaps you'd better begin at the beginning,' he suggested helpfully.

She nodded. 'Okay, but the beginning is *before* I met him.' She put her elbows on the desk and leaned toward him. Her swollen eyes looked into his.

'I feel so guilty,' she whispered, anguished. 'I feel I could have prevented this, if only I had tried a little harder, been more assertive ... but Ed wouldn't listen.'

Camelia sat back. He would let her get on with it, say what she had to say.

'It began in late October,' Zelda said. 'My friend, Harriet Simons, and I had started this house-moving company about a year ago. *Moving On*, it's called.' She smiled modestly. 'Actually it's just a forty-eight-foot truck and a small office in an old warehouse in Venice Beach, California. The truck was brand new,' she added, sounding regretful. 'I'd gotten a small inheritance from my Aunt Hester and used it as a down payment. I was in hock up to my eyeballs for it.

'It was our first big job, relocating an executive and his family from Beverly Hills to North Carolina. We drove across country, completed the job on time, then went out to dinner to celebrate. Harriet got food poisoning. The oysters, I guess. She ended up in hospital. They said she would have to stay there for a couple of days, so I decided to drive the truck back myself. We needed it in LA, you see, for another job later that week.

'It had been raining hard all day. A "tropical storm," they called it on TV. I wasn't going to let a drop of rain hold me up, I had to get back. So I set off . . . Oh, God, I remember it as clearly as if I were there now . . .'

Chapter Thirteen

Mel was driving the forty-eight-foot, sixteen-wheeler cautiously along the narrow road. The night was dark as a toad's mouth and the howling wind rocked the high-sided vehicle scarily. Toppled trees and debris littered the deserted road and the rain slashed sideways, sending waves of water back and forth across her windshield.

Right now, driving was guesswork and instinct. She told herself she was crazy for even attempting this trip when the forecast had said clearly that a tropical storm was certain and a hurricane a possibility. But business was business, and she had to get back to LA.

Shivering with cold in her damp T-shirt and wishing she at least had a sweater, she ran a hand anxiously through her jagged blonde crop. She had been driving for what seemed like eternity. She could swear she should have connected with the highway intersection half an hour ago, but navigation was not her forte. She had been known to get lost two blocks from her own home.

She hadn't passed a house or a building in the past half-hour, and the prospect of being lost in the boonies in this storm terrified her. She would have turned back ages ago, but the road was too narrow for the big truck. She decided that as soon as she hit the next town, she would find a motel and spend the night. LA could wait. A cup of coffee, a sandwich and a warm bed sounded just great to her right now.

The road suddenly ended. Just in time, she stamped on the brakes and the huge truck shuddered to a stop. In front of her was a narrow bridge. She could hear the roar of surf, a bass note under the shriek of the wind, and was surprised to realize she was near the ocean. *Too* near. She couldn't see the end of the bridge, but she could see huge white-capped waves swirling beneath it. *Very close* beneath it.

There was no room to turn the truck round and go back. She could either stay here and be drowned by the rising waves, or risk crossing.

She drove cautiously onto the bridge, gripping the wheel tighter as the truck caught the full blast of the wind. *Dear God, what was she doing here? She was out of her mind. Only an idiot would get lost and attempt to drive over a bridge in a hurricane.* The big truck aquaplaned the last few feet then skidded onto a flooded road.

Mel unfastened her sweaty hands from the wheel. At least she was on *terra firma*, even if it was covered with a foot of water. Opening the window, she stuck her head out and looked back. Waves were sweeping over the bridge; it was already half submerged. There was no going back now.

The lane sloped gently uphill, and in a few minutes she was on drier land. She was driving through woods with the wind roaring through the treetops. And then, there was a house.

'Thank you, God,' she muttered. 'Civilization. At last.'

The isolated house was all gables and porches, dark and spooky-looking. No welcoming lights shone from the windows, no smoke curled from its chimney, no dog barked.

A shiver crawled up Mel's spine. She had seen *Psycho*, and this must surely be the Bates house. Instinct told her she should get right back into the truck and drive back the way she had come. Then she spotted the car parked beneath the trees. A nice normal-looking Ford Taurus. Telling herself that guys from *Psycho* didn't drive nice normal-looking Fords, she staggered through the wind and rain and up the steps.

Again, she hesitated. She was alone; the house was miles from anywhere; she didn't know who might live there. It *could* be a Norman Bates. Shivering, she wiped the rain off her face with her hand. If she turned back now, she would drown crossing the bridge. Or a tree could fall on the truck. Or a broken power line. And the wind would probably blow the truck over . . . *This was what was meant by being between a rock and a hard place . . .*

She pressed a cold finger on the bell.

Chapter Fourteen

Mel rang the bell again. Shivering, she pounded on the door. Still no answer. She tried the handle. To her surprise, it opened.

The house was in total darkness, not even a glimmer of a light.

'Hello?' Her voice echoed eerily. 'Is anyone there?' She waited, then called hello again. Her voice sounded thin and trembly in the dense silence. She felt with her hand along the wall for a light switch, found it, clicked it on, blinking in the sudden light.

In front of her, a staircase led to a galleried area above the hall. There was just one big room, sparsely furnished with battered old stuff. It looked as though no one lived there, and she guessed it was probably used as a weekend beach house. On a rough wooden coffee table was a beautiful, slightly sinister bronze of a crouching cat holding a terrified bird in its mouth. And a stone bowl filled with jellybeans.

Suddenly starving, she grabbed a handful and devoured them, still dripping water onto the bare wood-plank floor, considering what to do. If the owner found her here she could be thrown into jail for breaking and entering. Except she hadn't broken in, the door was open. She shrugged resignedly: what the hell, she was a victim of the storm, surely they would forgive her.

Catching sight of herself in a mirror, she had second thoughts about that. She looked a wreck. The cheap red dye from the *Moving On* logo on her white T-shirt had run, and she thought now she would probably have the logo embossed permanently on her chest. Her nose was red, her T-shirt clung to her like a second skin and her sodden work boots squelched as she walked to the wall of windows fronting the ocean.

A solid sheet of rain obliterated the view, but she could hear the roar of the ocean surging over the rocks below. She shivered. Somehow, the violence outside made the silence inside the house even creepier.

A sudden noise sent her heart lurching. She froze to the spot, hardly able to breathe. Had that been a door slamming? The house shuddered under the impact of a gust of wind and she heard the timbers groan. She told herself it was just the wind. Still, she wished Harriet were with her, so they could laugh about all this.

She stepped cautiously back into the hall, calling hello again, though she would probably have had a heart attack if anybody answered. God, but she was wet. She needed a bathroom to clean up. She saw the door across the hall, opened it, switched on the light.

The glazed, dark eyes of a dead man stared up at her. His head was a mass of blood, there was a great red pool of it beneath him, blood and flesh splattered all around . . .

She knew she was screaming but the sound that came out of her throat was a howl. She wanted to run, but she was frozen to the spot with terror.

Then the light went out.

Panic spilled like molten lava into her veins, sending her running. *Right into a man's arms.*

A gun jammed hard into her ribs. Without pausing to think, she slammed her fist into his belly, heard the air woosh out of him as he staggered back. Then she was skidding across the floor. She was running, running for her life . . . out into the night.

The wind slammed her back against the wall, the rain was coming down in sheets, she couldn't even *see* the truck. *Oh, God, soon he would be after her . . .*

Clinging to the porch rail, bent double, she staggered down the steps. But the wind knocked her off her feet. It snatched her breath, flung the rain at her, hard as hailstones. Gasping, she dropped to the ground, slithered on her belly across the streaming blacktop.

She had to make it, she just had to . . . think of Riley . . . oh, God, she had to make it.

Then she was under the truck, wet as a seal and still trying to catch her breath. Sobbing with fear, she crawled out the other side, hauled herself upright, tugged frantically at the cab door. *It must be locked . . . but she didn't remember locking it.*

It flew open suddenly, almost knocking her off her feet. 'Oh, thank you God, thank you,' she muttered, pulling herself up into the cab. *Thank you . . .*

And then a hand slammed across her mouth.

He jabbed the gun into her ribs again. 'Shut the fuck up. One fuckin' sound and I'll kill you. Understand?'

His hand stank of stale cigarettes. Fear and nausea swept over her and she gagged.

Instinctively, he let go and in that split second she threw herself at him, raked her nails down his face, jammed her thumbs in his eyes . . .

'Shit.' There was a sickening crack as his fist hit bone, and Mel slithered slowly to the ground.

He stared angrily down at her. His eyes watered painfully. He put his hand to his face, felt the blood where she had dug deep into his flesh. He wanted to kill her right now, but he still needed her.

He took the expensive Ericsson from his pocket and dialed Mario de Soto's number. Miraculously, the call went through.

He explained that Ed Vincent hadn't shown up; that he was here in the middle of a fuckin' hurricane; that de Soto shouldn't worry, he would get him next time. Vincent was as good as dead. He did not mention the woman nor the dead Cuban.

'Get up.' He hauled Mel to her feet, pushed her into the driver's seat. 'You are gonna drive us out of here.' He aimed the Sigma at her head.

Mel stared straight ahead. Her head swam and her cheek-bone felt as though it had dissolved. She had no hope of escape, she would do as he said. Trembling, she put the key in the ignition. To her surprise, the engine caught immediately.

The gun was icy cold on her temple. 'Okay,' he said, 'let's go.'

She drove the big truck down the driveway out onto the lane that led to the bridge.

The bridge! Oh my God, it was surely under water by now. She wouldn't be able to get across, he would kill her then, she knew it . . . Oh, Riley . . . my darling daughter.

She heard the squeak of the wiper blades on the suddenly dry windshield. As abruptly as if someone had turned off the tap, the rain had stopped. The wind had dropped. And there were no waves. Just a sullen expanse of black water with the submerged side rails of the bridge poking out of it, marking its position.

Now the sky was clear, it was growing lighter. She could hear *birds* singing . . . *She must be hallucinating.*

From somewhere in the past, she recalled hearing about being in the eye of a hurricane. That though the storm still swirled all around them, here in the 'eye,' all was calm, and the birds that had been caught up in it and carried hundreds, sometimes thousands of miles from their habitat, had suddenly found themselves deposited in a strange new terrain. That is, until the circling storm caught up with them again and carried them even farther away. Or killed them. *And her.*

She stared at the sullen black ocean. There was no way to

gauge how deep the water was, or even if the bridge was still there. It was suicide.

The gun pressed harder against her temple. 'Drive,' he said.

Chapter Fifteen

'I guess you made it across,' Camelia said caustically, rolling an unlit cigarette between his fingers, foot tapping impatiently. Was Zelda-Melba some kind of nut? Or was she just putting him on? Whatever, she was surely a great storyteller.

Mel caught his skeptical glance, and glared angrily back at him. 'Thankfully, yes I did,' she answered primly. Then with a sudden flare, 'Dammit, I'm spilling my guts to you, Detective. Do you want to hear this or not?'

He grinned, her face was pink with anger. 'May as well.'

'Ohh!' Exasperated, she sank back, or at least sank as well as she could in a straightback wooden chair. She stared balefully at him. 'This man had a gun to my head,' she said, speaking slowly and distinctly, separating each word as though speaking to a child. 'I did not want to be dead. I wanted to be home, with my kid. I wanted to work some more with Harriet, moving families. *I wanted my life.*'

She was looking into his eyes and he stared back, coldly.

'So I just said sorry to Aunt Hester who had paid for my lovely truck – and drove it head-on into a tree.'

Camelia let out a low whistle of admiration. 'Good thinking,' he said. 'Never thought a woman would think that way, though,' he added, half to himself. 'Too worried about a scratch on the new vehicle.'

Mel propped her elbows on the scarred table and leaned her aching head in her hands, too exhausted, too gosh-darn bone-weary to argue the point.

'Next thing I knew it was two days later. I was in hospital. And Harriet was sitting by my bed, staring at me with that is-she-going-to-make-it look . . .'

Harriet's face swam into view as Mel's eyes focused. It was like being underwater, everything blurred and opaque – until she blinked twice and there Harriet was.

Her best friend and business partner, Harriet Simons, was in her early thirties. She claimed to be an 'ex-actress,' but she wasn't really 'ex' anything yet. Petite, whippet-thin and with a distinctive gravely voice, she was still always on the phone to her agent, still hoping for that break.

It had been Harriet's idea to call their moving company *Moving On*. She said it fit not only the lives of their clients who were moving house, but also their own, moving on from the unsatisfactory, itinerant jobs they had held previously and moving on with life. Except the truth was, Harriet had not really moved on yet. She still hit every audition and every casting call, still read *Variety* and the *Hollywood Reporter* as though they were her Bible.

Mel thought the only thing unfamiliar about her now was the anxious expression on her face. And that was worrying because it took a lot to scare Harriet.

'Am I alright?' Mel asked in a throaty voice she hardly recognized as her own.

'Of course you are.' Harriet's face lit with relief as she added tartly, 'For an idiot who drove our one and only brand-new truck into a tree.'

'Well, there was a hurricane,' Mel explained meekly.

'You've been here for two days,' Harriet retorted. 'You have a hairline fracture of the skull, as well as concussion, plus a broken cheekbone . . .'

Mel put her hand to her face, felt the gauze pad and suddenly it all came back to her.

'Harriet,' she grabbed her arm urgently, 'he tried to kill me ... that guy really tried to kill me ... he'd already killed someone else, the man in the library ... *oh, God,* I have to get out of here, we have to tell the police ...'

She was already half out of bed when Harriet caught her and hauled her back. 'Stay where you are, kiddo,' she said firmly. 'As they say in the movies, you ain't goin' nowheres. Yet, anyway.'

Mel glared at her, uncomprehending. *'Didn't you hear what I said?* The man had *a gun*, he held it to *my* head ... That's why I drove into the tree ...'

Harriet's face registered disbelief, then concern, then the fact that maybe, just maybe this was not the hallucination of a concussed woman, and that what Mel was telling her might in fact be true. 'Begin at the beginning,' she said, practical as ever. And so Mel did.

She told her story from A to Z, and then retold it as she recalled extra little details, like the scarlet pool of blood under the dead body; the yellow lumps of flesh; the light going out; the way the man had punched her; being forced to drive across the submerged bridge and not knowing if they were going to make it ...

'I could *almost* believe you,' Harriet said when she had finished, 'except nobody else was found in the wrecked truck. There was no man. And no gun. You were alone. The rescue squad had to use the jaws of life to cut you out of there. Look at it this way, Mel,' she added soberly, 'you're lucky to be alive, so forget all this bad dream stuff. You're just confused from the concussion.'

'Damn it, I did *not* dream it.' Mel was already out of bed and rummaging in the closet where her dufflebag, also rescued from the truck, was stashed. Flinging off the hospital gown, she dragged on underpants and sweats and thrust her feet into her sneakers. She turned to Harriet who was watching her, her mouth agape. 'Okay, let's go,' she said.

'But *where* are we going? You're sick, you're injured, you're medicated. You only just woke from the concussion, the doctor will kill me if I let you move out of this room. In fact, I'm going to call him right now this minute ...'

'You do that.' Mel was already through the door and running, rather wobbly, down the shiny polished linoleum corridor. 'I'm checking out of here.'

Grabbing the duffle, Harriet puffed after her. 'But *where* are we going?'

Mel half-turned. She gave her a withering glance and said, 'To the cops, of course,' as though there was any other course of action she could be taking.

The medicos fought her on it, but Mel checked herself out of the hospital, and with Harriet at the wheel of a rental car, drove to police headquarters.

'I'm sure I needn't tell you what happened there,' she said now to Marco Camelia.

'They told you you were crazy?'

She leaned closer across the table, looking into his eyes. 'Do you think I'm nuts?'

He shrugged. 'I think you tell a good story, Miss Zelda.'

Her gaze turned to a glare. 'Melba to you.'

'Oh, excuse me, Miss Melba. So? What did the cops say if they didn't tell you you were crazy?

Her shoulders slumped and she stared down at the table with a puzzled frown. 'They told me that no one had died in the storm. No bodies had been found. That the area had got off lightly, apart from a few road accidents, like myself.

'I told them where I thought the beach house was, that there was definitely a body there. They said they knew the place, it belonged to Ed Vincent, the property dealer. Then they did me a big favor and called them. The housekeeper answered, she told them everything was in order, no bodies, no blood, everything was secure. And that though Mr Vincent usually flew down for the weekend, this time because of the storm he had not. He hadn't even been there. Nor had she. No one had.'

Chapter Sixteen

Walking out of the Charleston cop station with Harriet, Mel wondered if she really had just dreamed it, if this were truly a figment of her fevered imagination, the dreams of a bad concussion. After all, she had hit a tree head-on . . .

Back in the rental car, she slumped wearily into her seat, eyes closed, then suddenly the smell of stale tobacco was in her nostrils again – the smell of the killer's hands. She felt the cold hard steel of the gun at her head, hear him say, 'Drive . . .' in that faintly guttural accent.

Her eyes popped open again and she sat up. 'Dreams don't make you remember the way things *smell*, the way it *felt*. I did *not* dream this, I could not have.'

She scrambled her long length out of the tiny car and sprinted round to the driver's side. 'I'm driving,' she said, and there was something about the way she said it, a kind of scared urgency, that had Harriet out and into the passenger's seat before she could even question the safety of a recently concussed, medicated and wounded woman in charge of a car.

'Tell me this is a play and I'm acting and you are dreaming, and let's just go home,' she pleaded as Mel whizzed round a rotary heading north out of Charleston. 'Anyway, where are we going now?'

'Where d'you think?' Mel put her foot to the metal as she

left the traffic behind and hit the beach road. She was in a hurry, she had to see for herself. She had to prove that it had really happened.

She stomped hard on the brake, though, when the bridge came into view. It was out of the water again, the pavement was cracked and crumbling at the sides and most of the posts were missing. And there was a large sign that said, *Caution, bridge impassable until further notice.*

'Well, that's that,' Harriet said thankfully. This whole thing was getting a little out of hand, and anyhow she wasn't sure she wanted to go looking for murder victims.

'No, it isn't,' Mel put her foot down again and rolled onto the flimsy bridge. 'I've driven across this in worse conditions, and at least this time I'm not in a sixteen-wheeler in a hurricane and I can see what I'm doing.'

Harriet held her breath, one hand on the door handle ready to bail out, the other covering her eyes, as Mel maneuvered the little car gently over the bumps and holes. 'Just don't tell me we have to do that again on the way back,' Harriet's usually forceful voice was weak. 'I don't think I could take it.'

'Then you'll just have to swim. This is the only way in and out. Oh, look, there it is. You see, Harr, I was right.'

Mel's triumphant yell faded. The *Psycho* house looked immaculate, serene. The tamed ocean lapped sedately at the rocks and the sun shone. It didn't look the least bit like Norman Bates's place.

'You mean, this is it? The House of Horrors?' Harriet laughed in relief. 'God, I was expecting Dracula or something.'

But Mel was already out and up the steps, standing on the porch, her finger on the bell. Harriet got out and leaned against the car, watching her. Waiting.

Nothing happened; the house was empty. And this time the door was locked.

'Damn,' Mel grumbled, trying it again, 'damn, damn, gosh-darn and drat!'

Harriet giggled, 'Well really, Miss Southern belle, I don't think your mama would approve of suchlike cusswords.'

But Mel was already circling the porch, pressing her nose against the windows, shading her eyes against the reflection with her hands. 'This is it,' she yelled, waving an urgent arm for Harriet. 'Here's the room, the library room. This is where I saw the body, I remember it exactly . . .'

Harriet peered through the window. It looked quite normal to her, nothing out of place, no pools of blood. 'So where's the body, Mel?' she asked finally. 'Where is this so-called killer? *Who* is he?'

'I don't know.' Mel shook her head, totally bewildered. 'I just don't know. All I know is I'm not crazy, but this will surely drive me crazy if I don't find out.'

She slumped onto the porch steps, elbows on her knees, head in her hands, staring at the blacktop driveway over which she had crawled, and from where she had been abducted. She remembered the killer hauling her into the cab, her fighting him, scratching his face, jamming her thumbs in his eyes . . . and the brutal blow to her face that had sent her sliding onto the floor of the cab, dopey with pain.

But not so dopey that she had not heard what he said. 'He made a telephone call,' she remembered. 'After he hit me, he called someone. He told them Ed Vincent wasn't here, but he would get him next time.' Her blue eyes rounded with alarm, and she grabbed Harriet by the shoulders. 'Listen to me, Harriet, *believe me*. Ed Vincent is on that killer's hit list. And if I don't warn him, he will be the next one found dead in the library.'

'Should I "mark your words?"' Harriet asked with a grin, because somehow now she *almost* believed her.

'Darn right, honey.' Mel was already back in the car. 'You'd better mark my words – and so had Ed Vincent.'

'Where are we going now?' Harriet closed her eyes as they

approached the battered bridge. This time Mel scarcely even slowed, and they practically flew over.

'We're going to telephone Ed Vincent in New York,' Mel announced triumphantly. 'For sure, he'll believe me.'

Chapter Seventeen

'So? Did he?' Camelia asked.

'Believe me, you mean?' Mel drummed her fingers impatiently on the table. She glanced round at her 'prison,' a bare little room with a single blank window, a table, two chairs and a layer of dust. She had been so caught up in her story, she had almost forgotten where she was. 'Can a condemned prisoner get a Diet Coke around here? Please,' she added as an afterthought.

'Sure.' Camelia got up. He straightened his silver-gray silk tie and smoothed back his hair, Al Pacino-style, Mel thought, as he walked across the room and asked the uniform standing outside the door to get her a Coke.

'Make that two,' Camelia added, closing the door again.

Mel took a good look at him, taking him in as a man and not just a cop — and a cop who thought she had tried to murder her lover at that. This guy was quite the fashion plate; if he were not a cop she might have tabbed him as a member of the Mob.

'You must be married,' she said, fingers still drumming on the table.

'Why do you say that?'

He leaned back in his more comfortable chair, one leg draped lazily over the other.

'No cop living alone would be as smart as you — freshly ironed shirt, light starch only, pants pressed, shoes shined.'

ELIZABETH ADLER

He grinned. 'I shine my own shoes.'

'Well, thank God for that.'

He laughed then. Leaning across the table, he took hold of her hand. 'Stop that drumming,' he said. 'Anyone would think you were nervous.'

'Who, me?' She stuck her chin defiantly in the air. 'I'm not nervous, I'm just trying to find out the truth.'

'Like me.'

'Like you.' Their gaze locked and then, because she just couldn't help it, she cracked. Tears streamed down her face. Big fat tears that rolled down her cheeks, dripped from her chin, leaked into her ears. Gosh-darn it, she was bawling like a kid and all because her heart was breaking. *Ed was lying in that hospital bed, Ed was gravely wounded, Ed was dying . . .*

'I can't bear it,' she wept, still sitting bolt upright in the chair. 'I just can't bear to lose him.'

Camelia got up. He took a handkerchief from his pocket and offered it to her.

She looked at it and then up at him. A kind of giggle, or maybe it was a hiccup, interrupted her sobs. 'That's what I mean about the wife,' she said. 'A clean handkerchief. Anybody else would have offered a box of Kleenex.'

Officer Brotski knocked on the door, then entered, carying two cans of Diet Coke. 'With caffeine,' he mentioned to Camelia, who gave him a withering look.

Brotski took in the sobbing blonde, the clean white handkerchief, the tension in the air and with a muttered, 'Sorry, excuse me, sir,' quickly departed.

'You really love him that much?' Camelia flipped open the can and handed it to her. 'You haven't known him that long.'

'Long enough,' she hiccuped. 'And there again,' she added in a whisper, 'not long enough.'

Camelia tilted his chair. He sat, one leg over the other, arms folded, silently watching her. There was something so vulnerable, so gallant about her at that moment, he was almost tempted to

74

believe her. Then he reminded himself she was here because Ed Vincent had said she had tried to kill him. He took in the ragged crop of blonde hair, the earnest whisky-brown eyes, the wide, trembling mouth. And also the long legs and the extremely short skirt that suddenly, for some reason, reminded him of Sharon Stone in *Basic Instinct*. And nobody, he recalled uncomfortably, had been more wicked than her character.

With an embarrassed cough, he righted his chair and took charge again. 'And so did you?' he asked abruptly. 'Telephone him, I mean.'

'I tried, God knows I tried endlessly. But Ed's office was like a fortress with a barricade of secretaries and assistants placed firmly between me and the boss. They said Mr Vincent did not accept calls, and could I please tell them what it was I was calling about?' Mel lifted her shoulders and shook her head. 'How could I tell them? They would think I was some kind of nut. Mr Big Shot, I thought. So full of himself. Too important to speak to little people. I almost let it go at that,' she added soberly, 'but then I reminded myself. Ed Vincent was a big shot *in danger*.'

Camelia watched her closely, waiting for her to tell him what happened next. Her head was tipped back, her eyes closed, as though she had retreated somewhere inside herself and was reliving her story.

'So I got on a plane to New York,' she said finally.

Chapter Eighteen

The reception area on the fiftieth floor of Vincent Tower
Madison was spacious, discreetly furnished in soft grays and
taupe, and the receptionist was sleek and blonde in a matching
gray suit with taupe lipstick. Mel wished now that she had
dressed for the occasion instead of just flinging on any old thing,
she was in such a rush to get to New York to warn him.

'I'm sorry, but Mr Vincent doesn't see anyone without an
appointment.'

The receptionist was polite, dismissing her as she turned to
answer the telephone.

The hell he doesn't. Slinging her bag over her shoulder, Mel
was across the room in three quick, long-legged strides
and through the connecting door that led into the inner
sanctum. Startled eyes watched from windowed offices as
she strode along the corridor. A pair of tall double doors
dominated the end of the hallway. She could hear the
receptionist running down the hall after her, shouting at
her to get out of here. She flung open the doors and
marched in.

Ed Vincent was standing alone by the window, looking
down at the busy traffic crawling soundlessly along Madison
Avenue. Swinging round, he stared, astonished, at the young
woman with short-cropped blonde hair and very long legs,

wearing a very short skirt, very high-heeled ankle boots and a battered black leather jacket, standing in his office.

Melba's voice sounded high-pitched and squeaky as she blurted out quickly, before they could stop her, 'Mr Vincent, I came all the way from LA to tell you this. Honey, someone is trying to kill you.' He was staring at her, stunned. 'I just thought you should know,' she added, realizing how crazy she must sound.

The receptionist ran in, followed by security. 'I'm sorry, Mr Vincent, but she just barged her way through, she's some kind of nut . . .'

He lifted a hand. 'It's alright. Please leave us.'

Mel took a deep breath, suddenly intimidated. Ed Vincent was younger and more attractive than she had expected. And bigger. Tall and rugged, with deep-set, bright blue eyes under black brows, thick dark hair, a craggy face, and a short beard. He was well-dressed in a conservative dark business suit and a blue shirt. He looked what he was: a rich, successful, confident man. A big shot, lord of the grand offices in the incredible Manhattan building that he owned.

Ed waited until the door closed behind them. There was a glint of amusement in his eyes as he said, 'You may be right. I can think of a lot of people who might prefer me not to be around.'

Melba rubbed one foot nervously behind the other, balancing like an awkward heron on one high heel, suddenly uncertain about what she was doing here. He was checking her out, taking her in from the tip of her untidy blonde head to the toes of her black suede ankle boots. She could see he didn't believe her.

'It's *true*,' she persisted. 'I was in your beach house in Carolina. *I met the killer.* I heard him talking about you. He was going to kill me too . . .'

Ed Vincent held out his hand. 'I'm glad to meet you, Miss . . . ?'

'Merrydew. And I promise I'm not crazy. I really saw him, I saw the body in your library ...'

'Okay, okay,' he nodded. 'Well, since you came all the way from LA to tell me that, the least I can do is take you to lunch. We can discuss it there.'

She couldn't believe it, the idiot was coming on to her, asking her to lunch ... *Didn't you hear what I said?*' She banged a fist on his desk for emphasis. '*I was there.* In that *Psycho* palace you call a beach house ...'

Ed grinned at her description. 'Okay. So I believe you were there.'

'Well, thank God for that.' Mel flopped into the big green leather chair behind his steel desk, long, bare, suntanned legs sticking out in front of her. 'Honey,' she said, relieved, 'I thought I'd never get through to you.' She caught his amazed look and added quickly, 'Don't take any mind of me calling you honey. Southerners call everybody honey. It's just the way we are.'

Her stomach rumbled loudly. She hadn't eaten since the plane last night. 'Come to think of it, I didn't have time for breakfast this morning ...'

Ed held out his hand and pulled her gently to her feet. She was as tall as he, and for a second they looked into each other's eyes.

Mel took a deep breath. *Woah*, she warned herself, *this guy is really something, better watch your step, honey ...*

The assistants and the secretaries were lined up outside the door, but she didn't give them a second glance. 'Bye, hon,' she called airily to the glossy receptionist as she sailed out on Ed Vincent's arm. Sometimes even petty revenge was sweet.

'Do you mind if we walk to the restaurant? It's such a nice day.' Ed took her arm, guiding her through the throng of pedestrians as they walked south on Madison.

Thank God he hadn't suggested a limo, she thought. That would really have put her off the big shot. It *was* a nice day though, bright and sunny and crisp.

'You're seeing New York at its best,' Ed Vincent said, thinking, amused, that she looked like a lofty Valkyrie loose on Madison Avenue with its elegant women dressed for fall in coats and scarves. She strode along, a golden Californian alien, bare-legged, head up, oblivious to how she looked. She was certainly different, and that's why he was intrigued, even if she was zany. Besides, she had certainly been to the beach house – only a woman would have described it that way . . . 'the *Psycho* palace . . .' He grinned again, thinking about it.

Her battered black leather jacket and bare legs got her a few sideways looks at the Four Seasons, though. She glanced uncomfortably at the Bill Blass-suited women who lunched. 'I feel out of place here.'

'You needn't,' he said easily. 'Besides, you're probably half their age.'

'I wish,' she said with a perky grin. 'You are looking at a thirty-two-year-old woman, the single mother of a seven-year-old daughter, who is the love of my life.'

'That's an admirable thing to be. I remember being the light of my own mother's life, and how good it felt.'

'Is your mother still with us?'

He smiled at the euphemistic way she phrased it; it was so very LA. 'Sadly, honey, she is not.'

'I'm sorry.' She lowered her eyes, twisting a piece of bread in her fingers. 'And I'm sorry I asked that. I didn't mean to pry.' The she grinned at him. 'That "honey" thing is catching, isn't it?'

Ed Vincent was different from what she had expected. There was something in the eyes, a wariness, a memory of deprivation imprinted on his craggy face. Despite his wealth and success, he was certainly no fat cat. She wondered about his past . . .

Over lunch and a bottle of wine, she told him her story, and about the conversation she had overheard where the killer named him as the intended victim. 'And he said he wouldn't miss next time,' she finished breathlessly.

'You must believe me,' she clutched his hand urgently across the table. *'I was there. This happened.'*

'Why didn't you go to the police?'

'I did. They didn't believe me either. Even my friend Harriet didn't believe me, so how could I expect the cops to? Nor did the doctor. He said it was the fractured skull and that I was confused and I'd been dreaming.' She shrugged. 'So I went back to the beach house with Harriet. I had to see for myself.

'The door was locked and we couldn't get in, but we looked through the windows. There was no dead body in the library. "See," Harriet said to me, "I told you you were dreaming."

'But, Mr Vincent, I swear it's *true*,' she said urgently. 'I saw what I saw. The killer made me drive him across that flooded bridge *at gunpoint*. I *know* what he looks like, I know his voice, his *accent* . . . I *couldn't* have dreamed all this.'

She took a deep breath, then glanced at her watch. 'So there,' she concluded briskly. 'I've told you. And now I'm catching the six o'clock back to LA.'

She gathered up her bag, spilling its contents in the process. Ed knelt beside her, retrieving the jumble of lipsticks and notebooks, photographs, pens and car keys, old shopping lists, store receipts and sunglasses. He said, 'You really did come all this way just to warn me?'

'I did. But you're a big boy. Now I'll leave you to take care of yourself. You have been warned.'

He laughed so heartily people turned to look. Impulsively, Mel leaned across and took his hand again. 'I know I sound like the voice of doom, but Mr Vincent, honey, you have to protect yourself.'

Her fingers were smooth and warm on his. She was a long, lanky streak of lightning, but she had an off-the-wall appeal that got to him. 'If I promise to do just that, will you help me find the killer?'

She groaned. 'I knew there was a catch to this smart lunch. I've done my part, I'm out of here, on my way home . . .'

'Only you know what the killer looks like,' he reminded her.

She thought about that. 'Okay, so I'll help. But remember, I'm a working woman and a mother. I live in LA. I can't just take off and play detective.'

'We'll employ a private eye.'

He was holding her arm as they walked from the restaurant. His strong hand beneath her elbow made her feel small and cherished instead of the tall, klutzy female she really was. A limo pulled into the kerb. 'Where are we going?' she asked, suddenly suspicious.

'Bill is taking you to the airport. I'm afraid I have to get back to the office. Order up that PI.'

He was laughing at her now, and she said sternly, 'Don't forget, this is serious.'

'I won't forget. And I need your address and phone number. To report progress.'

She pulled a cheap spiral-bound notepad from the tangle in her bag and wrote on it. 'There.' She tore the page off and handed it to him. 'That's me.'

'Melba Eloise Merrydew,' he said. He looked at her and grinned. 'Honey,' he said, 'you are straight out of Fitzgerald. They should have called you Zelda.'

'Huh, Zelda indeed,' she sniffed.

'I'll be in touch, Zelda,' he said, closing the car door.

She turned to look as the limo pulled away. He was still laughing.

'Zelda,' she snorted, snuggling down into the soft leather seat as she was wafted off to Kennedy Airport. But there was a pleased smile on her face. And at least he hadn't called her Scarlett.

Chapter Nineteen

Mel said to Detective Camelia, 'Ed hired that private investigator. The PI checked with the Charleston police and the hospital. The police accident report said I'd skidded into a tree that had then toppled onto the truck, completely wrecking it. The hospital report confirmed that I'd suffered a hairline fracture to the skull, and severe concussion that had caused memory difficulties and confusion. Plus a cracked cheekbone. So far, I had checked out.

'But then the PI went over the beach house with a special laser that caused "invisible" or "hidden" traces of blood – he said that was the residue left when blood has been cleaned up – to show up as fluorescent white marks. It showed bloodstains on the rug in the library. There were more leading out to the garage.

'Ed knew then that I was speaking the truth about the dead man. And he also found that there was money missing from the wall safe.

'The PI deduced that it was a simple robbery gone wrong – one robber shot the other and took off with all the money, and that there was no murder conspiracy against Ed. Ed wouldn't tell the cops about it because he didn't want to involve me. He told me he was worried because I could identify the killer. He thought it was *me* who might be in danger, not him.'

Despite his better judgement, Camelia thought she was speaking the truth.

'Now will you let me see Ed?' she begged.

Chapter Twenty

Mel was perched on the edge of the chair by Ed's bed. Camelia had given her ten minutes with him, that's all. *Ten minutes for the rest of his life.* She was recalling what happened after the PI had completed his investigation. Private stuff she hadn't told Detective Camelia. About Ed – and her. About the next time she had seen him. It seemed light years away now, with Ed dying in a hospital bed right in front of her eyes, and the end so near. But then it had seemed like just the beginning . . .

She and Harriet were sitting on the front porch of her tiny Santa Monica cottage, drinking Miller Lite from icy bottles, relaxing after a tough couple of days. They had just gotten home and were still in their work 'uniforms' – black shorts, sweaty white T-shirts, crumpled black socks and work boots. A brand-new forty-eight-foot silver truck with 'Moving On' in lipstick-red script on its sides had replaced the crashed one and was parked across the street.

Mel loved that truck like her own baby – well, not quite, but she knew what she meant. It was the product of her own brains and body and hard labor. And of the insurance company who had reluctantly forked over the money after she had wrecked the first one. 'Isn't that just the greatest truck, Harriet, honey.' Mel eyed it with a pleased smile.

Today, using that truck, they had moved an eccentric old woman from one expensive condo to another on the same block. The woman had complained all the while about the cost and why she needed such a big van and so many crew, she was sure she could have gotten everything cheaper elsewhere. Nerves frazzled, they had done their job and left her, still grumbling, with her bed made up, fresh towels and soap in the bathroom, her refrigerator stocked, coffee brewing, and flowers in a vase on the hall table. Their signature.

'The old bitch never even said thanks,' Harriet sighed wearily. 'Oh, 'scuse me, Riley, I forgot you were there.'

Mel's seven-year-old daughter, Riley, laughed, a hearty, rollicking sound that infected those around her with laughter. She was lying in the hammock strung between two beams. Lola, a feisty little tan-and-white terrier-mutt, lay on her chest, eyes blissfully closed as she swung gently. 'S' okay. I've heard worse,' she replied calmly.

'No, you have not.' Mel was indignant. 'There is no cursing in this house.'

'Only when you think I'm not listening.' Riley grinned at them, showing the double empty space where her front teeth used to be. 'Visitors,' she added, staring at the black BMW that had just pulled into the parking spot in front of the house.

'I'm not expecting anyone.' Mel propped her feet on the porch rail, fanning herself with one hand. She took another swig of the cold beer. The Santa Ana winds were blowing in from the desert and it was hot as hell, even at seven-thirty at night.

'It's probably the old bitch, come back to complain some more.' Riley giggled.

Lola leaped off her chest and onto the front steps. The terrier stared, tense as a trigger, at the man emerging from the BMW.

'Some guard dog.' Ed Vincent was standing on the sidewalk, hands shoved in his pockets. 'How're y'doin', Zelda?'

'*Zelda?*' Harriet's eyes met Melba's in a question. 'Who's he talking about?'

'Oh, oh my gosh.' Mel thrust the Miller Lite bottle hastily behind her chair and leaped to her feet. She tugged down her black shorts and tried vainly to smooth the sweaty T-shirt.

Ed had to smile at her astonished look. He knew that whatever she was feeling it would show in her eyes, and whatever she wanted to say, she would come straight out with it. There was no guile about Zelda Merrydew. Even if she did hide beer bottles behind her chair. 'Love the new truck,' he said, smiling as he imagined Mel behind the wheel. It was quite a picture.

'What are you doing here?' she demanded.

'I just happened to be in the area. Thought I'd stop by, take my partner in crime out to dinner, if she would let me.'

'*Wow,*' Riley clambered out of the hammock, inspecting him closely. 'A *date*, Mom.' Mel threw her a withering look and she giggled.

'What does he mean, *partner in crime?*' Harriet asked in a loud whisper.

'Melba is my "detective" partner.' Ed bent to pat the dog, who promptly nipped his hand. He pulled it back fast.

'Don't mind Lola, it's just her way of saying hello,' Riley gave him her gappy smile. 'Lola never draws blood. Not unless she really hates you.'

'That darn dog is just plain uncivilized,' Harriet said. 'And Mel, your mother would be ashamed of you. Where are your manners? Aren't you going to ask your visitor in?'

'Oh ... yes, of course.' Mel was suddenly nervous. 'Riley, grab the dog. Won't you please come in, Mr Vincent? This is Harriet Simons, my friend and partner. And my daughter Riley.'

'Are you going to have dinner with him, Mom?' Riley demanded. 'He asked you a question and you always told me I should answer when I'm asked, and so should you.'

'Oh, oh ...' Mel threw Ed an embarrassed smile. 'Okay.

Yes. I guess so. Thank you. I mean ... well, I guess I have to change ...'

'That would be a good idea, Mom,' Riley said drily. 'Now,' she said, taking charge, 'would you like a cold drink, Mr Vincent? A Diet Coke, or lemonade?'

Mel hurried to take a quick shower, leaving him with Riley and Harriet. He looked around, pleased. Mel's home was a mixed bag of pretty antiques, probably from that antebellum Merrydew plantation house, and scruffy overstuffed pieces. An ancient baby grand was squashed into a corner, and the sea breeze wafted the gauzy cream curtains at the open windows.

Bunches of mixed flowers in jolly yellows and oranges wilted in pottery jugs; there was an unfinished sandwich on a plate on the window-seat, and Riley's schoolbooks were spread out on the old pine table in the cheery blue and white kitchen. The hardwood floors bore many scratches, and dust motes floated in a beam of sunlight. It looked comfortable, lived-in. It was exactly right, he thought, satisfied. *Exactly Zelda.*

The dust got in his nose and he sneezed, accepting a lemonade from Riley, who proceeded to question him closely about where he lived and what he was doing in LA.

'A proud mama could not have interrogated you better,' Harriet told him afterwards, with a grin.

Ed hauled himself out of the big sofa as Mel appeared, wearing what looked to him like a dress made out of black elastic bandages stitched together. It fit closer than any glove. It was low-cut, short, tight. Stunning.

'It's the latest thing,' Mel explained, catching his look. She hiked up the neckline, tugged down the skirt. 'Tight as a corset, but it pulls a girl in and pushes her out in all the right places. And I guess I have to suffer for beauty, or whatever I can catch of it, fleeting as it is.'

'You mean when you take it off all that's left is a shapeless sausage?'

He was laughing at her and she grinned back at him.

'Some days that description fits. However, this dress is to your advantage. Because of it I'm what's known as a cheap date. I can't possibly eat more than a hint of soup, a touch of salad ...'

'Or else the dress bursts and all you're left with is that sausage,' Riley finished for her, with that great rollicking laugh that Ed thought must come from the gut. 'Don't you think Mom looks like a tart?' she added *sotto voce* to Harriet, but loud enough to be heard by all.

'Thanks, child, for your vote of confidence.' Mel dropped a kiss on her daughter's copper curls as she said goodbye.

Chapter Twenty-one

'So, where are we going?' she asked, settling into the spacious front seat of the parked BMW.

Ed shrugged. 'LA's your town, not mine. Where would you like to go?'

Her eyes slid sideways and she looked at him, considering what kind of place might please him. He looked such a dude, she thought, all LA-casual in a gray cashmere sweater, chinos and loafers. On an impulse, she decided to take him to Serenata, a funky little Mexican-style place where she was a regular, along with other young wannabees, writers and actors as well as just locals. It was low-key and busy and they served a terrible conconction they called a wine Margarita, of which she was secretly fond.

She ordered two and smiled at him across the table. 'You'll like it,' she assured him when he raised his eyebrows. 'Besides, they don't sell the hard stuff.'

He laughed. 'Then I guess I'd better like it. And since I don't know my way around a Mexican menu, maybe you'd better order the food as well.' Her wide, slightly lopsided smile reminded him instantly of Riley. Like mother, like daughter . . . he thought.

'It's nice, being here with you,' he told her.

'On my terms, this time,' she said. Then, remembering the Four Seasons and the ladies-who-lunch and the chauffered limo, she added, 'I hate to tell you, but this is reality, honey.'

He nodded. 'I know, I've been there.'

'You have?' She was astonished. 'I thought you were the heir to a fortune, rich kid makes good and all that, empowering the family's old millions and turning them into billions with your marketing genius.'

He grinned modestly. 'It wasn't quite like that.'

'No? Then tell me what it *was* like.'

'You first,' he said.

So she told him how she was Melba Eloise Merrydew of Merrydew Oaks, an old Georgia plantation house, with a mother who thought she was a modern-day Scarlett and a hard-drinking father who definitely was not Rhett.

'That lasted all of five years,' she informed Ed. 'By then Daddy had lost all the family money, so Mommy took charge. She hocked the plantation, put Daddy into rehab and moved us into a condo in Atlanta. She put me in a private school she couldn't afford, and, still acting the Southern lady, got herself a job as a saleslady in Brown Jordans. Actually, she did quite well there. Unlike me, she always did have style. She ended up running the designer department. Quite a feather in her cap, she called it.

'Anyhow, somehow I got through school, worked as a waitress to pay my way through college. Dad never came home – I mean, he quit rehab and just disappeared. We never heard from him again until we were notified by the police that he had died in a car wreck, out in Montana somewhere.

'Mom couldn't imagine what that old Southern gent was doing up in the wilds of Montana, but she wasn't surprised to hear that there were two causes of the accident. One was his alcohol level – the other was the moose he hit.'

She took a sip of the wine Margarita and made a wry little face. 'I can't imagine why I like this,' she complained.

'Nor can I,' he agreed, taking a sip. 'So what happened to your mother?'

'Oh, she's living in comfort, if not exactly splendor, in a retirement condo in Chapel Hill, North Carolina. Playing bridge – she's a killer at bridge – and having a wild social life. And though she's never cooked in her life, she's always e-mailing me old Southern recipes. And *I* live on power bars and Diet Coke! She's still playing the Southern belle, though I guess it's a bit tougher being a Southern belle in a Chapel Hill North Carolina condo than it was at Merrydew Oaks.'

She laughed, still thinking about her mother, and Ed said, 'She's quite a character.'

'She is, and I love her. And now it's your turn, Mr Vincent.'

'Mmm,' he turned his attention to the nachos and salsa, 'maybe later. First, I want you to look at this.'

Mel took the letter he handed her, scanning it quickly. It was the report from the PI, saying that the laser had detected traces of bloodstains that had been cleaned up.

'So now you believe me,' Mel said triumphantly, glad that she hadn't been dreaming after all. Though come to think of it, it might have been better for Ed if she had.

'I believed you before. This is evidence, though we still don't know what happened to the body.'

'What do we do now?'

She was looking expectantly at him, as though he was sure to have all the answers. He hated to disillusion her. 'You are the one who can identify the killer. I think you might be in danger.'

Mel gulped the Margarita. '*Me?* What about *you?* He missed you once, he's sure to be around for another go. Anyhow, who *is* he?' She glanced suspiciously at Ed from under her lashes. He hadn't yet told her about his past, and now she wondered. 'Tell me *why* someone wants you dead.'

'They don't. The PI believes it was just a robbery gone

wrong. One robber killed the other and took off with the money. There's a hundred thousand missing from the safe.'

'*A hundred thousand!*' Her eyes bugged and he laughed.

'When you've been as poor as I was, you kinda like to have a bit of chump change around. Just in case.'

'Chump change. Huh. The rest of us should be so lucky.'

'It wasn't all luck,' he reminded her.

'I know, I know, hard work and all that. I believe you, thousands wouldn't. Not when you start as the heir to millions.'

'About those millions . . .'

'Yes?'

'We'll talk about it later,' he said, tucking into a plate of beans and rice with guacamole, chicken tacos and a green sauce that almost blew his head off. He gasped, agonized. 'You don't need a gun, this is a killer.'

She ignored the food. 'But someone wants to kill you. I heard him say so, on the phone.'

'You're dreamin,' honey,' he grinned. 'What we do know is that the robber was an expert. Or at least, he was certainly expert at getting rid of the body and cleaning up the place. Even the safe had been re-locked, as well as the front door. The flooding obliterated any tire tracks or footprints. So, as they say, Zelda honey, that is that. Now, why don't you enjoy some of this killer food?'

'There is nothing,' she said, picking at her tamale, 'so foolish as a man. Especially a rich man. And you still haven't told me that story.'

'I will,' he promised. 'Later.'

'I'll drive,' she said when they left the restaurant. 'I've never driven a BMW, and besides, I want to take you somewhere special.'

He climbed into the passenger seat and she streaked off, heading west down Pico to Santa Monica, then north on Pacific

Coast Highway, driving alongside the ocean, through Malibu until she finally made a sweeping U-turn and parked on a rough verge on the ocean side of the highway. She pressed a button and the windows slid down. A mere sliver of moon failed to cast any light on the dark waters, but the soft slur of waves on the shore wafted gently into the car, along with the cooler night air.

'Peace,' she sighed, lying her head back against the cool black leather. She turned her head slightly and her eyes met Ed's.

'Now, tell me about your childhood,' she said quietly.

Chapter Twenty-two

It was not easy for Ed to talk about his family. And in fact, he had done so only once before. And that was to another woman.

Ed was the youngest of a brood of six, born in the wooded upslopes of Tennessee's Great Smoky Mountains, in a two-room shack with a corrugated tin roof, and plank walls patched with tarpaper on the outside and wallpapered with newspapers on the inside.

For the first fourteen years of his life, Ed never went more than fifteen miles from his homestead. His daddy's ancient Dodge pickup barely made the trip into Hainsville of a Saturday, loaded with the root vegetables he grew for market. The locals said his pa could grow anything on his small but fertile five acres, but still and all, he barely made enough to keep a roof over their heads and feed his hungry family, who craved more meat than potatoes.

Trout, small-mouth bass, and rock-bass from the streams were not enough to stave the eternal hunger of six growing kids, who endured squash and beans only because they had no choice, and who were sent out to scavenge the woods for the plentiful wild mushrooms, seasonal berries and nuts to add to the family's larder.

Like his three brothers and two sisters, Ed was a skinny kid, always hungry, always on the alert, and handy with a rifle, scouting for quail and squirrel or woodcock, anything to bring variety to the eternal stewpot his mother had constantly on the stove.

Ellin was a once handsome woman, so thin her skeleton showed through her translucent flesh, every bone apparent, the sinews knotted like ropes in her work-weary body. Her meager breasts had nourished six children in quick succession; her callused hands had soothed their fevered heads when they were sick. She had sung them to sleep in a tired soprano, and smiled as she kissed them goodnight, promising that one day, soon perhaps, things would be better.

'Then I'll buy you a new dress, Ma,' young Ed had promised.

And no doubt I would have also promised her a diamond ring, Ed said to Mel, *had I known about diamonds then. Which, being only an ignorant young hillbilly, I did not.*

All six kids looked like their ma: narrow, hard-boned faces, deep-set blue eyes sunken beneath strong black brows, ears set flat against the head, strong white teeth that flourished without the aid of a dentist. Thanks, their daddy told them, to their diet of vegetables and pulses, and to their little milk-cow and the few scrawny chickens that provided tiny eggs. Steak was an unknown, boiled fowl an occasion to be savored and remembered, and hog killin' a wondrous annual feast of pork and cracklin'.

All the kids had their ma's luxuriant black hair, straight as a plumb line and thick as hay in a summer meadow, and they all spoke with a Tennessee Mountain accent, so dense it sounded like a foreign language.

They ran barefoot from spring to autumn, by which time their feet were Indian-hard, their skin berry-brown from the sun, hair streaked a dozen shades lighter. In September, they filed reluctantly to school again, wearing roughly cobbled shoes that rubbed the skin off their heels. Reluctantly, that is, except for Ed and his eldest brother, Mitchell, who, for entirely different reasons, couldn't wait to get there.

'My two intellectuals,' Ma called them, smiling as they pored over geography books and history, and math. Ed didn't know what an intellectual was, and neither did Mitch, but each had his own urge to learn. Both wanted something more than this rough, deprived existence.

'Not that I knew then I was deprived,' Ed said to Zelda. 'When you're a kid you don't. It's all there is. If you don't know about any other way of life, how can you miss it? Yet somehow, somewhere, I believed there was a better life. And it wasn't a tidy little three-bedroom house with indoor plumbing and a picket fence in Hainsville I longed for. It was a far bigger dream; a wider world.

'I was already in love with the idea of travel and adventure. I didn't know how, but one day I would spring like a bird from the cage of those forested green foothills and fly around the world on a jet plane. I would dine in Paris and saunter through the London parks, maybe even shake hands with royalty.' Ed smiled. 'Nothing seems impossible when you're just twelve years old.'

Ed's brother Mitch was different. Narrower eyes half hidden behind prominent cheekbones gave his face an almost Cherokee cast. Of course those eyes were his mother's family blue, but the rest of him was closer to his father. Huskier, with muscular shoulders, a tapering back, strong neck and jutting jaw. He was the odd man out in a sapling-growth family, a full-grown tree before he was even fifteen. Sure, he had that same mark of deprivation, the pinched look of almost-hunger, the wariness about the eyes, the quickness with the rifle. But it was different with Mitch.

Privately, his ma believed she had a changeling on her hands. Though she told herself she loved him equally with the others, she didn't understand Mitch. There was a streak of cruelty in him. He enjoyed killing animals even if they were not for the pot. He liked tormenting his brothers, using his superior weight and strength to wrestle them, screaming, to the ground. And he teased his sisters to the point of tears. He beat up other kids in school and in church, scrapping in the woods after the sermon and shaming his family. He'd even been caught by the Deputy, brewing moonshine in the forest, reeling about, drunk as a lord.

'Mitch didn't care what anyone thought,' Ed said to Zelda. 'He was a bully who swaggered his way through life. Whatever was bad, he seemed to find it. To our poor mother, it seemed he even sought it out. And no matter how hard Dad whupped him, it didn't daunt him.

'At seventeen, Mitch towered over our daddy. He could have killed him easily, with just one blow of that powerful arm, one crazed shot from the rifle. And he was an expert marksman. Living with Mitch was like living on the edge of a volcano. You never knew when it might erupt.

'But Dad was so proud of the fact that he owned his five acres and that he owed nobody. The four hundred dollars needed to purchase that strip of land had taken him twenty long years to accumulate.'

'Mitch wants too much,' his daddy said to Ed one day when they were riding into Hainsville in the rusting old white pickup, taking the produce to Saturday market. 'Mitch ain't content to be no scrabble-farmer, even though we own our own piece and ain't share-croppers no more.'

'Hard work is the only answer, son,' he told Ed as they descended through the wispy morning fog, splashing through sparkling streams and over polished rocks. Through meadows waist-high with wildflowers, where orange and black butterflies unfurled their wings as the early sun warmed them. Down the rutted lane onto the narrow blacktop road that led into the local town, fifteen miles away.

'But mark my words, Mitch ain't one for hard work. He wants it all and he wants it now. No matter what it takes to get it.'

'And that's the way it was, growing up.' Ed's tone was deliberately light, but Mel heard the undertone of despair.

She said in a choked voice, 'I'm sorry.'

He shrugged. 'No need to be. I wasn't the only kid to grow up poor.'

'But you fought your way out of that poverty.'

'Not for a long time after that.' He paused. 'A long, long time,' he said softly, and there was such a note of sadness in his voice that Mel was afraid to ask what he meant, so instead she leaned over and kissed him. A sweet nothing of a kiss, light and airy.

While he was still dazed, she started up the car and breezed slowly back down PCH, back home to Santa Monica.

'I'm returning to New York tomorrow morning, early,' Ed said reluctantly. His eyes linked with hers.

She nodded. 'And I have to move Mr and Mrs Barton Forks from Encino to Sherman Oaks. My, how full life is.' She dropped another kiss, on his cheek this time. 'Honey,' she said with a wicked grin, 'I surely enjoy playing detectives with you.' Then she was out of the car, slamming the door, waving goodbye.

Ed watched her take the front steps in a giant leap, then she turned and waved to him from the door. He was still laughing as he drove away.

They met many times after that – he just couldn't keep away from Santa Monica. He chartered a small jet, and every Friday evening he would be there. They went to dinner; took Riley to the Lakers games; and to the Kings, freezing in the ice-hockey stadium, eating hot dogs and laughing. They *always* seemed to be laughing. And Riley held onto Ed's hand as though she never wanted to let him go. Neither of them wanted to let him go ... even Lola was coming round, and didn't bite him anymore. 'And I have the scars to prove it,' Ed had said, laughing. Mel had taken him to all her favorite places; he had met her friends, though she had never met any of his.

'Don't you have any friends?' she had asked.

'Not too many,' he'd admitted. 'I'm a cautious man.'

'I wonder why?' she'd said, puzzled, and he had looked back at her with that strange expression in his blue eyes, sort of faraway, a remembered pain ... she didn't quite know what he was thinking.

'Maybe some day I'll tell you,' was all he had said. And then he had changed the subject and whisked her and Harriet and Riley off to the Bel Air Hotel for a sumptuous Sunday brunch, outdoors in the pretty courtyard. But he never talked about his past again, after that night.

Chapter Twenty-three

Mel was in the hospital, sitting next to him, watching over him.

Ed could sense that she was there, he could smell her sweet, fresh scent — thank God he still had one of his senses still functioning . . . But he needed to touch her, to hold her . . . With a mighty effort he reached out for her.

Mel watched as his hand crept, agonizingly slowly, across the tight white hospital sheet toward her. She took it in both hers, bent her head and kissed it. *He knew she was here . . . Ed knew.*

Standing in the doorway, Art Jacobs knew he was looking at a miracle.

'She can stay,' he told the nurse. 'In fact, she can stay as long as she likes.'

You're here, Ed thought, you've finally found me. Please, don't ever take your hand away from mine. As long as you're holding me I'll know I'm still in the land of the living. I can feel your blood pulsing; maybe it'll inspire mine to get to work again, pump this old heart . . . which always pumps twice as fast when you're around anyway. Right from that moment I first saw you . . . That's sentimental, I know. But if a man can't get sentimental on his deathbed, then when can he? I wish you would kiss me again, I just want to feel those sweet, chapped lips on mine, I want to hold you, Zelda, make love to you . . .

I remember the first time. I had invited you to New York for the weekend. I went to meet you at the airport. I was waiting for you at the gate and you strode out of that corridor, gazing round, searching for me. I could tell from the expression in your eyes you were afraid I hadn't shown ... that I'd left you in the lurch. When you saw me, it was as though someone had lit a candle in your eyes. You just glowed. I thought you looked wonderful ... a golden girl. Except your nose was red.

'Don't kiss me or you'll catch my cold,' you warned, turning your face away. As if I hadn't gotten you to come to New York with the express purpose of kissing you. Boy, you can be a hard woman when you choose ...

So I held your hand instead, all the way to Manhattan in the limo. You were so impressed by Vincent Towers Fifth you insisted on walking all the way around it. You inspected the lobby from corner to corner, saying, 'Wow, this place must have cost a fortune. And you built it all by yourself.'

I was modest. 'Well, not quite ...' I replied.

You were even more impressed when we got into the elevator and I pressed the P for Penthouse button. You were all wide-eyed with wonder ... Sometimes you are so like Riley, I don't know which is the kid, you or her ...

When we got there, you ran to the floor-to-ceiling windows and looked out at the view, all Manhattan spread in front of you ... 'Central Park,' you said, awed, and I wanted so badly to throw my arms round you and hug you. But I didn't want you to think I had brought you all the way to New York just to seduce you ... though of course, I had. Except there was more to it than just that. I knew it, even then ...

He felt her moving away from him. *Oh, baby, don't take your hand away ... please don't go ... oh, Zel, I need you, now more than ever ... I'm scared of leaving you, Zel, I don't want to die ...'*

He could smell her familiar scent as she leaned over him, felt the softness of her lips on his and the cool wetness of her tears. 'I'm here, honey,' he heard her whisper. 'I'm never leaving you. Detective Camelia would have to drag me away. Except I'm bigger than he is.'

She giggled through her tears, that intoxicating giggle that erupted at all their most serious moments, breaking him up . . . Had he been able to, he would have heaved a sigh of pure happiness, but the machine was doing his breathing for him . . . *Damn these machines . . . he had to get out of here . . .*

She was saying something. He strained his ears to catch her words, spoken softly, almost as if she were talking to herself . . . remembering . . .

'I walked into that penthouse,' Mel said, 'expecting – I don't know what – the Taj Mahal, the Sultan's palace. I mean, there was this huge space, and just these few old sticks of furniture. A table, a couple of chairs, an old rug and a sofa that looked as though it came direct from the thrift. I guess my jaw must have dropped because you were laughing.

'I said, "I didn't know you were just moving in."

'"Actually, I've lived here for five years," you said. "This is it."

'"Mmmm, definitely not the nesting type," I said. I was laughing, too, as I inspected your bedroom. It was just what I'd expected by now. A bed, a chair, a lamp. My, but you were basic. Except for the hi-fi equipment. I'd never seen anything like that. "The latest and the best," you told me proudly, putting on a CD of Eric Clapton singing *The Way You Are Tonight*. I'll never forget it . . . it became our song . . .

'I walked to the windows. The lights sparkled down Fifth Avenue and it was snowing. You came and stood beside me . . . not touching, but it felt as though you were, with those little electric vibrations zinging between us like morse code. I was so aware of you I swear my hair stood on end. I had never felt anything like it before . . . never . . .'

Mel looked sadly at Ed, so still, so silent, in the white

hospital bed, kept alive by machines. 'I hope you remember too, honey,' she said wistfully.

'Oh, I hope you remember, my love . . .'

I remember. I was looking at you, storing you in my mind for just such a time as this, when I couldn't see you. I guess the right description for you would be 'gamine,' but that implies someone smaller, and you were my Valkyrie. I remember thinking I'd never be able to run my hands through your hair, it was barely a couple of inches long except for the jagged golden bangs falling into your eyes. And I remember those huge, urgent copper-brown eyes that I melted into when they met mine. Did I ever tell you I liked that you didn't wear mascara? I loved those long, curling golden lashes, they made you look so innocent, like a fawn. And I liked your nose, too. Straight, rather long — kind of arrogant if you want the truth, but it went with the bone structure. And your mouth, oh, boy, your mouth was special, it really got to me, even if your lips were chapped. Full and kind of pouty. 'Vulnerable' was the word that came to mind.

'Let's go out,' you said, just as I was about to take you in my arms . . . 'I want to walk down Fifth Avenue in the snow.' So I took my California alien out walking in the blizzard . . .

'Heaven,' Mel remembered, smiling. 'It was sheer heaven. The snow covered our hair and got stuck on your beard. The horses outside the Plaza had on little bonnets and blankets, and there was even the smell of chestnuts roasting. It's magic, I said to you, and you laughed and said only you could think so; just take a look at the traffic. It was crawling along, bumper-to-bumper. We could see the drivers' angry faces and feel their frustration, but we were outside of it. Get out and walk in the snow like us, I yelled at them, laughing.

We were in our own magic circle. Even the little diner on East 49th with the windows steamed and the smell of bacon and burgers and hot coffee was wonderful. The snow melted off our hair as we shared a toasted ham and Swiss on rye, and drank coffee so hot it burned our throats.'

I'd meant to take you out to dinner someplace fancy, woo you with fine food, champagne, roses. Impress you with my savoir faire and the fact that the maitre d' knew me. Hah, I didn't even get a chance ... and you didn't care, you loved walking in the snow, you practically danced along on those wondrously silly high heels. And you insisted on eating at the diner ...

'We window-shopped all the way back up Fifth Avenue,' Mel said, laughing. 'Saks, Gucci, Bergdorf, with me planning what I would buy when Moving On finally made some money. And you telling me you would buy me anything I wanted ... until I had to remind you that my Southern mama would definitely not approve. Well, she certainly would not have approved of what happened next ...'

We melted in the elevator, he thought, only this time into each other's arms. We couldn't even wait until we got to the top. When I stopped kissing you for a second, you said, what if somebody else gets in? Let them, I said. Like Rhett, I don't give a damn ... and then you were giggling so hard, I couldn't get my mouth over yours again ...

'We were still kissing when the elevator doors opened,' Mel remembered. 'Somehow we managed to get out of there without removing our mouths from each other's. God, we were so hot for each other, we could have melted that entire blizzard ... You unfastened my coat, and I slid my arms out of the sleeves, letting it fall where it may. Then I was unbuttoning your coat. "Naked," I said triumphantly, throwing it to the ground and laughing. "Not yet," you said. Then you put *The Way You Are*

Tonight on again ... You were setting me up with sweet music, soft lights ...

You said, 'I should offer you a glass of champagne, give you the roses.'

'Forget it,' I murmured. Then my eyes popped. 'What roses?' I asked, astonished.

'You took my hand and walked me to the bedroom. And there were roses everywhere. White roses, cream roses, pale pink, peach, apricot ... in the couple of hours we had been out, that bedroom had been transformed into a veritable bower. "I just thought it looked a bit sparse," you said apologetically. *And I knew then may I loved you ...'*

I knew I loved you, Ed remembered, *when I saw that look in your eyes when you looked at the roses. Awe and wonder and astonishment, and then that melting again ... 'How did you do it?' you asked, shaking your head in amazement. I just shrugged. You're in New York now, baby, I said, grinning like a fool.*

'And you are its King,' you cried, throwing your arms around me. Which, you being as tall as I am in those heels, you could do very easily. In fact, I'm not sure whether you wafted me off my feet or whether it was the other way round ... We were so hot for each other, we just tore off our clothes, stepped out of them. We stood looking at each other. You were exactly as I had known you would be: the ribcage curving into a narrow waist, the flare of the hips and the smooth line of your flanks, the deliciously soft golden mound, the long, tapering legs. And those high, round breasts that I knew would feel like satin under my hands ...

Mel was smiling. 'I looked you up and down. Down and up again. You were fit, muscular, and ready for me ... Oh, boy, were you *ready* for me ... I was unable to tear my eyes away. I couldn't help it, I had to laugh. Why do I always manage to laugh at the wrong moments, just when it should have been so ... so intense ... so sexy ... *"And they say size doesn't matter,"* I remember saying, amazed.'

Ed remembered it too. He remembered his great shout of laughter as he snatched her to him and fell backwards onto the bed, helpless with laughter. He could taste her mouth now, sweet and juicy as strawberry jam.

Your arms were twined around my neck, pressing my face to yours. 'More please,' you murmured when I came up for air. And I laughed again as I obliged.

'I could feel you, pressing between my thighs, hard as a baseball bat, and hot. I wanted you, Ed. Oh, I wanted you as I had never wanted anyone before. I wanted you to devour me, to enfold me, to enter and claim me as your own. I wanted everything. I could feel your heat sleeking deep inside me, sending unstoppable shivers through my entire body. Your kisses were soft as butterfly wings on my face, so sweet, so loving, while you rocketed me to heaven.'

We were one, Zelda, Ed remembered. And surprisingly, his body remembered too, recalling the way she had felt, the scent of her, her heat and passion ... 'You threw back your head at the final moment, 'Oh, God,' you gasped, and then your cry matched my own.*

Mel remembered opening her eyes; she had needed to see him ... 'I looked at your face, still contorted with passion,' she whispered, 'and I was awed that all that emotion was for me ... for us. Your body was heavy on mine, but I never wanted to move. We were as slick with sweat as a pair of sumo wrestlers. I remember even now the smell of the roses and sex, the magical aroma of our love. I'll never forget it, Ed, never ...'

Her tears ran onto his face as she kissed him, and the reality of the hospital bed took over. For a moment, she had been transported back in time, and that time had seemed their reality. 'Not this,' she thought, agonized. 'Not Ed lying here, hooked up to a machine that keeps him breathing ...'

'You will *not* die,' she said, gripping his hand urgently. 'I will not let you. Do you hear me, Ed Vincent, you great oaf?'

I hear you, he thought with an inner smile. *And if anybody can keep me alive it's you, baby. Only you. Though I'm trying my darndest ... It's win or lose time ...*

'I wanted to tell you, back then, that I loved you,' Mel said aloud. 'But I didn't dare. I mean, you can't just go saying that to a man, even one who's just taken you to heaven and back. He might think you were looking for a commitment.'

And I was looking at you. Your eyes were closed and I was wondering what you were thinking ... hoping you would say I love you, because I dared not, in case I scared you away ... I mean, you were so ditzy I didn't know how you felt. Whether I was just a one-night stand or what. Then you opened your eyes and said, 'You've got to be careful what you do with that thing. It could get you into a lot of trouble ...'

'I shouldn't have been joking,' Mel said. 'I know it now, but I was scared of that much emotion. And then your great bellow of laughter almost crushed my chest, and I was laughing along with you, helpless. And I felt you grow hard again.'

I've never laughed when I made love before, Ed remembered saying to her, I just want to eat you up.

'Now don't go telling me about all the others,' you said in that firm no-nonsense voice. 'I want to believe I'm the only one.'

You are the only one, I told you. And I meant it, Zelda, I meant it. You will always be my only one. I was kissing your mouth again by then.

'Great,' you said. 'So are you. My only one.'

A giggle erupted from your throat and I kissed it away. Then we're even, I said. Life starts from this day. This moment. I raised myself up on my arms. Our eyes locked. I was inside you again, and your body reacted. You swore it had nothing to do with you, nothing to do with your head at all. Your body wanted me, and it was not going to say no.

'I knew you would always be ready to oblige a lady,' you murmured, running your hands across my naked butt, making me laugh again, even as I moved deep inside you.

Oh, Zelda, Zelda, it was a night that should never have ended . . .

'It was our beginning,' Mel said sadly. 'Who would have dreamed that this could happen? But they can't take you away from me. I'll find those bastards and I'll kill them. I swear, Ed, that if you die, I'll kill them with my own hands.'

Another reason not to die, Ed thought with a sigh . . . he couldn't let her become a murderer, just because of him . . . Don't be crazy . . . he wanted to say, but telling Zelda not to be crazy was like telling a canary not to sing.

Standing in the doorway, Detective Camelia heard Mel's final words, and he knew without any doubt that he had been accusing the wrong woman. Unaware that he was there, he had heard her speak the truth.

She turned and looked at him. She was haggard from lack of sleep, drooping with fatigue, devastated by Ed's fight with death. Camelia's heart lurched.

'How about a cup of coffee,' he said.

Chapter Twenty-four

Camelia sat opposite Mel Merrydew, aka Zelda, in the steamy little deli round the corner from the hospital. Another sleepless night had not enhanced her appearance. Her skin had lost the peachy California glow he had noticed when he first saw her. Now it looked dull, grayish, with shadows big as bruises under her eyes. It hurt him just to look at her.

'You look like hell,' he said bluntly. 'You can't go on like this. You know, not eating, not sleeping. Ask yourself, what good is it doin' him anyways?'

Mel lifted her head from her coffee cup. She stared at him, stunned.

The waiter came over. 'What can I get you guys?' He was brisk, efficient, no time to spare, like all New Yorkers. He looked inquiringly at Mel, but she just shook her head and turned away.

Camelia said, 'The lady will have scrambled eggs, bacon and a toasted sesame bagel. I'll have the lox and cream cheese on the same. And make those bagels well toasted, will ya.'

'I'm not hungry,' Mel protested wearily.

'Oh, yes you are. You've just forgotten about food, is all. Kinda need retraining into the food mode.' Camelia grinned at her, but she did not smile back. 'Look,' he said gently, 'I know what you're thinking. That it's none of my business. But Ed

Vincent has become my business. And right now I need you more than he does.'

Suddenly panicked, Mel pushed back her chair, and grabbed her bag, ready to run. 'I shouldn't have left him.'

'He's not going to die, y'know, just because you're not around. In fact, he may just not die at all. Did you ever consider that fact, Miss Melba?'

'Mel,' she corrected him, automatically. She sank back into the chair, then added, off the cuff, as though he needed to know. 'I always hated my name. Melba Eloise Merrydew. Like a marshmallow Georgia-peach sundae, all whipped cream and froth. And there was I, this great galumphing lanky kid. A long ways from my mother's idea of a genteel Southern belle.' She grinned suddenly. 'I always told her you can't win 'em all, honey.'

She fixed him with a sudden glare, but her bottom lip was trembling. 'And what d'you mean, have I considered he might not die? What the heck d'you think I'm fighting for, every minute I sit there by his bed, holding his hand, talking to him, urging him to fight back, to wake up and look at me?'

'One thing I can tell you is when he does wake up he's in for a hell of a shock when he looks at you. He's gonna say, who the hell is this old broad sitting on my bed ... where's my Georgia peach?'

Mel's laugh rang out, and Camelia grinned at her in relief.

'Do I really look that bad?'

He nodded. 'That bad.'

She sighed as the waiter placed the scrambled eggs in front of her. 'That's what happens when you're not a true beauty. A girl can only fake it so much with lipstick and blusher.' She looked at the eggs, realized she was starving and took a huge forkful. 'So how long have you been married?'

He bit into the bagel piled high with cream cheese and lox. 'Twenty-six years already. Almost your entire lifetime, I'll bet.'

'I'm thirty-two.'

'And I'm forty-six,' he noticed, satisfied that she was enjoying the eggs. He didn't know why he felt pity for her but he did. She was different from the women he usually encountered. For starters, she was dead honest, and in his job that was not a given. Plus she left herself wide open to being hurt, like now, with this guy Ed Vincent. Lord knows what Vincent had been up to for someone to want to take him out this bad, but he'd bet his boots it was something that involved deals gone wrong and a lot of mazoolah. Money and sex were at the root of all evil. He had found that little fact out in twenty-six years of police work.

'You have kids?' She held a strip of crispy bacon in her fingers, nibbling on it. It was the best thing she had tasted in what seemed like weeks.

'Four.' Always the proud father, he told her their names: Gianni, Daria, Julio and Maria. 'A combo of Italian and Puerto Rican,' he added.

'I'll bet you've got photos.' She smiled as he quickly fished in his inside jacket pocket for his wallet.

'This is my eldest, Gianni, we call him Johnny. He's a senior at MIT. Daria works as a production assistant on the *Today* show. Julio – known as Jules – is in his junior year at Rutgers. And this is my baby, Maria. She's sixteen and still wondering what to do with life.'

Mel studied the photos carefully, not just skipping through them the way most people did when you showed off your kids' pictures. 'Pretty good-looking family you've got there. You're right to be proud of them, Detective Camelia.'

'Marco,' he corrected her.

Their eyes met for a long moment. Mel was thinking she didn't understand him, but she instinctively liked him. Camelia was thinking she was way out of his league; he had never known a woman like this before. And she touched him in some deep, troubling way.

'I have a daughter, Riley.' She pulled her wallet out of her handbag and showed him the picture. 'This was taken last year. Now she's missing her two front teeth.' She smiled, recalling Riley's cheeky toothless grin. Oh, God, she hadn't even called her yet ... Harriet must be frantic ...

'She looks like you, though. A pretty girl.'

Mel made a little face. 'Thank you, kind sir, but I don't think pretty was ever in my vocabulary.'

He thought about it for a second or two. 'Then maybe you should add beautiful to your vocabulary, Miss Melba.'

A breathless silence hung between them. Then she said, smiling, 'Why, Detective Camelia, I do believe you're flirting with me.'

He grinned, amazed to find he was enjoying himself. 'I make it a practice never to flirt with married women.'

She shook her head. 'I'm not married. Never was. When I knew I was pregnant with Riley, I realized that the guy wasn't good enough to be my kid's father. He would never have stayed around.' She shrugged. 'So I said goodbye to him. Decided to bring my baby up on my own. Take full responsibility. Lots of women do nowadays, you know,' she explained, seeing Marco's shocked expression. 'It's better than chasing after a deadbeat dad.'

He nodded. 'I guess you're right. But I'm just an old-fashioned guy.'

'What's your wife like?' She reached across and took a bite out of his bagel. 'Mmm, that's good.'

'Here, have the other half.' He pushed the plate across to her, signalling the waiter for more coffee. 'Claudia? She's great. Nice, y'know, a good woman.'

Her eyes were mocking him over the rim of her coffee cup. 'Go on, you're crazy about her, aren't you? I'll bet she's gorgeous.'

He shrugged, smiling modestly. 'How else d'ya think I got to have kids that look like that? It surely wasn't from the Camelia genes.'

'But they got their brains from you then, as well as your good sense. And your kindness.' She finished his bagel. 'I'll bet the sex is great, too.'

He choked on his coffee and she laughed. 'It's okay, Marco, I'm a grown-up girl, you can tell me.'

'Okay, so it's great. And I swear to God I've never told anyone that before in my whole life.'

'Well, I certainly hope you told Claudia.'

She was impossible, he thought, laughing.

Mel contemplated the bagel crumbs on her plate. 'It was great with Ed, too,' she said quietly. 'I didn't know it could be like that ... you know, so ... so filled with love. I really love him, Marco.'

'I know. Believe me, I know. No married-in-church wife could have sat such a vigil. And I apologize for ever believing you might be involved.'

He did not tell her that he had overheard the final part of her whispered words to her mortally wounded lover. He felt guilty even thinking about it. But because of it, he knew her as he never could have. Knew who she was. And that made a world of difference.

'I said I needed your help.'

'I'll do anything, you know that.' She took out a tawny-color lipstick and applied it without the benefit of a mirror.

'That's quite an art.'

'Years of practice. Not that it'll make much difference, considering I look like hell.'

'I'm sorry I said that.'

She shrugged. 'It's probably true. I haven't looked in a mirror since I got here. Anyhow, you're right: when Ed wakes up I should be looking beautiful. Or at least my best.'

'Just look the way you usually look and he'll be a happy man.'

'Then you think he's going to wake up, Marco? Seriously.'

Her huge brown eyes had that urgent look again; he could

see the fear lurking behind them. 'I'm no doctor, Mel, and I can only tell you this. Any other guy woulda been dead. Four slugs from a Sigma .40 semi at that close range would fell an ox. But he's a strong guy, a fighter. I believe he's got a chance.'

She nodded, lips tightly compressed to stop from crying. 'Thank you for that,' she said softly. She really liked this man. Sure he was tough, but that was his job. Compassion was not, and she knew that must come from his Italian soul. She reached across the table for his hand again. 'Friends?' she asked.

'Friends,' he agreed, meeting her eyes.

Chapter Twenty-five

Camelia finished his coffee. Clearing his throat nervously, he was suddenly all business. 'Ed's PI faxed me the report, said he was sure some incident had taken place at the house. He confirmed what Ed told you about the missing money. Now, a hundred thou is no small change, so somebody out there has to be livin' it up good by now.'

Mel stared blankly at him. 'But who?'

'I was kinda hopin' *you* could tell me that.'

She groaned. 'Are we back to square one again? With me as chief suspect?'

'No. You didn't do it, but I want you to help me find who did. Let's start with the body in the library.'

'Just like an Agatha Christie novel.' This time Camelia looked blank, and she added, 'You know, the mystery writer. Somehow there always seemed to be a body in the library.'

'And the butler always did it.'

They laughed together, and for a moment Mel felt her heart lift. If she could laugh, there was hope . . . hope for Ed . . . *Oh, Ed, Ed, I'll do anything to help you . . . anything . . .*

'The killer, your attacker . . .'

'More like assassin,' she retorted, remembering.

'The killer and your would-be assassin. Now, I know it was dark, it was raining cats and dogs, the wind was howling and you didn't get a good look at him. But you must remember something. Anything at all. Come on, Mel, *think.*'

She slumped back in her chair, eyes closed, and Marco signalled the waiter to refill their coffee cups.

Mel was concentrating on the sensory memories, how she had felt when he touched her, the way he had smelled, sounded . . .

And Marco was thinking how innocent she looked, just a babe herself . . . though 'babe' was hardly the right word. Or was it? With those legs, those lips . . . Her eyes flew open, she was staring into his . . . and oh, my God, those eyes, deep and round now as twin shots of single malt . . . what the hell, he wasn't a poet but he knew what he meant . . .

'I think he was foreign,' Mel said. 'He had a guttural accent. You know, kind of like spies do in James Bond movies. And he's a heavy smoker, I smelled it on his hands. I almost threw up, and that's when he let me go. I stuck my thumbs in his eyes, I felt my nails digging into his flesh. A fat face . . . no not fat exactly, but big, and a big neck. I'm tall, but he was a good bit taller, maybe six four, a really big guy, his hand covered my face from ear to ear . . .'

She sighed as she sat back again. 'That's about it,' she said soberly, taking a sip of the newly hot coffee. 'I really didn't get a good look at him. It was dark in the house, dark outside, dark in the cab . . . although, wait a minute.'

She closed her eyes again, shivering as she relived the moments when she thought her end had come. There had been a flash of light as she aimed the huge truck at that tree, her own headlights bouncing back at her. The gun was still at her head, she could feel its icy coldness even now. The coldness of death.

Marco watched the tears slide down her face. Her eyes were still tight shut and he had to hold himself back from grabbing her there and then, and just holding her tight, telling her it was okay, not to worry, he would take care of her. God, what was he thinking! He was a cop, a professional. He took a gulp of the hot coffee, burning his mouth in the process, welcoming the jolt it gave him that brought him back to his senses.

Mel remembered swiveling her eyes, just as she slammed her foot on the gas, that sideways glimpse of her would-be killer . . .

'He looked like a pit bull,' she said softly, almost whispering as the memory came to her. 'A lowering forehead, sort of bulbous. Narrow eyes, a tight mouth, clean-shaven, a lot of dark hair. And he was wearing a business suit and a tie . . . I remember thinking I didn't know killers wore ties . . .'

She sighed and took another sip of the coffee. 'That's all.'

Camelia nodded. 'It's enough, to start. You'll talk with the photofit artist, tell him what you remember while he constructs an image. And we'll get a language expert to play some tapes for you, try to identify the accent.'

'Okay.' She nodded, eager to help.

'So tell me, Mel, what exactly do you *know* about Ed Vincent?'

Again, her eyes widened and she stared blankly at him. 'Why, I guess just what *you* know. I mean, everybody knows who Ed Vincent is.' Then she had the grace to laugh. 'Except me, I guess. I seemed to be the only one who didn't know he was the New York developer guru, rich and handsome and . . . and oh, so kind. He's a good man, Marco, if that's what you want to know. I can't believe there's a reason someone would want to kill him.'

'And yet someone did. Does, in fact.'

Alarm bells rang in Mel's head; she was already on her feet. *'I've got to get back.'*

'Take it easy, take it easy, no one's gonna get to him in the hospital. There's a uniform outside his door twenty-four hours, and another standing by the elevators. Plus we have surveillance set up outside the hospital.'

She sank back into the chair with a troubled sigh. 'Then what do you mean, what do I know about Ed?'

'Well, for a start, who *is* he?'

She shook her head, puzzled. 'I don't get it.'

'Where does he come from, his family, his life before he was the famous Ed Vincent? I thought for sure you would know.'

'I knew he had been poor. *Really* poor. It's a media myth about him being an heir to a fortune. He told me he'd been brought up in a two-room shack in the Tennessee Mountains. Hainstown, I think, or something like that. He was proud that his father owned his own piece of land. They were farmers. And he had brothers and sisters.'

'Brothers and sisters, huh?' Camelia said, thoughtfully. 'Now, Ed doesn't strike me as the kind of man who would abandon those poor brothers and sisters when he'd made himself a pot of money. What d'you think?'

Mel thought, surprised, that he was right. 'But he never mentioned them by name, never really talked about them, except one. His eldest brother, Mitch. I've no idea where they live, or if he ever saw them.'

'A family fallout,' Camelia said, then added wryly, 'It happens in the best.'

'Yes, but Ed's not like that. I mean, he's not the kind of man to hold a grudge. He's the giving type, he helps strangers, gives to charities. I can't believe he would just ignore his own family, especially knowing how poor they were.'

Camelia said soberly, 'Then I guess it's up to me to find out the answer to that riddle. Hainstown, Tennessee, here I come,' he added with a grin. 'But first I have to find it on the map.'

'Maybe it was Hains*ville*,' she said. 'And you can bet it'll be a mere pin-dot on the map,' she added. Then she realized that Camelia was going to find out about Ed's life, a life she had hoped to share with him, a life that he had kept a secret, even from her. 'I wish I could come with you,' she added wistfully.

'Think you'd be of any help?' Camelia's voice was deliberately casual as he picked up the coffee cup. Dear God, he thought, here she was, the one woman on God's earth who could probably seduce him by just batting those golden eyelashes, or smiling at him with those pouty lips, and she was offering to go on a trip with him.

Visions of a rustic motel room, with pine trees and soaring mountains, of dark black nights with the stars a trillion miles away, of foggy, dewy mornings and a warm tumbled bed pushed their way into his mind. He took a deep breath, downed the coffee and signalled for more.

Mel looked doubtful. 'I can't leave Ed. He might . . .' She couldn't bring herself to say *he might die*, though she knew the odds. Besides, she wasn't going to let him die without her there. *'Ed needs me,'* she said fiercely.

Camelia pulled his wits together, cancelled the coffee order and asked for the check. 'Better put you in touch with the photofit guy and the accent expert, see if we can get tabs on this killer,' he said gruffly. 'I'll go to Hainsville in search of Ed's past, while you do what you can to come up with an ID.' He pushed back his chair, stood, held up his hand. 'Deal?'

'Deal,' she said, smiling as she gave him a high-five.

Chapter Twenty-six

Brotski was on duty again, prowling the gray corridor outside Ed's room, looking, Mel thought, too young to be a cop, with his ginger-spice cowlick and peach-fuzz cheeks. He also looked bored to death, and she guessed this wasn't exactly what he had expected of police work. Still, his presence calmed her fears that the worst might have happened while she was in the deli. Brotski being there meant that he still had a man to protect. Ed was still alive.

'You look like a guy in need of some fresh air and a cup of coffee,' she said, smiling. 'Tell you what, why don't you take time out and I'll guard the fort?'

Brotski's baby-blues narrowed and his jaw firmed right up. 'Sorry, ma'am, but I'm on duty here,' he said stiffly.

'Oh ... right ... I'm sorry.' All of a sudden Mel had the feeling that she was the suspect again, and she hurried past him. Her hand was on the doorknob when she felt him behind her, then his hand was on hers, preventing her from opening the door. Surprised, she turned and looked at him.

'Sorry, ma'am,' Brotski said again, 'but Mr Vincent already has a visitor. He particularly asked that they should not be disturbed.'

A frown creased Mel's brow, followed by a shiver of foreboding. 'You mean you let somebody go in there — *alone* with him?' Her voice was squeaky with fear. It might be him. The killer. Somebody who wanted to harm him . . .

'It's Mr Vincent's business partner, ma'am,' Brotski said patiently, but his hand was still over hers on the doorknob and she knew he wasn't about to take it away until she stepped back. 'Mr Estevez is on Detective Camelia's list of permitted visitors.'

Mel flung her hand away, impatiently. 'Well, I surely hope Mr Estevez had a photo ID,' she said, still uneasy.

'Yes, ma'am, he did.' Brotski was so straightfaced and earnest, Mel almost wanted to laugh, except this was serious.

She eyed the door longingly. 'Why does he need to be alone with Ed? It's not as though they could have a private conversation.'

'That's Mr Estevez's business, ma'am.'

'Oh, for heaven's sakes, call me Mel,' she said with a sigh that seemed to come from her boots. 'Mind if I borrow your chair for a minute or two?' Despite the caffeine, exhaustion was claiming her and she could have fallen asleep in a second, even on the hard chair, if it were not that a Mr Estevez was alone with Ed. And *she* was outside, the guardian at the gate, praying he wasn't the killer. Then she remembered: Camelia had said Estevez was *persona grata*, and if Camelia said that, then he must be okay.

A ghost of a smile touched her lips as she thought about Detective Marco Camelia. He was like a character in a movie, the dark-haired, smooth, tough detective, complete with the heart of gold. But he was also a tender man, a man who loved his wife and adored his kids. *A man who was attracted to her.*

The door opened and a tall, silver-haired, distinguished-looking man stepped out into the hallway. She was on her feet in a minute and he turned, surprised. Their eyes met for a long moment, then he said, 'Miss Merrydew, of course,' and held out his hand.

'Mr Estevez,' she said, taking it. His hand was cold, as

though he had been in the presence of death, and again that shiver of foreboding trembled up her spine. She had to stop herself from running into that dim, monitored room with its flickering, humming machines just to check that this man hadn't killed him. 'How is he?'

'He is just the same. Unresponsive. I talked to him, about business, about the restaurant he likes, about people we know.' He shook his head. 'But nothing.' His glance was sharp. 'Perhaps you will be able to do better, Miss Merrydew.'

'I hope so.'

In the uncomfortable silence that followed, they sized each other up. Estevez was wondering what Ed saw in her. And Mel knew he was wondering exactly that.

'Might I ask where you are staying, Miss Merrydew?' he said at last.

'Staying?' Mel looked blankly at him. 'Oh. Right here.'

His brows rose. 'You mean the hospital gave you a room?'

'No. I mean I stay right here. With Ed.'

That accounted for the circles under her eyes, purple as Van Gogh's *Irises*, Estevez thought, astonished. He found himself unexpectedly touched. 'Then you have had no sleep. It's not good for you, Miss Merrydew. You need rest. I can arrange a hotel room. The hospital can call you if you are needed.'

She shook her head. 'I know Ed's not going to die as long as I am here with him,' she said stubbornly. 'I won't let him,' she added fiercely.

Estevez sighed. He understood that feeling: that as long as you were there, giving Ed your lifeforce, surely he could not die. 'I only wish that were true,' he said quietly. 'Unfortunately, my dear, we are all, in the end, in the hands of our medical scientists. The doctors, the nurses, the machines, the drugs – they are the ones keeping him alive.'

'His body, you mean. But I am here for his soul.'

Mel felt her eyes brimming. Great waves of exhaustion washed over her, her legs buckled and she slumped into the chair again. Officer Brotski took one glance and hurried to fetch her some water.

'I'm so sorry, Miss Merrydew.' Estevez crouched beside her, holding the paper cup to her pale lips. 'This is terrible for you, but I want you to know that I and my family are grieving also. It would be our pleasure to invite you to stay with us while you are here in New York.'

Was he doing it for her, Mel wondered? Or for Ed? She knew nothing of this man, nor of his family. Only that he was Ed's business associate, and that Camelia approved of him. She was half tempted; it would be so easy to sink into a soft bed, to be looked after, to be pampered with hot tea and a cool shower; so nice to be with people who loved Ed too . . . But then she remembered.

'Thank you, Mr Estevez, that's a very kind offer, but I'm okay. And when I really can't take it anymore, I'll just go to Ed's place, lie down there for a while. I'll feel closer to him, in his home.'

Estevez's brows rose. 'Ed's penthouse? You have a key?'

'Ed gave me one.' She smiled, remembering. 'And I gave him the key to my house in Santa Monica. Kind of a trade-off, though I guess he got the worst of the deal.'

Estevez was remembering the lavish share transfer, and now the key to the penthouse. This odd young woman was either a masterful schemer – or she meant much more to Ed than he had thought.

'As you wish.' He nodded gravely. Then he shook her hand, and with great courtesy said goodbye.

A gentleman, Mel thought, watching him walk briskly away. A handsome gentleman at that. Her Southern belle mother would have approved of him.

Meanwhile, she was feeling like death herself – but it was Ed who was still lying there, still attached to those machines and catheters. She opened the door and peeked inside.

Ed looked just the same: pale, gaunt, propped up by pillows, eyes firmly closed. The ventilator still breathed for him and they had shaved his chest where the electrodes were attached. Shaved his jaw, too, where the stubble was growing in. Odd, she thought, how the small things of life went on, when life itself seemed to be ebbing away. Quietly, she took a seat beside the bed, took his cold hand in hers. She rubbed it gently in an effort to get the circulation moving.

Ed tossed restlessly and Mel got out of the way as the nurse came hurrying, checking the machines and tubes that were Ed's lifeline. Mel wished she were the one looking after him. She wanted desperately to do everything for him. Wash him, feed him, hold him. She would treat him tenderly as a babe.

'He's restless,' the nurse said, stating the obvious.

Mel caught her disapproving glance and looked away. She wasn't going to let the nurse throw her out of here. No way. She was here for the duration, holding his hand, keeping him alive. If she took that hand away for more than a few minutes, he might die on her.

'He really should be alone, get some proper rest,' the nurse said meaningfully, but Dr Jacobs had given the woman permission to stay and there was nothing she could do about her.

She's staying with me, Ed thought. *God bless her. But what about Riley, though? She must be missing her mother; I don't have the right to keep her here* ... The sheet felt like a ton weight on his legs, and he shuffled impatiently. *Riley,* he thought. *You could have been my little girl, my own child. Maybe even had a little sister and brother to keep you company. If only I had asked your mother to marry me* ...

Why didn't I? I like everything about her, her looks, her laugh, her child, her dog ... *I would ask her right now if I didn't have this tube in my throat and could open my darn-fool mouth. Tell her right now, Zelda Merrydew, I love you and I want you to be my wife* ...

But first he would have to explain a thing or two about himself. So she knew exactly who he was. What she was getting. The reality behind the façade of the Manhattan entrepreneur . . .

He had come close to dying twice before. The first had been planned, though not by him. The second had seemed inevitable. He had beaten both, but he didn't know if he could beat this.

Chapter Twenty-seven

It seemed a long time before Ed stopped his thrashing around, and each second dragged like hours ... days ... weeks ...

'I have to ask you to leave for a while,' the nurse said frostily to Mel. 'There are things we need to do and the doctor is due for his visit.'

Mel knew the nurse was right; she shouldn't be here to see the indignity of what they had to do for Ed: change catheters, run tests, sponge down his body ... the body that had loved her so wildly and so well.

Overwhelmed, she drifted out into the hallway, hardly noticing the new young uniform on duty, though he noticed her alright. Pulling herself together, she headed for the payphone and dialed her own number.

'Hello?' Riley's voice was breathless with unspoken questions.

Whatever happened, however bad she felt, the sound of her daughter's voice would always flood Mel with a particular happiness that nothing could touch. That was the beauty of being a parent, she thought, gratefully. There was always Riley.

'Hi, baby, it's Mom.'

'Oh, Mommy, we've been waiting for you to call.'

'I'm sorry, honey, I've just been so caught up, I forgot ... I mean, I didn't forget *you*, it's just that ...'

'I know, Mom, it's okay, really it is. Is Ed alright?'

She sounded so understanding, so grown-up, Mel could have wept. But she didn't want what had happened to Ed to force Riley to grow up, to face things she should not have to face. Not yet. She was only seven.

'Ed's doing okay, honey, he's holding on. You know what a big strong guy he is.'

'I know, Mommy. But on the TV news, they said he was still in a coma. Does that mean he can't speak to you?'

Mel's sigh was dredged from her guts. 'I'm afraid it does.'

'But, Mom, d'you think Ed can hear you? Hear what you're saying? Because I want you to tell him something from me. That I love him. That when he's better he can come on our private Sundays anytime he wants. *Anytime*, Mom. Will you be sure to tell him that?'

Mel could see her daughter as though she were there: phone clamped anxiously to her ear, a finger twisting a strand of copper hair into a ragged curl, brown eyes wide and earnest. Riley had said she loved Ed, that she would share her precious private Sundays with him. It was an important moment, something Mel would treasure forever, something she would be sure to tell Ed, perhaps even see him smile ... maybe Riley could do what she couldn't.

She choked up as she promised Riley she would be sure to tell Ed in just a few minutes, when she went back into his room.

'I'm right here, at the hospital, honey,' she said, 'and I wanted to tell you how much I'm missing you. I hate being away from you, baby.'

'I hate it too.' Riley's voice was small, and Mel thought she detected a faint sob.

Oh, God, she thought despairingly, I don't have the right to do this, I should be home with my child. But how can I leave Ed? I can't, I can't ... and yet I can't bring Riley here, to sit vigil at a dying man's bedside.

'School okay, honey?' she asked, trying to bring the conversation back onto an even keel.

'Okay. Except Jason Mason drives me nuts, always tagging along after me, sending me silly notes in class. He even tries to sit next to me at lunch,' Riley added indignantly, making Mel laugh.

'It must be love, honey. He just can't resist those sparkling brown eyes and glorious red curls.'

'I hate my glorious red curls. I'm gonna iron my hair straight and bleach it blonde. Then I'll look like a real California babe.'

'Oh, sure. Like on *Baywatch*. Just what every mother wants her daughter to be. Thanks a lot, pal.'

Riley giggled and Mel heaved another sigh, of relief this time. 'You take care, my daughter, you hear me?' she said, smiling. 'I miss you and I love you and I'll see you soon. Now, is Harriet there?'

'Thanks Mom, and I love you too. Yes, she's here, hanging onto every word.' Riley giggled again, then suddenly serious, added, 'You won't forget the message, to Ed?'

'I won't forget, honey. And when he hears it, nor will he.'

'Love you, Mom,' Riley yelled, and then Harriet was on the line.

'So?' she asked, cryptically.

'A woman of few words, I see,' Mel retorted.

'You want me to ask in full? When y'know exactly what I mean? This is family shorthand, so quit being wise and give me the answer. And better make it a good one.'

'He's still alive. That's about it.' There was a silence, and Mel rushed to fill it in, bringing Harriet up to date.

'Not good,' was Harriet's verdict and, in her heart, Mel agreed with her. 'You want me to come out there, give moral support?' Harriet asked.

'Thanks, but one wrecked woman is probably all Ed could

stand right now. And believe me, I am a wreck. I don't think I've slept since I got here.'

'Then you'd better get to bed right now.' Harriet's voice was sharp with anxiety. 'You're not doing Ed, or yourself, a favor, driving yourself into the ground.'

Weariness suddenly enveloped Mel like a fog, and she knew that what Harriet said; that what Estevez had said; that what Camelia had said; was right. She could not go on. She slid to the ground, propped against the wall, the phone still clutched in her shaky hand. Sleep and oblivion were claiming her.

'Take care of Riley for me, Harr.'

'You know I'll always do that. And you take all the time you need. We love you, Mel.'

Mel replaced the receiver. She was too tired even to cry. Somehow, she got to her feet and trudged back down the long, empty, silent gray corridor. She didn't even see the cop at the door, nor the nurse, hovering. She went directly to Ed's bedside, took his cold hand in hers, leaned closer.

'Riley sent you a message, Ed. She said to be sure to tell you that she loves you. And Ed, she wants you to know, specially, that you can share her Sundays anytime you want. Isn't that great, honey? Riley loves you. And so do I.'

She stared down at him. Not a muscle moved, not a flicker of acknowledgement that he had even heard.

Her heart was back in her boots – where it seemed she kept a supply of sighs these days – as she trudged wearily from the hospital room into the elevator and took a cab to Vincent Fifth.

Ed's penthouse had the forlorn air of an abandoned home. No roses, no music, no magical evening lay ahead of her. Instead she lay down on his bed. Sleep didn't even describe the sensation overtaking her. She was sinking into it, wheeling downwards into oblivion. This must be what Ed feels like, where he is, she thought. And then she was out.

Chapter Twenty-eight

The subdued purr of a phone penetrated Mel's subconscious. Eyes still tight shut, she groped for it. It wasn't where it usually was, and, bewildered, she forced her eyes open, shading them with her hand from the subdued glow of the bedside lamp that seemed like a glare in her semi-awake state.

But this wasn't her lamp. It wasn't her bed. It wasn't her phone . . .

It came to her in a rush. *Oh, God, it must be the hospital calling . . . oh, God, Ed, wait for me, wait for me . . .*

Adrenaline catapulted her from the bed. She stared wildly round, looking for the phone. There wasn't one. But she could still hear it ringing. *Oh, God, oh, God, Ed, my darling, honey, sweetheart . . .*

Now she remembered: Ed hated telephones in the bedroom. He'd refused to have one, said there was no need for anyone to call him in the middle of the night, business could wait . . . *But not the hospital.* She was already racing through the lofty living room, grabbing up the telephone . . .

It stopped ringing.

Jesus! She sank into the sofa. Her hands shook and she bit her bottom lip hard to stop it from trembling. She couldn't fall apart, not now. This was urgent, mortal . . . she needed to keep her wits about her . . . she needed to call the hospital. Right now.

It rang again. She picked it up on the first bleat.

'Mel? Are you there?'

Her stopped breath came out in a quick gasp. 'Oh, God, it's you, Camelia. What is it, what's wrong ... Is it ...?'

He finished her thought for her. 'Ed's still the same. It's you I'm worried about. Nobody has heard from you in twenty-four hours.'

Twenty-four hours ... she had been away from Ed all that time ... anything might have happened ... anything ... But it hadn't. She put a hand to her fast-beating heart, willing it to calm down.

'I've been calling you for the past three hours. I was just about to come over there and break down the door.' Camelia's voice dropped a notch. 'Don't scare me like that,' he said softly.

Mel clutched the phone tightly to her ear, her lifeline. 'It's okay. I mean, I'm okay. I was just out of it, I guess. Completely out.'

'I'll bet you feel like a new woman.'

There was a smile in his voice that made her grin too. 'I wish,' she said ruefully. 'Maybe after a shower and a cup of coffee ...'

'Wanna have that cup of coffee with me? There's some things I'd like to talk to you about.'

'Sure. Yes, of course.' She caught sight of herself in the mirror, grimaced and added, 'Just give me half an hour.'

'There's a little diner on forty-ninth, between fifth and Madison. Meet you there.'

Mel swung through the door into the steamy little diner. The very same diner where she and Ed had dined that magical snowy night, the first night they had made love. Wild, raving, spectacular, funny, erotic love. She felt the memory of it in the smile on her face, the forever imprint of it on her body, the sensual images she would carry in her mind, always.

Camelia wasn't the only man to turn and look at her. There was something about her, poised there in the doorway, her short blonde crop ruffled by the wind. Something about the way she stood, so tall, so erect, so lanky and yet so graceful. And so goddamn sexy it took Camelia's breath away. Which also made him think twice about what he was gonna say to her.

'There you are.' She smiled at him, a big smile that gave him a shock. The golden glow had returned, and she was back to the Georgia peach again. All it took was sleep, he guessed. Just like with a kid.

He held the chair for her, sank back into his own, signalled the waiter for coffee.

The table was tiny, the place jammed. She leaned on her elbows, still smiling. Her face was so close Camelia could have kissed it. But that wasn't what he was supposed to be thinking about.

'You look better,' he said, guardedly, instead.

She nodded, sending her long, freshly washed bangs bouncing. 'Sleep and a shower will do it every time,' she agreed. 'Not great, but anyhow, better.'

Camelia thought she looked great, but he wasn't about to argue the point. Besides, she smelled subtly of roses, or maybe it was jasmine. It certainly wasn't Claudia's familiar Arpège, he thought with a guilty pang, but whatever it was, he was loving it. He groaned again, inwardly. Maybe he should ask to be assigned to another case, ask them to put someone else on this Ed Vincent affair. He thought *affair* was definitely the wrong word to use.

He smoothed back his already sleek black hair, straightened his silver-gray tie, stirred sugar into his coffee, ordered a ham and cheese on rye for himself and a bacon and egg sandwich on a Kaiser roll for her. She laughed, said he looked after her like a father, and he grinned back and said, 'Yeah, sure, everybody's dad, that's Marco Camelia.'

'That's not what it said in this morning's *Post*,' she said, suddenly serious. 'It said you were one of New York's finest, and also one of its toughest. They said if anybody could get Ed Vincent's shooter, it would be you.'

He contemplated his coffee, still swirling slowly in the thick white mug. 'I hope they are right,' he said finally.

So far, there were no clues, nothing to indicate who was involved. Nor why. The wall safe at Ed's penthouse had contained only money – a couple of hundred thou, to be exact. He guessed that Ed was right: once you had been dirt poor, you needed that security blanket of greenbacks.

Mel's heart skipped a beat, she had felt so full of confidence in Camelia, and now here he was, talking like something was wrong. She reached across, grabbed his arm, stared anxiously into his eyes. 'What d'you mean? Are you saying you won't be able to find the shooter? Why? Surely somebody must know him, know who did it?'

'It's *why* they did it,' he said quietly. 'We've got the cart before the horse, Mel. And my feeling is we have to get it the other way round before we can find the truth. We have to go in search of Ed Vincent's past before we can find our killer.'

The word killer struck a knell in her heart. 'Ed's not dead yet,' she retorted fiercely.

'No, and the doctor reported to me this morning that he was in a more stable condition. Not out of the coma and certainly not out of the woods, but he's holding his own.'

Mel had gotten the same report over the telephone half an hour earlier. 'Is that good news?' she asked doubtfully, because she had been expecting more, to hear that he was awake, asking for her.

'It's better news,' was all Camelia could think of to say. 'And it gives us time.'

'A breathing space,' she said, helpfully.

The waiter put the two orders on the table, asked if there was anything else, refilled their cups and departed.

'Twenty-four hours is a long time to sleep, you must be starving,' Camelia said, though he was suddenly not hungry himself. Still, he enjoyed the way she wolfed down that sandwich, and the way that, with every bite, she seemed to come back to life. This was a far cry from the gray, shadowy woman he had dined with in the deli around the corner from the hospital.

'I take you to all the best places,' he said, taking a bite of his own ham and cheese.

'Story of my life,' she said with a mischievous grin. 'I guess I'm just not the type guys take to Le Cirque 2000. Maybe it's something to do with the way I dress, the boots and all.'

She stuck out a foot for him to see the little black suede ankle boots with the teetering heels that added four inches to her already considerable height. Her bare legs were still faintly tanned from that California sun, and she was wearing a black leather jacket over a tight white stretch tank top, and a California-short skirt.

'Looks fine to me.' He dragged his eyes away and took another bite.

'Tasteful, huh?' She gave him that wide ear-to-ear grin, the one that defied you not to smile along with her. 'With my Southern background, my friend Harriet says I should know better.'

'Talking of Southern backgrounds, I found out where Hainstown is. And it is Hainsville, you were right the second time. And you were right again, it is a pin-dot on the map, though from what I hear, it's surely a prosperous pin-dot nowadays. Golf courses, sub-developments, quite the little resort, so they say.'

Mel's brows lifted. 'You think Ed had something to do with that?'

Camelia shrugged, took another bite. 'That's what he does, so I assumed he did have something to do with it. But I got in touch with the local police and they told me the place was developed by a man called Haines.'

'Huh. That figures.' Mel had finished her own bacon and egg, and now she helped herself to a bite of his ham and cheese.

Like they had known each other forever, Camelia thought, watching her. 'The cops know nothing about Ed Vincent, never heard of him down there.'

'That figures, too, out there in the boonies,' she agreed. 'Fame is where you find it.'

He thought about that for a minute, smiling, then he said, 'Okay, but Ed told you he came from Hainsville, was brought up there in the two-room shack. He must have gone to school there. So why, I ask myself, is there no record of him?'

Mel looked doubtfully back at him. Could the story Ed had told her have been a lie? Her heart sank. Then, no, she told herself, he would never lie to her. But Ed's life had suddenly assumed many more complications.

'Maybe he was the rich-guy-heir after all,' Camelia said mildly. He pushed his plate across to her, but Mel had suddenly lost interest in food. 'Perhaps he just didn't want you to think of him that way.'

Mel shook her head, lips compressed, brow furrowed. 'Not true. I believe Ed.'

'Then somebody else down there in Hainsville has to be lying.' Camelia's dark brown eyes met her single malts across the narrow table. Hers grew suddenly fierce.

She slammed a fist onto the table, sending the mugs reeling, spilling coffee onto his immaculate dark gray pants. 'Then, darn it, let's get down there and find out,' she yelled.

Chapter Twenty-nine

Mel was back at the hospital, holding Ed's hand. She stared hard at him, willing him to open his eyes, but the miracle did not happen, and her heart felt as weighted as her heavy sigh.

'I slept in your bed last night, honey,' she said, rubbing her fingers lightly up and down his arm, praying that he would respond to her touch. 'I slept there without you. Without our magic. Without our love to keep me warm. I fell into a bottomless pit of sleep and as I did so, I thought, this is what Ed feels like. This is where he is too. Maybe I will meet him there, in both our dreams.' She shook her head sadly. 'But there were no dreams, just . . . oblivion. Is that what it's like for you, Ed? Just . . . nothing?'

No, he wanted to yell out. *No, no, no . . . I know you're here, I want to say I love you but somehow I can't . . . Just don't leave me, baby, don't give up on me. Don't let them pull the plug on me . . . I'm still here, still alive . . .'*

'They showed me your brain scan this morning,' she whispered. 'They showed me how the blood supply was still working, that there is brain activity, that somehow you are still here with me. I'll never give up on you, honey. I'm yours forever, I know that now. And Riley misses you. Did I tell you she said she loved you, that she wants you to share her Sundays? Oh, God,' she gave a choked little laugh, 'I must be losing my mind, I can't remember from one day to the next. Maybe I need some of that ginkgo biloba to perk up the old memory cells ...'

Just remember me, honey ... remember us, that's all I ask ...

'Ed,' she said, serious again. 'The detective who's looking for the shooter. His name is Marco Camelia. He checked into your home town — you told me about Hainsville, remember?' She bit her lip; of course he didn't remember, how could he ...

I remember Hainsville ... oh, I remember alright. Hot panic flared in his head, sent his heart thunking again ...

'Ed, the police there say they don't know any Ed Vincent. They say you never lived there. Somebody is lying, Ed, and I know it's not you. Detective Camelia thinks its someone connected with the shooting. I need to go with him, to Tennessee, to your home town. I'm going to find your roots, Ed, honey, and then we'll find the truth.'

Don't go, he wanted to scream ... *Don't go there ... oh, Mel, please ... don't go ...*

The monitor bleeped. Mel eyed it, alarmed, as the nurse came running.

It was a different nurse; they changed all the time depending on the shift, and this one was gentler, with a softer heart.

'He's okay,' she reassured Mel. 'Just a little agitated. At least he's showing some response.'

'Then it's good?' Mel was scared.

'It's good. He'll be okay, nothing to worry about.'

'Then I'll just sit here quietly with him, until he calms down.' She took his hand again, stroking his arm gently, but now Ed lay still as death.

He could not push away the memories — his past was crowding out the present, taking away his future. Life had seemed so simple once ... when he was just a hick little kid with big dreams ...

Don't go, Zelda, he begged silently ... *Please ... don't go there ...*

*   *   *

It had been on his fourteenth birthday when he had his first brush with death. In that single year it seemed he had grown from a boy into a man. Already touching six feet in height, he had broadened through the chest and neck, and gained extra poundage on his lean frame. New muscles rippled on his arms from hard work in the fields and from felling trees for winter logs, and he was as swift and light on his feet as a boxer from hiking up and down the mountains.

His mother, Ellin, knew, though, that agricultural work was not for him. His nose was always in a book, his mind on things far from her and from their tiny farm. She had bought him a birthday gift, a new shirt from Hains Haberdashery in Hainsville, in a checked flannel in a deep blue that matched his eyes, and a pair of denims that were too long now but she bet in two months would be reaching up around his ankles. And she knew that on his next birthday, when his schooling was finished, he would leave her. He would set out for that wider world he had always longed for.

'Happy Birthday, son,' his pa, Farrar, punched Ed's shoulder lightly.

Outwards displays of affection, hugs and kisses and such, were not part of mountain folks' lives. They were a reserved people, and the punch on Ed's shoulder from his father, the shy birthday embrace from his mother and her smile as her rough hand sleeked back his thick dark hair, were enough to fill his heart.

As the youngest boy, he had always been the final recipient of hand-me-downs. Inevitably, by the time clothing descended from the eldest, Mitch, on through Jared and then Jesse, even hard-wearing denims were worn into pale ragged areas at the knees and seat, which his Ma had to reinforce with patches. Not that that made Ed the scruffiest lad in school. There were others from even poorer handscrabble families, and at least his ma kept their clothing scrupulously clean, despite the fact that there was no running water in the house.

She would scrub away on a metal washboard perched over the galvanized tub out on the back porch. Her two daughters, Grace and Honor, helped her, one feeding the clothes into the heavy iron wringer while the other turned the handle. Then they would hang them on the line to dry in the wind, and later fold them carefully, ready for ironing.

Today, being a Monday, was meant to be a washday, but Ellin had been stymied by the rain falling in torrents from a low, leaden sky. The wind had gotten up too, gusting through the tall pines, the mountain ash and poplars, rattling the branches and sending early cascades of leaves onto the rough ground. She was surprised, therefore, to hear the sound of a car's engine coming up the hill. She wondered who would turn out on an evening like this, with the wind now threatening to topple trees it was that fierce, and the rain so hard the streams overspilled, turning the steep lane into thick mud that grabbed a vehicle's tires and hung onto them, tight as kudzu.

His ma and pa and Ed turned as one, as the vehicle crowned the hill and jolted over the rutted yard. Ellin recognized the forest-green jeep immediately. She threw an apprehensive glance at her husband. 'What'll Michael Hains be wanting now?'

'Guess,' Farrar replied laconically.

'But you already told him no.' There was a worried note in her voice, an uneasiness. Hains wanted to purchase their land. Her husband had told him no twice already, but Hains was not the kind of man who took no for an answer. He operated on the principal that what he wanted, he got. It had worked all his life, and he saw no reason why it should be different now.

Michael Hains owned the town of Hainsville, which he had renamed after himself. He owned the gas station, the hardware store, and the grain and feed, as well as Hains Haberdashery where she had purchased Ed's birthday shirt and denims. Plus the grocery store, the pharmacy, the barber shop, Hains Auto-Body Repairs, and the Dew-Drop-In drive-in. He even owned the red-brick town hall, for which the town paid him an annual rental. But Hains's influence extended much further than his own personal town. He also owned all the land surrounding Hainsville, some two thousand acres of it, share-cropped by men who worked their lean bodies too hard in order to pay his annual dues. Only one person came out of Hainsville a winner, and that was Michael Hains.

Now he wanted their land. They had been mystified as to why until they had heard the rumor, whispered in Farrar's ear by Mule Champlin, the blacksmith who also ran the hardware shop. Mule never got Farrar's business in the blacksmith shop; most men around here shod their own horses – they couldn't afford to pay Champlin's prices. Anyhow, Mule had told him that Hains and a property development company were planning on a new purpose-built community, with a shopping mall and a golf course, as well as cheap thrown-up-in-a-hurry housing. Mule also told Farrar why they needed his land. It was to be the center of the new golf course.

'Evenin', Mr Hains,' Farrar said now, hands thrust in his overall pockets, rocking back and forth on his heels. A sure sign of nerves, Ed knew.

'I've come to you with my last offer.' Hains stood on the rickety porch out of the rain, arms folded over his barrel chest. He was a big man, bigger even than eighteen-year-old Mitch, who hovered in the background, ears wagging as he strained to catch the dialogue.

'Ahm wonderin' just why you want my land so bad, Mr Hains.' Farrar shoved his hands even deeper into the pockets of his overalls.

'Simple.' Hains glance shifted to Mitch. 'I want to increase my farm holdings. I've bought all the surrounding land. Your acres will complete my parcel. And I'm willing to give you a fair price for it.'

Ellin folded her arms across her chest, unconsciously mimicking Hains, only hers was a defensive gesture. The man made her uncomfortable, wary.

'And if ah might consider your offer,' Farrar said, 'and ah'm not saying ah will — exactly what would that offer amount to?'

Hains's dark, unreadable eyes met his. 'I'm offering you more than one-hundred-percent profit on your land. Much more. Two thousand dollars.'

Ellin sucked in her breath. It was a lot of money. But Farrar was already doing quick calculations in his head. He had paid four hundred. Two thousand would take him years to earn, but most of that would be gone on just livin'. Meanwhile, he owned his own land, his family lived off it, there was a roof over their heads and food in their bellies. Without the farm, he would be back share-cropping, working for Hains for a pittance, and his sons like him. He'd be darned if he'd worked from being ten years old to end up back where he came from. Besides, if the rumor were true, his land was worth a lot more than two thousand.

'Ah thank you for your offer, Mr Hains,' Farrar said. 'But ah reckon ah'll keep my farm.'

Hains's fleshy face grew mottled with frustration and anger, but he kept his voice under control. 'I'll add a sweetener. I'll take your boy, Mitch, into my firm. Apprentice him, y'might call it. He'll learn the business, learn how to manage my land. I'll pay him a fair wage and he'll be off your hands. One less mouth to feed.'

'Aye, and one less son to work my own land.' Farrar shook his head, adamant.

Ed heard Mitch's angry gasp and glanced sideways at him. His narrow eyes were slits of fury, his mouth turned down, his jaw clenched.

You knew about this, he thought, astonished. *You'd discussed it all with Michael Hains, plotted how to get Dad's land away from him.* He felt an ache of betrayal in his heart. *Traitor,* he thought. *You would have traded your family, your birthright, for a few thousand dollars and a chance to work with an immoral man like Michael Hains.*

Hains unfolded his arms and stood, legs spread, hands

on his hips. Arrogant, contemptuous. Powerful. 'Is that your final word?'

'It'll be my last word, Mr Hains.' As always, Farrar was polite.

Hains turned on his heel. He stalked down the rickety porch steps, bulling his way through the mud and torrential rain.

Farrar swung round, confronting Mitch. 'What d'you mean, going behind my back to Michael Hains, plotting how to get my land from me? *Our* land. *Our family's* land. All ah've worked for. *All ah have to leave you.* What kind of son are you?'

Mitch took an angry step towards his father. He towered over him, his big hands clenched into fists. For a second, Ed thought he was going to punch his father, and he stepped quickly between the two.

Mitch's anger exploded. 'You just cost me the best job any man could have. Mah one chance at a different life. All for what?' Mitch flung his arms wide, staring furiously around at the dripping trees, the rutted yard and the sodden land beyond. 'So ah can be like you? Live in the boondocks for the rest of my life? Break mah back to earn enough to do what? Put food on the table? Barely clothe us? Educate us? Bah!' He spat contemptuously at his father's feet. 'That's what I think of you and your precious land. It was worthless before Hains offered you the money. Now it's worth nothing. *Zero.* Get that into your head, *Father!*'

He stared murderously into his father's eyes for a full minute before turning on his heel and, like Michael Hains, stalking out into the rain. Except, unlike Hains, Mitch had no forest-green jeep to drive into town, and his ma wondered where he could be going on such a night.

She looked at her husband. His shoulders stooped as though he had acquired a new and heavier burden, and she pitied him his son's cruelty.

'It's okay, Pa.' Ed badly wanted to hug his father, but the

unspoken rules meant he could not. 'Mitch didn't mean nuthin'. He's just disappointed about the job, is all.'

'Disappointed?' Farrar's expression was weary as his eyes met Ed's. 'Somehow, I don't reckon it's just that. I reckon Mitch would sell his soul to hitch up with Michael Hains.'

By the time they all went to bed that night, Mitch had still not returned.

'He'll be drinkin' in Hainsville Saloon,' Ellin remarked, sadly.

'It's Mary Hannah James he's interested in, not the liquor,' Ed said, trying to get his mother's thoughts away from the saloon.

His sister, Grace, gave a snort of contempt. 'He'll be after both, the liquor *and* the girls.'

'More likely he's with Michael Hains, plotting his next move.' Farrar's voice grew weary at the thought of his son's treachery. 'He'll not make it back tonight, to face me again.'

As the girls drifted off to the only bedroom to sleep, Ed glanced anxiously at the ceiling. Rain drummed on the tin roof and the wind wailed at the windows and doors, sending chilly gusts through the many cracks.

Ellin opened the old iron stove and poked the coals into a hot glow before throwing on another couple of logs. 'There,' she said, satisfied, letting the door clang shut, 'at least we'll be warm tonight.'

'All except Mitch,' Ed thought, lying warm and cosy in the bunk, built into a sort of cupboard near the stove. Ellin slept with her daughters in the bedroom, and he and Pa and the boys slept in the main room. The others were soon asleep, but Ed lay awake, worrying about Mitch.

Why had he done what he'd done? Mitch didn't have to sell his birthright, like Esau, to get a job. He was clever, he'd educated himself, he was a whizz at math. Mitch could do anything, get a job anywhere. Not just here in Hainsville.

Ed tossed and turned, agonizing over what Mitch had done

to his father. When he could stand it no longer, he got up, slipped on his old denim shirt and boots and put on Pa's black oilskin slicker. He hesitated, thinking how muddy and bedraggled he would be by the time he reached his destination. Realizing he would make a sorry sight, he quickly thrust his new jeans and shirt into a backpack. He would change into them when he got there.

He crept past his sleeping brothers to the door. It creaked as he opened it, but they were all sound asleep, and anyhow, the roar of the wind in the treetops drowned out any other sound.

Slipping and sliding in the mud, he began to jog down the lane. He was heading for Hainsville. He had to find Mitch, confront him, try to reason with him. He would help Mitch any way he could, but he couldn't allow him to destroy their father, no matter how all-powerful Michael Hains might be.

Chapter Thirty

Mel had been in a precinct house only once before, when Camelia had taken her there for questioning. From what she saw now she wasn't sure she ever wanted to be in one again. Gray walls, steel filing cabinets, worn-looking chairs, cheap tables serving as desks, paper coffee cups, the odd box of donuts, piles of thick files, wire baskets brimming with paperwork, shrilling phones, yelling felons, wailing relatives, crackling tension, and a lot of tough-looking guys in blue wearing weaponry that scared the hell out of her. She knew the world was a safer place because of them, but she would prefer to keep that side of the world at a distance, thank you very much.

Camelia took her elbow and shepherded her into a tiny room, already occupied by a handsome Hispanic with the build of a weightlifter and the liquid dark eyes of a Casanova. Except now he was all business.

He shook hands, took a seat at his computer and got right to questioning her, boosting partial images of a man's face onto the screen as Mel described what she knew.

'I'm not being very helpful,' she apologized nervously, 'it's just that I'm not sure what I *really* saw — and what I *think* I saw.'

'Just give it your best, ma'am,' he replied. 'I'll try to fill in the rest.'

So Mel scanned the separate images carefully. Yes, that was exactly the way his forehead had looked, exactly like a pit bull, kind of brutal, half hiding his eyes. Narrow eyes, she thought, but that could have been from the glare. No, she didn't know the color. And so it went on.

She gasped when he finally showed her the finished composite. *It was the killer.* She gulped back the nausea, twisted her clammy hands nervously, bit her lip to stop the tears though she couldn't tell whether they were tears of fear, or of joy, because at least now they had someone to hunt for.

'It may not be exact,' she said, still worried that she had got it wrong. 'I mean, I think this is who I saw.'

'Good enough, ma'am. We'll run it through the national computer, see what we come up with.'

'Thank you,' she said gratefully, edging out the door. 'Thank you so much.'

She wanted out of there so bad, she almost made a run for it, but Camelia hadn't finished with her yet. Next she had to sit in another gray windowless room, listening while an expert played various tapes for her, all of men speaking with foreign accents. The coffee in the paper cup tasted like it had been sitting in the machine for a week, and even the Krispy Kreme donut, offered by Camelia, couldn't tempt her.

They must have been on the thirtieth tape, her head was whirling and she knew she had lost it, when suddenly a voice rang a bell. A smooth voice, but with that low, guttural sound, throaty, harsh . . .

'That's it.' She was out of her chair, excited. 'That's exactly the way he sounded. Oh, thank God, I've finally got something right.'

'Ukrainian,' the expert informed them. 'From the Caucasus region, near the Black Sea. A lot of real bad guys drifted into that area, got out of Russia via the Bosporus and Turkey, took on new identities, came into the US as political refugees, along with the decent folk.'

'Terrific,' Camelin said, 'we'll add it to the photofit, see what comes up.'

And then they were out of there, walking along in the sunshine, breathing the fumes that in New York passed for fresh air, sighing with relief as they headed back to Vincent Fifth to pick up Mel's duffle, and then on to the airport.

Camelia had already seen Ed's home; he had personally gone through the place with a finetooth comb, and found nothing. At least, nothing personal that could lead him to a killer, or even a motive for killing. He waited downstairs in the lobby for Mel, thinking that the only scrap of a motive so far was the fight over buying the expensive Fifth Avenue airspace. His team was working on that, but so far had failed to penetrate the myriad layers of corporate identities that masked the real buyer. The investigations now involved Interpol and Scotland Yard, and, given time, he knew they would come up with the answer.

The elevator pinged and Mel emerged, pink-cheeked from where she had just washed her face to clean off the smoke and smell of an alien world, unsmiling because she was about to leave Ed, and with an anxious look in those whisky-browns that brought out the protective animal in Camelia.

She strode toward him on those ridiculous heels, towering over him as she slipped her arm through his. 'Let's go,' she said determinedly.

And they were off to the airport in Camelia's police Crown Vic, hustling through the thick traffic to make the afternoon flight to Nashville.

Chapter Thirty-one

Mel slept on the plane, then slept through the long drive to Hainsville in the rented Ford Explorer, curled up on the back seat with her head pillowed in her arms and Camelia's jacket slung over her for warmth.

'Didn't you ever think of bringing socks, or a sweater? Y'know, something warm?' Camelia said, astonished that she had shown up, bare-legged, in the tank top and black leather jacket. 'This ain't California, y'know what I mean.'

She did know, now. It was cold and it was also raining. 'Feels to me like there could be snow flurries,' she muttered, half asleep, and he sighed. She was a true Californian, despite her Southern background. Come to think of it, that was another good reason she was with him on this investigation. That good ol' boy Southern accent might go down a sight better with the locals that his own Bronx twang. Of course, it wasn't the only good reason she was here, and he knew it.

It was late, but as a kind of penance, instead of driving straight to the Inn, where he had been looking forward to a leisurely dinner with her, he drove instead to the local Sheriff's station.

Red-brick, low-rise with a dark slate roof, it sat squarely on the corner of Main Street, immediately opposite the grandiose Town Hall, the white-columned porticos of which were trimmed with red, white and blue bunting, topped with a medallion showing a man's head in silhouette. The name MICHAEL HAINES was strung in separate scarlet letters over the lofty double doors.

'No doubt who owns this town,' Camelia said drily to Mel, who by now was sitting up and taking notice.

It was a small town of flower-filled window boxes and white picket fences; of stern warnings against the throwing of litter and don't even think of parking here, and of the need to clean up after your dog, with the mention of substantial fines for violators. The street lights were copies of iron filigree lamps from the turn of the century, a time when, Mel suspected, this had still been a one-street place with wooden sidewalks, and the only lighting had been the moon. Bedding plants were laid out in perfect circles on the velvet lawn outside the Town Hall. There were white-painted storefronts with cute Dutch doors, and the immaculate red-brick and white clapboard houses had gingham café curtains on gleaming brass rods at their windows. And though it was only nine p.m., there wasn't a soul in sight.

'Oh, my God, it's Stepford,' Mel whispered, awed.

'Or Disneyland.' Camelia was already out of the car and striding toward the Sheriff's station. She hurried after him.

There were two guys manning the station, both big burly fellows, both wearing cream stetsons with their sand-colored uniforms, even though they were indoors, and both drinking coffee out of mugs with Michael Haines's silhouette on them. They glanced up in surprise as Camelia swung through the door. They took in his smart gray suit, his silver tie, and his big-city look. An expression of distaste spread over both their faces, followed by matching false smiles.

'How can I help ya?' the taller Deputy asked, without getting up. 'Sir,' he added, with a knowing smirk.

Camelia got the feeling that if you didn't come from Hainsville, you didn't count. Then Mel raced into the room, and he heard the squeak of chair legs on wood floors as the two beefy rednecks lumbered to their feet. She might be different, but Mel was all woman, and even these lurches recognized it.

He flashed his NYPD badge and saw them take a mental step backward. 'Detective Marco Camelia,' he said smoothly, knowing he had thrown them for a loop. NYPD was light years away from the Hainsville cop department. 'And this is Ms Melba Merrydew, my ... er, my assistant.'

Mel flashed him an amazed glance that he deliberately ignored. Getting the message, she stuck her hands deep into the pockets of her leather jacket and tried to look as butch and cop-like as she could – though remembering poor little pink-cheeked, carrot-haired Brotski, who looked as though he was still in high school, she had to hold back a giggle.

'Yeah, er, well ... and what can we do for you, Detective?' They shook hands cautiously across the counter.

'A quiet night here, huh?' Camelia glanced round the immaculate room, nothing out of place, no teetering piles of paperwork on scuffed-out desks, no styrofoam cups of cold coffee, no Krispy Kreme crumbs. And not a sound to disturb the silence, except his own voice.

'Hainsville's a quiet place.'

'Law-abiding, huh?'

'Yes, sir. And proud of it.'

The redneck's steely-blues met Camelia's Sicilian browns in a hard stare.

'Er ... coffee, ma'am?' The other Deputy waved a hand toward the smart chrome Coffee Master.

'No, thank you.'

Mel flashed him her beaming smile and Camelia swore he saw the guy's knees go weak. He watched him sink back into his softly padded office chair as though he'd been poleaxed. Camelia grinned. 'I could sure use a cup of coffee, it's been a long trip.'

No one moved a muscle, and he leaned both arms on the counter, unsmiling. 'I said, I'd appreciate that cup of coffee,' he repeated softly, but there was something about the way he said it that suddenly had them both jumping.

'Yes, sir. Won't you please come into the office, take a seat? Jeb, see if you cain't rustle up some cookies. Or Ma Jewel's muffins. Ah believe there's still some left in the box on top of the refrigerator.'

The flap on the counter was lifted to allow them through, the frosted-glass office door thrown open, chairs pulled back, coffee quickly placed in front of them, with sugar in a bowl that matched the Michael Hains mugs, and proper cream in an identical pitcher.

'Smart,' Camelia commented. 'We don't run to matching teasets in New York.'

'Hainsville is a tourist destination, Detective Camelia,' the burly one said. 'We aim to keep it looking real nice, even down to the cops.'

'Right to the last detail,' Mel said, ignoring the coffee which she was far too tired to drink anyway. She was, as they said, past it. She wondered anxiously how Ed was, and she longed to get out of here so she could call the hospital. But then she reminded herself that she was now Camelia's assistant, and Ed was the reason they were here. She sat up and began to take notice.

'Ah'm Sheriff Duxbury, and this here's Deputy Higgies. Now, sir, how can the Hainsville police be of help to the New York PD?'

They sat on the opposite side of the table, looking, Camelia thought, as interchangeable as twins. Both still wore their hats, both had wide red faces, both had pale blue eyes and blond moustaches. If you put black stetsons on them instead of the cream, they could have been the bad guys in any old western.

'You ever hear of a guy called Ed Vincent?'

'Vincent?' Duxbury answered for both. 'No, sir, cain't say as we have. Ain't nobody with that name lives round here, though of course we do get a fair number of tourists, for the golf and all. One of the best par seventy-two courses in all Tennessee,' he added proudly.

Camelia nodded. 'I'm not a golfing man, myself. Ed Vincent claims that he was brought up here, in a two-room shack in the foothills. Had a big family, brothers and sisters. This man is in his forties. He lived here before Mr Hains developed the town.'

'Ah don't recall the name,' Higgies said, puzzled.

'So, here's a picture of him. Maybe it'll help jog your memory.'

Mel watched as each man studied the picture, then handed it back to Camelia. Her heart was in her mouth. Surely they must know him. How could they have missed him, growing up? He was so tall, like them; God, they must grow them all big around here ...

Duxbury handed it back to Camelia, shaking his head. 'He some kinda New York big shot?'

'Kinda.' Camelia put the photograph back in his wallet. 'But you guys never heard of him, huh?'

'Ain't no big shots round here, Detective. I guess Michael Hains was the biggest shot we know. Been dead ten, eleven years now. Still carry his picture on everything, though. Kind of like a symbol. Like a coat of arms, that old family-tree stuff in England. Yes sir, Michael Hains had no title, but he was surely Lord of the Manor around here. Without him, there'd be no Hainsville.'

'I resisted saying "and who would miss it,"' Mel said to Camelia as they hurried back through the rain to the Explorer. 'This place gives me the creeps. I can't even imagine Ed living here.'

'He didn't. He lived in the old Hainsville, before it became Stepford.' Camelia looked grim. He had gotten exactly nowhere. He needed to regroup, rethink his tactics. Goddammit, he had thought it would be so easy. He glanced at Mel, slumped next to him in the passenger seat. She looked as dispirited as he felt. 'What we need,' he said, 'is a drink. And then some food.'

'Yeah,' she said, in a small, frozen voice. 'I can go for that.'

The Hainsville Inn & Country Club looked like the rest of Hainsville. Pristine red-brick with white clapboard, verdant lawns and soldierly rows of flowers that, Mel thought, must be too scared to even droop their heads in the torrential rain, for fear somebody might annihilate them.

Camelia checked them in and then they headed for the bar, a cosy red-plush-booth affair, with a faux log fire blazing as merrily as a faux fire could in the massive river-rock fireplace.

They ordered drinks from the bland-faced young man behind the bar: she a Cosmopolitan, he a beer. Perched on stools, each contemplated his and her own thoughts.

Mel took a sip of the Cosmopolitan. The young bartender had got it right, exactly the way she liked it: light on the cranberry juice and even lighter on the lime, and the vodka was Belvedere. It was the first good thing to happen that day, and she gave him a smile. Then she got on the phone and called the hospital. And Camelia got on his phone and called the precinct.

No news on either count: Ed was status quo, neither worse nor better. And no progress on the Ed Vincent killer situation.

Camelia downed the beer and ordered a single malt. He stared moodily into the glass. The color reminded him of Mel's eyes, and he stole a glance at her. The purple shadows were back and she was yawning. She looked beat, and he heaved another sigh.

'I'm too tired to be hungry,' she said, nibbling on a handful of peanuts. 'All I want is to fall into bed and sleep.'

He nodded. 'Maybe tomorrow will be a better day.'

She didn't say anything, but he knew she was hoping so too. She finished her Cosmopolitan, slid off her stool, dropped a light kiss on his cheek, said goodnight, and was half-way across the room before he realized it.

'So? What time shall I wake you?' he called after her.

'Wake me? Ohhh, whenever you're up. You call the shots here, Camelia. I'm just your assistant. Remember?'

He was smiling as he watched her lope fluidly across the hall to the elevator. He wished she had stayed and had another Cosmopolitan. He sighed as he ordered another single malt, just so he could remember the color of her eyes again.

Then, pulling himself together, he quickly dialed his home number.

Chapter Thirty-two

Early the next morning, Camelia was breakfasting alone in the perkily decorated dining room, surrounded by potted plants and piped music, and a young blonde waitress in a wide, rustling red skirt and a white organdie apron. She had the same bland look and perfect white smile that seemed to be the norm in Hainsville. He wondered where they recruited them from.

'You from round here?' he asked as she took his order.

'I sure am, sir. My family have lived here for three generations.'

He nodded. 'Then maybe you've heard of this guy, Ed Vincent?'

'Vincent? No, I don't think so, sir. It's not a local name, and believe me, I know them all.' She laughed, showing her pretty white-on-white teeth, reminding him, uncomfortably, again of *The Stepford Wives*.

Well, everyone's real nice here,' he said, accepting a copy of the local newspaper she handed him. The *Hainsville Gazette*. What else would it be called, he thought with a wry grin.

He glanced through it while he ate the perfectly cooked, perfectly bland eggs and bacon and a boring Stepford bagel that bore no resemblance to the hard chewy New York type he was addicted to. He washed it down with unbitter coffee, sadly lacking in caffeine, and slightly too cool for his taste, and thought again about the newspaper.

He checked the masthead. *Fifty years of bringing Hainsville its news,*' it boasted, and gave an address on Third Street.

He got to his feet as Mel appeared, looking refreshed and energetic and totally out of place among the potted palms, in her black leather and her short skirt and her high-heeled little boots.

'At least I know where we start this morning,' he said by way of greeting.

'You do?' Mel gave him that grin. 'Okay, honey, let's go.' And she linked her arm in his and they were on their way. One more time.

The *Hainsville Gazette* occupied what must have been the oldest premises in town and, in fact, looked as though no speck of dust had been disturbed in its entire fifty years of business.

Camelia explained his quest to the gray-haired woman behind the counter, who was definitely not a member of the Disneyland cast assembled to greet the tourists. This one was sharp, and sour with it.

'Ain't niver heard of the fella,' she said briskly, shuffling papers on the counter.

How small fame was, Mel thought sadly. No one here had even heard of Ed. Nobody knew what he had accomplished, nobody knew how good he was. And nobody cared.

And even though Camelia insisted they search the records, going back forty years, they found the woman was right. There was no mention of a Vincent family.

'Ah told ya so,' was her parting shot as they left, sneezing from the dust and her venom.

'Seems to me that if Ed really did live here, the best thing he did was get out,' Camelia commented as they stepped across the street to the Explorer. There was a pink parking ticket stuck under the windshield and he snatched it up, irate. 'So much for love and goodwill toward tourists.'

Mel giggled. 'You're a cop, you can fix it.'

'I'm a law-abiding cop,' he said in a steely voice, 'I pay my tickets.'

Her eyebrows rose and she pursed her lips to stop from smiling. 'Where do we go next?'

'Follow me,' he said, climbing back into the car.

The Town Hall had a parking lot, so at least he wouldn't run the risk of another ticket. Inside it was as elaborate as out: pale oak paneling, black-and-white checkered-marble floor, Doric columns and a wash of gold leaf. The receptionist told them where the Land Registry department was, and they strode down the endless corridors of small-town power until they found it.

As Camelia now expected, a brief look revealed no 'Vincent.' But then he got down to business in earnest. He searched the names of all the previous landowners in the area, and the dates on which they had sold their parcels to Michael Hains.

'It seems like every single person in this town sold out to Haines,' Mel finally said, exhausted.

'Except one. Farrar Rogan. His tract of farmland – four acres – was picked up by default, for the sum of one dollar. Now, don't you think that's a tad strange, when everybody else got a couple of thou?'

'So what d'you think happened to Farrar Rogan?' she asked, not hoping for much of an answer.

'Let's ask around and find out,' was what he said.

Back at the *Gazette* the gray-haired woman did not look pleased to see them. No bland, warm, white smile here, Mel thought, glancing at her watch, longing to call the hospital again, though she had spoken to them early that morning. And she wanted to hear Riley's voice so bad. And Harriet . . . God, she was missing out on her life. What was she doing here, chasing wild geese when she should be with the ones she loved, even if it meant being bicoastal?

The woman flinched when Camelia flashed her his badge. 'I didn't know you was cops,' she whined. 'Sure, I remember the name, Rogan. There was an accident, I don't recall what. Yes, sir,' she added with new respect, 'I'll show you where to look in the archives.'

It didn't take her long to find the relevant newspaper. And there it was in big, bold headlines.

Farrar Rogan and his family were front-page news.

Chapter Thirty-three

The blurred photo in the *Hainsville Gazette* showed a pile of smouldering ruins with the caption, *Rogan Family Perishes In Tragic Fire*. Then underneath it read:

Fire destroyed the log cabin of Farrar Rogan, killing him and his entire family, wife Ellin, daughters Honor and Grace, sons, Jared, Jesse and Theo. Only one son, Mitchell, was saved, due to the fact that he was at the Hainsville Saloon at the time.

How the cabin caught fire remains a mystery, though the Sheriff says it might have had something to do with the old stove, since Mitch says his ma was in the habit of stoking it up real well on such cold nights. The cabin burned so well that not even the torrential downpour could extinguish the flames.

Services for the Rogan family will be held at the Memorial Chapel on Saturday morning at ten a.m. Mitch says to say that everybody knew his pa and ma, and everyone is invited to pay their last respects.

Michael Haines has stepped into the breach to offer the only surviving Rogan son, Mitch, a job in his company.

The Saturday newspaper had another photograph, this time of a crowd standing respectfully bareheaded next to a row of seven plain pine coffins. A huge bouquet of calla lilies rested atop each one, and the caption said that the flowers were courtesy of Michael Hains.

'Where are we heading now,' Mel asked, back once more in

the Explorer. The rain had started again, long slashing drops that careened across the windshield, hard as buckshot. She shivered, remembering the night of the hurricane.

'To Hainsville Cemetery,' Camelia said. 'Just to make sure they are all still there and Hains didn't dig 'em up so he could resell the plot.'

'You think he was that bad?'

'Rotten to the core, I'd bet my life on it.'

'So what happened to Mitch? You think he had something to do with the deaths of his family?' Her eyes bugged as a thought suddenly occurred to her. 'Oh God, you don't think that Mitch is really Ed, and that he changed his name because ...'

'Because he killed them?' Camelia lifted his shoulder in a shrug as he swung the Explorer through the ornate iron gates of the cemetery – or The Hainsville Resting Place, as was euphemistically inscribed in large gilt letters on the twin stone pillars beside the gates. 'What can I tell ya, baby? What you want to hear? Or what I think might be the truth?'

Mel stared blankly in front of her. Ed? *Her Ed*, a possible killer? She slumped back in her seat. Her stomach churned at the thought; her mind pushed it away; her whole being resisted the concept. 'No,' she cried, 'damn it, Marco Camelia, you'll never convince me of that.'

He nodded. 'Okay, okay. Let's just wait and see which way the cards fall.'

She was silent as she stood next to him, staring through the downpour at the plain black marble headstone. The names were engraved into the stone, but the gold had worn off long ago and now it was hardly possible to make them out. Only the ROGAN stood out boldly at the top.

'Seven names,' Mel said, sniffing back a tear and mopping her runny nose. 'And not one of them is an Ed.' She felt terrible: cold, wet, hopeless. She wished she were anywhere but here. And anywhere but with Camelia, who was telling her things she didn't want to know. *The truth*, her brain insisted, but again she denied it. *No, no, no, never. Her Ed was not a killer . . .*

Back at the Sheriff's station, Duxbury was not thrilled to see them. However, he nodded when they asked about the Rogan family tragedy, and about the surviving son, Mitch.

'Everybody knew the Rogans. Nice family,' he said thoughtfully. ''Ceptin' that son, Mitch. Quite a character he turned out to be. There was rumors round town he had some'n to do with it.'

'With his family's deaths, y'mean?' Camelia was all ears.

'They was just rumors, y'know, but some said it had been murder. Nothin' came of it and he went to work for Michael Haines. He was quite a boy, that Mitch. Ripped off Mr Hains but good. Stole everything he could get his hands on. Lit out of here leaving Hains with the creditors. Served time, too, when they finally caught up to him, though I did hear he was soon back in business. And with money in his pocket. Yeah, quite a boy, that Mitch Rogan,' he repeated, half admiringly.

They were silent on the drive back to the Hainsville Inn, each busy with his and her own thoughts.

'I'm sorry,' Camelia said, as the Inn's lights loomed through the murk. 'I didn't mean to malign Ed. It's just that right now, events are pointing in that direction. It's only circumstantial; it could be all wrong.' He flung his arms wide with another shrug. 'Then it's my mistake, and I'll apologize all over again.'

'That's okay,' Mel said, stiffly. But he knew it wasn't, and he sighed.

'Have a drink with me,' he said abruptly. 'We need to talk.'

They headed for the bar, frozen, wet, miserable, and apprehensive. They ordered the same drinks, a beer and a Cosmopolitan. Again, the young ever-smiley bartender got the Cosmo right. Again, Mel got on the phone, called the hospital.

Status quo. Again, Camelia got on the phone, called 'the office' to check what was doin'. This time, quite a bit, it seemed.

He listened intently while Mel sipped the Cosmo and nibbled on peanuts. Somewhere along the way they had forgotten all about lunch, and she was starving.

She heard Camelia give them the information on Mitch Rogan, and ask them to run it through the computer. She watched him, trying to guess the other part of the conversation, but his face was impassive and his responses noncommittal. Finally, he had finished. He turned back to the bar, took a good sip of his Bud and ordered a single malt.

'Ever hear of a George Artenski?' She shook her head. 'The national computer came up with a reasonable match for your photofit picture. We think he's our man.'

Color flooded her face, and she clutched a hand to her heart. 'You've caught him.'

'Not yet. But we have a pretty good idea of who he is. Of course, by now he'll be using a different ID, living somewheres else, probably have created a whole new life for himself. But Artenski was a hitman and this was a contract, I'd bet on that now.'

'But why? *Why* would anyone want Ed dead?'

She still didn't get it, didn't want to know that Ed might not be the nice, kind, loving, guy he seemed to be. Camelia let her off lightly, though, this time. 'That's what we still have to find out. Meanwhile, we don't want to scare our hitman underground, we want him to think he's gotten away with it.'

'Well, he has,' she retorted, spiritedly.

'So far, he has,' Camelia admitted. 'But not for much longer. We're not gonna show his picture on TV yet, but it's on every police computer in this land, and someone, somewhere, is bound to recognize him. It won't be much longer, you can count on that.

'Can I really, Marco?'

She reached for his hand. A thrill shot like a warm arrow

into his groin. He glanced away, and took a good slug of the single malt.

'*Really* count on it?' she added, pleadingly, thinking of how much safer she would feel with the hitman behind bars. How much safer Ed would be, despite his bodyguards around the clock.

'You can bet on it.' He squeezed her hand, then deftly removed his own without making it look too obvious. 'And we want him alive and kicking.' He didn't add *so we can get to know the truth about what happened*, but then, he didn't have to.

She was sharp as a tack and so goddamn beautiful, with her long neck tilted, her head drooping, her skin so pale and cold-looking. He wanted desperately to reach out, stroke the nape of her neck where the soft golden hair grew into a little downward point; he wanted to inhale her scent . . . Jesus, he was a cop on duty, what the hell was he thinking . . . yet, why else had he brought her here? He pushed the thought to the back of his mind. Like her, he didn't want to know the truth.

'Ever hear of a Mam'zelle Dorothea Jefferson Duval?' he asked. She shook her head, again. 'Me either. Apparently there was a call from her, from a nursing home near Charleston. She said it was urgent, that she wanted to talk to me about Ed Vincent. Wouldn't talk to anyone else.'

'How did she know about you?'

'Saw me on TV, perhaps. Or read about the case in the newspapers. Anyways, its worth a shot. We'll go to Charleston tomorrow, check out the beach house and speak with the Sheriff there. And also pay Mam'zelle Dorothea a visit. See what she has to say.'

'Okay.' It was getting late. Mel's head was throbbing, her nose was raw from the wind and she was sniffling with cold. All she wanted to do right now was go to bed, or go back to New York and Ed. *Oh, Ed, honey, I'll find out who did this, trust me . . . all I know it wasn't you . . .*

She said, 'Sorry, Marco, but I can't make dinner. I'm sending for room service. Chicken soup and cheese grits. Exactly what my mother used to give me when I was a kid and felt bad.'

'That's okay. Goodnight, baby, sleep well.' Again she dropped that light kiss on his cheek, but there was no smile tonight. Camelia sighed. He was the guy who had smashed her dreams.

And this scenario was so far from his own dreams of starlit nights and warm tumbled beds, that he grinned. He was in a one-horse pseudo-tourist town; it was pitch-dark and raining like hell; and the woman he was enamored with had gone off, sniffling and clutching a box of Kleenex, with a room-service order for one.

Chicken soup and grits. Camelia wished that was all it would take to make him feel better.

Chapter Thirty-four

They were on the flight to Charleston. The legroom was almost nonexistent and Mel sat with her knees practically under her chin, her eyes tight shut, her face pink with fever. The few times she spoke, in response to Camelia's questions about how she felt, her voice was a hoarse whisper.

So much for romance, Camelia told himself with a grin. You might say it was God's punishment to a would-be erring husband. Only, it seemed to him, she was the one suffering.

He asked the attendant for some hot tea and insisted she drink it, and also take the Tylenol Flu tablets he had bought at the airport.

'Thanks,' she whispered throatily.

'A magical sound,' he replied, drily.

'What is?'

'Your voice. Kinda like sandpaper on rusty iron.'

She giggled, then took a sip of the tea. It was *almost* hot, airline-style. 'I was just beginning to hate you, y'know that?'

He caught her sideways, glossy brown-eyed glance. 'For what?' he asked innocently. 'For taking you to Stepfordville, treating you to the best they had to offer? Buying you as many Cosmopolitans as you like? Treating you like a lady?'

'Thank you for that,' she whispered in that hoarse voice

that only made her seem sexier, in that oddball kinda way that appealed to men like him and Ed Vincent.

'For which one?'

'The lady part.'

Her eyes met his again, then he looked uncomfortably away. 'You're welcome,' he said, but he guessed she knew how he had been feeling. He crossed his fingers and thought of Claudia, the love of his life, the mother of his children, the woman who meant everything in the world to him. What was he doing, thirty thousand feet up in a plane with another woman? What was he thinking? He had never understood infidelity, particularly the casual sort. Never believed that the momentary physical pleasure it brought could ever equal the terrible pain it might bring to the one who had loved and trusted. He still didn't understand. All he knew was what he felt.

The sun was shining when they got to Charleston. There was the tang of the sea in the air, a blueness to the sky and a softness to the breeze that lifted both their spirits, and Camelia went completely mad and rented a Chrysler Sebring convertible. Then, top down, hair whipping in the wind, and feeling like a couple of teenagers, they drove through the outskirts of the city.

The Fairland Nursing Home was a residential unit for the elderly and infirm, expensive and a class act. It sat regally atop a hill, a pleasant stonefaced building with magnificent views over the countryside and a gravel driveway that swept in a circle to an imposing portico. The tall double doors stood open to the sunshine, revealing a polished hallway flooded with light from the long windows on either side.

Camelia sat for a moment, contemplating it. 'You don't get this on Medicare,' he observed. 'This costs. Our Mam'zelle Dorothea must be rolling in it.'

They went inside, walked to the end of the hall and tapped on a glossy blue door marked 'Office.'

'Come on in,' a pleasant Southern voice sang out.

The pleasant voice belonged to a pleasant-looking middle-aged woman, with a cloud of gray hair held back by a blue velvet Alice band. She was small and comfortably stout, wore no make-up, had pink apple cheeks and smiling greenish eyes behind little wire glasses.

'Definitely not a Stepford wife,' Mel whispered.

'That's because you're in Realville, not Hainsville,' he whispered back. 'Hi, how are ya, ma'am. I'm Detective Marco Camelia, of the New York Police Department.' He flashed his badge and she took it in her stride, with a little gasp of recognition.

'Oh, but of course. You men are so wonderful, so brave, and such an exciting job. Always putting your lives on the line for others.'

Camelia heard Mel's choked laugh and he coughed, embarrassed. 'That's only on the TV, ma'am. In fact we live a pretty quiet life.' It wasn't exactly true, but he wasn't a man to take credit where it wasn't due. He heard Mel giggle again, and said quickly, 'This is my assistant, Ms Melba Merrydew.'

Remembering her new role, Mel stuck her hands in her pockets and assumed what she hoped was a detective's assistant's stance: back straight, chin up, eyes steely, expression stern.

This time Camelia laughed. With her short skirt and long legs, she looked more like a showgirl than a worthy member of the force.

'Merrydew?' the woman said, thoughtfully. 'I remember a Merrydew Oaks, from when I was a girl, in Georgia. A wonderful place it was. I don't suppose you're from the South, my dear?'

Mel's eyes widened. 'I certainly am,' she said, astonished at what a small world it was. 'And Merrydew Oaks was my family's old place. Until the hard times came upon us.'

She sounded so like Scarlett, Camelia cracked another grin and she shot him a glare.

'Well, my dear, how lovely to meet you. And I'm sorry to hear about your hard times. But didn't that happen to all of us? The good Confederate families, from the old days? Now, better introduce myself.' She bustled out from behind her elegant antique desk, 'Rhianna Fairland.' She shook hands warmly and offered them a seat. 'How can little old me possibly be of any help to the New York Police Department?'

She beamed expectantly at them, and Mel found herself automatically beaming back. She *knew* this woman. She was exactly like her mother, Southern to the core and smart as all get-out under that sugary smile.

'You run a lovely place here, Ms Fairland,' Camelia laid on the compliments before getting down to business, softening her up so she would be more forthcoming. 'And that's quite a view. It must cost families quite a bit to place their loved ones here.'

'Of course it does.' She smiled back at him, fluffing her cloud of gray hair and adjusting her sixties John Lennon-style glasses. 'There are some families who have managed to hang onto their money, y'know. And quite a few more who've made recent fortunes.' Her sugary laugh tinkled merrily through the sunlit, Persian-carpeted office. 'We welcome them all here, of course, old money or new. Can't affort to be snobbish. After all, I am running a business.'

Her face softened, and her eyes had a faraway look as she said, 'It wasn't always like this, y'know. Who would have thought that I, Rhianna Fairland, born to genteel Southerners, and a true flower-child of the sixties, would have ended up running a home for the aged. I was at Woodstock, y'know,' she added proudly. 'Body-painted, free love, Acapulco gold and all. Ooops, maybe I shouldn't be admitting this to the police, but it was all so long ago. Everybody was doing it then. Anyhow –' her smile was bright again – 'how can I help you, Detective?'

'Mam'zelle Dorothea Jefferson Duval is one of your guests?'

Mam'zelle D? Well, of course she is.' A flicker of amusement crossed her face. 'But what can Dorothea possibly have been up to that could involve the NYPD Blue?'

Mel stifled a giggle, and Camelia ignored her. 'She telephoned my department, Miss Fairland. The Homicide Department,' he added quietly, and heard her little gasp.

'Homicide? Oh, *no* ... how can that *possibly* be? I mean, Dorothea didn't *kill* anyone. She hasn't left the place in *years*.'

'No one is accusing her of anything, ma'am.' He soothed her down quickly. 'But Mam'zelle Dorothea did telephone my department.'

'She *telephoned*? But how could she? None of the guests – we call them all guests here, though stricly speaking many are patients and under strict medical care – none of our guests has access to a telephone without supervision.' She tapped her head with a knowing look. 'Some are a bit what I used to call "wigged out." You never know who they might get on the phone. My guess is that Dorothea must have been watching too much TV, though how she got to the phone I can't imagine. She's one of our oldest residents, you know. Been with us almost twenty-five years now.'

Hand over her mouth, she added in a whisper, 'The poor dear came here with a severe alcohol problem, though we managed to straighten it out. But she's old now, very old. Ninety-three, y'know. Never thought she would last that long, but she confounded all the medicos.'

She paused to take a breath, and Camelia took advantage of the moment to get a word in.

'Is Mam'zelle Dorothea ...' he hesitated, not wanting to say *sane* ... 'is she of sound mind?'

'She most certainly is. Well, she's a bit, you know, doddery. Her mind's here one minute, gone the next. You can't take everything she says as gospel, I'm afraid. Hence my scepticism over the mysterious phone call.'

'She claims to know a man called Ed Vincent.'

'Of course she knows him. He pays her bills here, visits her every weekend.' Her smile faded and she added, 'Until recently, of course.'

Mel stared at her, stunned. Ed took care of this old lady? He had never mentioned her. But then, Ed was a charitable man, he took care of a lot of people. People she knew nothing about. And how much did she really know about Ed, after all, she wondered, bewildered.

Camelia's face was cop-impassive as he waited for Rhianna Fairland to continue.

Realization dawned on Rhianna. 'Dorothea called because she wanted to talk to the police about *Ed?* I guess she wanted to know who did it. Poor Dorothea. She missed him last weekend, she so looked forward to his visits, and he never skipped them. Oh, no, he was always here, every Sunday, except for the weekend of the hurricane. And now, of course.'

Her eyes met Mel's. 'I'm so sorry,' she said quietly. 'Mr Vincent is a very nice, very generous man. We shall all miss him.'

'He's not dead yet,' Mel shot back, alarm bells ringing. *She had been away too long, anything could happen, people were already talking as though he had gone . . .*

'Of course, I didn't tell Dorothea about it. Far too upsetting. And I don't know how she found out what happened. The TV-viewing is strictly supervised, and I understand she doesn't see well enough to read the newspapers. And anyhow, all her bills are paid via a private trust.'

She flipped back her long hair again. Like a sixties teenager, Camelia thought. He guessed some people just got stuck in a comfortable timewarp, when they were happiest.

'Ms Fairland, I need to question Mam'zelle Dorothea. I believe she has information about Ed Vincent that might help in our search for his attacker.'

'*Dorothea* does? Well, I'll be darned!' She flopped back as though the stuffing had gone out of her, limp with shock. 'But how can Dorothea possibly know who tried to kill Mr Vincent?'

'She claimed in her message to have information we would

be interested in.' Camelia shrugged. 'I'm afraid I must insist on seeing her, Ms Fairchild.'

'Well, I don't know . . .' she hesitated.

'It's official police business, ma'am,' Camelia warned.

'Oh. Official police business. Well, yes, then I suppose it's alright. But she's a very frail old lady, I'm warning you to take care.'

Chapter Thirty-five

Mam'zelle Dorothea's room was spacious, with double french windows leading onto a flowered terrace. The scent of gardenias drifted in on the breeze, along with the trickling sound of a fountain, reminding Mel of a hundred such lazy, sunny days in the South, when she was a child.

It had been a long time since Mam'zelle Dorothea had been a child, though, and every day of her life seemed written on her corroded face. Sharply jutting cheekbones propped up the withered flesh, and eyes of the palest winter blue, brimming with intelligence, stared inquisitively at them as they entered. Her sparse hair was pulled back so tightly Mel thought it could have acted as a facelift, but at ninety-three, Mam'zelle Dorothea seemed beyond vanity. As proven by the fact that she was wearing a ratty fur coat from some indistinguishable animal that might easily have been prehistoric.

She wafted a scrawny arm at them, urging them inside. 'Come into my lair,' she called in a voice thin as cracked glass, following it with a throaty chortle that made Mel jump.

And it was 'a lair'; overstuffed floral chintz sofas with lacy antimacassars; ornate vases; porcelain statues of brightly colored parakeets and toucans; crystal knicknacks; embroidered foot-stools and carved whatnots. Mam'zelle Dorothea had brought her past with her to the Fairland Nursing Home.

There was only one photograph, though, in a large, simple silver frame on the nightstand. It was of Ed, looking so handsome, so alive, so *vital*, that Mel cried out in shock.

Ms Fairland introduced them and Mam'zelle Dorothea sank back against the huge leopardskin cushions propping her up in the chair that looked way too big for her fragile frame. She took a long look at Mel. 'You're the one Ed's in love with,' she said, at last.

Mel crouched by Dorothea's side. She took her sparrow-boned hand eagerly in hers. 'You know?'

'Ed tells me everything. *Everything*,' she added, with a wicked twinkle. 'Always has. Ever since we met.'

She glared beyond Mel at Rhianna Fairland hovering in the background. 'You may leave now,' she said, haughtily. 'My conversation with Miss Merrydew and Detective Camelia will be private.'

Ms Fairland hesitated. She glanced at Camelia. He nodded, and with a regretful sigh she exited, closing the door soundlessly behind her.

Long shadows reached across the room, leaving Mam'zelle in the half-light, a waxworks dummy, frozen in time.

'It took you long enough to get here,' she said sharply to Camelia.

'I'm sorry, Mam'zelle, but I only received your message last night. We were in Hainsville.'

'Huh. Hainsville.' She made a little face of distaste. 'You've been there?'

'Never. Thank God. But from what Ed told me, it didn't sound like the kind of place anybody should live.'

'And what exactly did Ed tell you, Mam'zelle Dorothea?' Mel was perched on a little round needlepoint stool, next to the old lady. She took her hand again, anxious for contact with this woman who obviously cared deeply about Ed. And who, in return, Ed obviously loved.

'Y'don't look like the kind of gal I would have expected

him to fall for.' Mam'zelle inspected her sharply, and looking into her water-blue eyes, unclouded by the cataracts of age, Mel knew that, at least today, she wasn't missing a trick. 'I would have thought he'd go for the Southern belle. Landed gentry, just the opposite of where he came from himself. That's what usually happens when a man is on the way up.'

'I don't think Ed is on the way up anymore, Mam'zelle,' Mel said. 'He is already there.'

'Ahh. Then he has no need of the trophy wife.' She looked shrewdly at Camelia. 'Trophy wives come in all shapes and configurations, Detective. The blonde bombshell, the nubile teenager, the star. The Southern girl-next-door.'

Camelia nodded uncomfortably. He had the feeling this old woman could read minds.

'I suppose I had better introduce myself. I am Mademoiselle Dorothea Jefferson Duval. Kin to the famous president on my mother's side of the family. And to the Creole Duvals on my father's side. And a resident of Charleston for my entire life.'

'Nice place to live,' Camelia murmured, wondering why he was here. Was she just gonna ramble on, tell them her life story, and that Ed Vincent was her hero because he paid her bills as an act of charity?

'Mam'zelle Dorothea, tell me about Ed, please,' Mel begged. She needed to know the truth so bad, she would have sat all night at this old woman's feet. She would have bathed her in tears and kisses, given her soul, to know what she had to say.

But instead, Mam'zelle Dorothea fished a bottle of bourbon from behind the leopardskin cushion. They watched, stunned, as she took a water glass from the little crinkle-edged, round oak antique table that was already liberally stained with white rings, and poured herself a stiff shot. Mam'zelle tipped back her head, took a slug, then sighed with satisfaction.

'They've been trying for years to wean me off this. Ed too. I told him he might as well try to take away a mother's milk.' Her wicked laughter was not a cackle now, but the gentle, refined tinkle of the Southern belle, a sound Mel knew well. 'They tell me I've been dying of drink for fifty years now. Hah, and here I am, outliving all the doctors. And there's always someone who can be bribed to break the law, get you what you need. But then I suppose you already know that,' she added to Camelia.

'Yes, ma'am, I do.' He guessed by this age the bourbon could do her no harm. Good luck to her, he thought.

'I called you here,' she said, looking contemplatively at them, 'because I thought you needed to know about the real Ed Vincent. And to know that his true name is Theo Rogan.'

Mel's sigh of relief echoed through the shadowy room. *Thank God*, she thought. *He is not Mitch. He's not the killer . . .'*

'But wasn't Theo Rogan killed in the fire?' Camelia asked.

Mam'zelle waved an imperious hand at him. 'Now, now, don't get impatient. I've known Ed for thirty years and I will tell you the whole story, but I must begin at the very beginning.' And she took another long slug from the tumbler, thinking about what she was going to say.

Chapter Thirty-six

He was missing her, oh, how he was missing her . . . the scent of her, the cool sexy scent that he would recognize even through the fog of Bloomingdales' perfume department, a seductive mixture of her soft flesh and lilies and jasmine and summer . . . A peachy smell . . . he smiled as he thought that one . . . Where had she gone, oh, Zelda, where have you gone . . . I hope you didn't go there, not to Hainsville . . . I can't even bear to think of it, to think of you there . . . that place where my life ground to a halt, where my guilt and shame will never leave . . .

He was back to that terrible night again. His birthday. The night Michael Haines had demanded to buy their pa's land, and Mitch had cursed him when he had refused. He had thought Mitch was going to punch Pa, he was that angry . . . but it was worse than that . . . oh, much worse . . .

He had slipped out of the cabin and was running down the road, his backpack bouncing against his shoulders. The fierce wind howled all around him. It snatched his breath, sent him gasping and reeling, clutching at the trees to keep his footing. The entire forest was alive with the sound of it. It shook and trembled as the wind tore full-grown trees from the ground and sent heavy branches crashing.

He was relieved when he was finally out in the open,

descending through the meadows onto the potholed blacktop lane that led to Hainsville. He picked up speed now, head bowed, running steadily through the rain with the wind behind him giving him a push, as though it knew of his urgent mission.

He had gone a couple of miles when he saw the gleam of headlights cutting through the darkness. Was Michael Haines bringing Mitch home? Unwilling to be caught, he dodged into the thicket of poplars bordering the road. Their slender trunks seemed to ripple in the wind, and the brittle, golden leaves covered him, the way they had the children in the story of *The Babes In The Woods*.

He held his breath as the vehicle approached, peering from his hiding place, half blinded by its lights. As it whizzed past, he saw it was a pickup truck with two men in it. He didn't know the truck, didn't know the men, but guessed they were itinerant laborers. He pondered on where they could be heading. The road ended at Sorrygate Farm, one of Haines's properties, but they weren't likely to be going there at this time of night. The only other place it led was to his own home.

A warning signal buzzed from his brain to his feet, and in a second he was running back the way he had come. Running fast down the center of the narrow road, oblivious to the rain, fighting the wind.

He was almost home when he saw it. A bright red glow against the lowering sky. 'No,' he screamed out loud, 'please God, no . . .' And then he was running again. Staggering, sliding, falling. *Desperate*.

He reached the clearing, saw the men throw more gasoline on the flames, saw the tarpaper-covered cabin explode in a ball of fire.

He was screaming. He saw the men silhouetted against the fireball as they turned and looked at him. Heard their hoarse cries of alarm. Saw one lift a rifle.

Paralyzed with shock, he let out a blood-curdling yell of fear and anguish before instinct sent him fleeing, deep into the forest.

That forest was his backyard: he knew every inch of it, all its secrets and hiding places. He found the tiny cave where he and his sisters had played hide-and-seek. He tucked his large bony frame into it, clutching his arms over his head, hiding like a hunted animal. He might be six foot tall, but he was only a fourteen-year-old kid, terrified and alone. Fear sent shudders through his body. He could scarcely breathe. A terrible feeling of desolation overwhelmed him as he waited for his family's murderers to find him.

A name zapped like an electric shock through his brain. *Mitch.*

His brother was not one of the men who had fired the house and murdered his family. But he knew for sure that Mitch had something to do with it.

Now he could hear the men crashing through the forest, hear their muffled curses as they tripped over fallen branches, heard them when they called it quits.

'Aw, *fuck this,*' one grumbled.

'*Whoever it was won't dare say nuthin' anyways,*' the other yelled, so close it made Theo flinch.

'*Whole family's gone. We did our job,*' the first agreed. '*Let's call it a night and git outta here.*'

The sounds diminished as the men made their way back to their truck. He heard faintly the sound of the pickup disappearing into the night. Numb with shock, he clambered from his hiding place. He ran back to the clearing, stood gazing at the smouldering ruins of his home. Ruins that held the remains of his entire family. *Except for Mitch.*

Tears coursed down his face, thick as the night's rain. He choked on his sobs as a deep sense of shame overwhelmed him. He had run away, hidden in the woods while his family burned to death. Even though he had seen the fiery explosion, and knew that they had already been dead and that there was nothing he could have done, it brought no respite from the shame. He should have tried to help. He should have strangled the men, broken their necks, run them through with a pitchfork. He should have killed them. *And now he would kill Mitch.*

He sat for a long time on the stump of the big mountain ash his daddy had cut down the previous year when it became too tall, thinking black thoughts of despair. Anguish lay heavy as a stone in his chest as he planned how he would go into town and find Mitch, imagining the dozen different ways he might kill him.

As dawn broke, he rose wearily from his seat and walked toward the still smoking ruin. 'God bless you, Ma, Daddy,' he whispered. 'God bless you, Jared and Jess, Honor and Grace. You are in heaven now, and safe from all this. The Lord will take care of you. *And I will take care of Mitch.*'

At that moment, he could have sworn he heard his mother's voice: calm, rational, speaking directly to him, telling him that he must not kill Mitch. That if he did, he would be a murderer too, and she wanted no blood on his hands.

He lifted his head, looked around, wondering. But of course she was not there. The voice in his head was his own conscience, telling him that he was no killer.

There was only one thing to do. Hefting the small pack containing his birthday jeans and new flannel shirt, he set out through the forest for the top of the mountain. He couldn't see the peak because it was wreathed in mist, but the rain had stopped and a weak beam of sunlight struggled through the clouds.

Carolina lay on the other side of that mountain, and he intended to put as much territory between himself and Tennessee, and his murdering brother and Michael Haines as possible. He guessed the killers were right. They would assume the entire family had perished in the blaze. He would never see his brother again.

Chapter Thirty-seven

'I didn't shed any tears when he told me what happened that night they murdered his family,' Mam'zelle Dorothea said. 'Nor did I cry when he told me the story of what happened afterward. I was a selfish woman. My parents had indulged me, spoiled me rotten, y'might say. I never cared what other people thought, and I lived my life exactly the way I wanted. But that young stranger touched my heart. Or what was left of it.'

She contemplated her glass, staring into the bourbon's amber depths as though looking for an answer as to why she had found Theo Rogan's story so heartfelt.

'He was so young,' she said finally. 'So pitifully young. And so thin and starved. Oh, not like me, which was, y'might say, by choice. That is, I chose to drink rather than eat. And he was so damned gallant with it. A young gentleman.' She was silent for a moment, then she added softly, 'I thought to myself, this could have been the son you never had. The boy who would have made your life worth living. And then I took another long look at him. And I thought, y'know what, Dorothea, he still can.

'And that, my dears,' she added softly, 'was the beginning of our lives together.'

Ed's body felt like a dead weight ... *dead* he thought, *how*

ironic, my body is dead but my brain is working overtime, crowding me with memories.

I lived the life of an itinerant, he remembered. *Hopping freight trains, dodging the law, bumming food from other hobos, hunching round their campfires. A thin, starved lad, looking older than my fourteen years. I lied about it, of course, always said I was sixteen, and no one questioned that. I took jobs where I could get them: picking tobacco or cotton, working in the fields. My life was worse than my father's. He had at least succeeded in owning his own piece of land, but I was lower than a sharecropper. I was an itinerant laborer of little value to anybody, except as an extra bent back in the fields. I hated it, but I saw no way out. Until Dorothea Jefferson Duval came along and saved me.*

Almost a year after he had climbed over the mountain into Carolina, he found himself in Charleston on a night of freezing rain when the temperatures dipped into the low thirties. He had only his denims, which true to his mother's words were now rising around his ankles, the worn blue-checked flannel birthday shirt, his old home-cobbled shoes and the oilskin slicker that had belonged to his father.

It was January, and the black fields lay hibernating and desolate under a coating of frost. There was no work to be had and Theo drifted, hungry and cold, with only a fifty-cent piece in his pocket, into the beautiful city of Charleston.

He had never seen such a place. Light from the tall windows of splendid houses spilled across the sidewalks into tree-filled squares. Shop windows glittered with an array of goods, the likes of which he had only seen on his rare visits to the Dew-Drop-In drive-in movies. Well-dressed people thronged the sidewalks, streaming into restaurants whose aromas nearly drove him crazy with longing, and shiny automobiles cruised the nighttime streets, heading, he guessed wistfully, for home.

The city was everything he had ever daydreamed about and more. Beautiful, rich, opulent and sensual. It was, he felt sure,

unmatched by Paris or London, though maybe not by Rome, with all its wonderful antiquities. Of course, he had no true way of comparing because Charleston was the first *real* city he had ever seen, but if he were a rich man, he knew he could want for nothing more than to live here, in one of those splendid houses.

Each pastel-colored mansion was hidden behind high walls and elaborate iron gates that offered a glimpse of gardens shaded by magnolias and ancient oaks, and secret courtyards where winter-silent fountains promised to lift next summer's humid air with their music.

Theo waited until the restaurants closed, then he scavenged in the garbage cans, fighting off the feral cats in search of the same meal, gulping down the scrapings from other people's dinner plates, gnawing on steak bones for the final tasty bits of meat, scooping rice and beans from the debris in the cans. He was still hungry when he left, drifting through the now quiet streets, a thin gray shadow unnoticed by the few pedestrians.

It must have been around midnight when he found himself in the area known as The Battery, with spacious lawns fronting the sea, dotted with huge oaks and old monuments and ancient cannons. The wind was edged with ice and he shivered under the black oilskin. A memory of his siblings flashed across his mind, huddled around the wood-stove, toasting their toes along with a few chestnuts, arguing and punching, rowdy as a pack of puppies confined in the tiny cabin with its newspaper-covered walls.

In that moment, Theo longed so badly for his home and his family, his knees went weak. He sank onto the frosty grass, head bowed, lost in grief and despair. He had nothing to live for.

Frozen, he finally stirred himself, drifting away from the water, seeking shelter from the wind. He wandered north of The Battery into an area of grand homes. The big houses were silent and dark, their lucky families asleep in warmth and comfort. Envy left a bitter taste in his mouth, though he would have traded any one of those grand homes just to put back the clock

and have his own little cabin and his family alive, all together again, safe in the lee of the Great Smokies.

He paused outside a pink-washed Federal house, just visible through the leafless trees. No lights showed at the windows, but he noticed that a small side gate stood ajar. He saw that it led into a courtyard and quickly stepped inside. The high walls cut off the wind and he stood for a minute, catching his breath, letting his eyes adjust. He was a country boy, he was used to walking hilly terrain at night and could navigate his way around in the dark easier than most folks did in daytime.

He walked cautiously past the frozen fountain, through a low wooden door set in the brick wall and into a neglected garden. Even though it was winter, he could see that no human hand had touched the place in a decade. Vines choked the camellias, leafless rosebushes spread thorny branches across the path, and box hedges that once bordered flower beds had now taken them over completely. Ivy swarmed over the walls of the house and across the garden, half hiding the many statues of angels and nymphs. And, at the far end of the garden, he saw another building. Dirt was so ingrained on its exterior that it was impossible to know, until he went inside, that it was completely made of glass.

When his eyes got used to the even deeper level of darkness, he made out the shelves of long-dead plants; withered orange and lemon trees, dead fig and espaliered peach. He knew it was some kind of hothouse he was in, except there was no heat. But there was a long table fashioned from wooden planks that he recognized as a place where seedlings were potted and brought on in the winter. His daddy's precious tomato plants had flourished in a makeshift version of this potting shed.

And on the table were a few old flour sacks. He did not hesitate. He climbed onto the table, covered himself completely with the sacks so that not even his nose peeked out, and curled up into a fetal position for warmth. He had found a home for the night.

As the temperature fell and ice crusted the glass panes of his shelter, he had the feeling it might be his second encounter with death. Winter would kill him, even if Mitch and Michael Haines had not. Death would be his companion this night, and he welcomed it.

He did not wake until the faltering rays of a wintry sun thawed his numb legs. Still beneath the sacking covers, he stretched out his full length, arms above his head, surprised to be alive. His first thought was that he was hungry again.

'Hot damn, you're a big fellow, whoever you are.' A female voice cut through the silence like a pistol shot.

Theo flung off the sacking and stared at the old woman sitting opposite him in a green canvas lawn chair. Faded eyes sunk in dark shadows gazed calmly back at him. Her silver hair was tugged fiercely back from a bony, lined face. She was scrawny, with sparrow-claw hands and tiny feet thrust into old boots, and she was as shabby as himself in an ancient fur coat that looked as though it had once belonged to a much larger person, and which enveloped her stringy body like a mangy shroud. An empty bourbon bottle was on the floor next to her feet.

He breathed a sigh of relief. She was a vagrant like himself, seeking temporary shelter and warmth. He felt a pang of pity as he looked at her. He couldn't guess how old she was, but he knew she was too old to be living rough like this. He wished he could help her, but he could not even help himself.

'Ahm sorry, ma'am, if ah startled you,' he said, remembering to be polite to his elders and betters.

A cackling sound came from her throat. It made his hair stand on end until he realized she was laughing. 'I think it's the other way about, young man. And do I detect a mountain accent?'

Theo felt himself blush. His almost impenetrable accent had caused him no end of problems since he'd left home. He couldn't

figure out why folks had so much trouble understanding him, until he realized they spoke different, and then he'd begun to try to copy them.

He slid hurriedly off the table, tucking his shirttails into his pants, running his hands through his thick dark hair until it stood on end like a cockscomb. 'Ah didn't see you when I came in last night. Ah'm sorry, Ah would've left you alone. Ah wouldn't want to interrupt your sleep.'

She chuckled again. 'At my age you don't care much about sleep anymore. It's all I've got to look forward to. *That long, last sleep.*'

They stared at each other in silence, neither understanding what they saw. He thought she was obviously as poor as he was, yet she spoke with an educated accent. She thought he was like a rough young animal, thin and wild.

'We are alike, you and I,' she said at last, reading the pain and fear in his eyes. 'But for different reasons.' She clambered slowly out of the lawnchair and Theo hurried to assist her. He flinched as he touched her. Her hand was icy, purple, bloodless, and her breath smelled of bourbon.

'Where y' headin', ma'am? Cain't ah do anythin' to help you?'

'Can you think of anything?' She stared up at him, tiny as his sister Grace had been.

He blushed again, bewildered. 'No ah cain't, ma'am. Ah ain't got nothin' to offer you. Cept'n my arm, to aid ya down the street.'

She nodded, thoughtfully. 'That's very civil of you. Thank you, but I can manage.' She shuffled slowly to the door of the conservatory, leaning heavily on a silver-banded cane. 'You must be hungry,' she said, turning as she reached the door.

'Ah guess so, ma'am. Yes ah am.' Theo's stomach rumbled loudly as she reminded him. 'Ah'll find something, though, sooner or later.'

'Sooner is better, I think,' she said, nodding to herself. 'Wait here, will you.'

She closed the glass door with its broken panes as carefully as if it were crystal from Venice. Theo stood where she had left him, shaking his head in wonder. A call of nature brought him back to this world and he found a discreet corner of the garden in which to empty his bladder.

Buttoning his filthy old denims, he found a metal bucket of water, cracked the ice on it and dashed the water over his face. He didn't flinch. All his life he had washed in cold water, even ice water like this, in winter. He smoothed his hair as best he could and adjusted his clothing until he was as neat as a lad who had slept in his clothes for several months could be.

The old woman returned a few minutes later, pushing an ancient perambulator that had once been very grand. Its glossy navy coachwork and soft creamy leather interior had once been suitable for the baby of a very rich family. Now it contained a fresh baguette, a dish of butter and a pot of very hot coffee, the smell of which almost brought Theo to his knees.

'Where d'y' git all this?' He was afraid she had stolen it.

'Oh, the people here know me.' She smiled at him. 'They take pity on me, sometimes. Think I need feeding up. When all the time it's young fellows like you who need nourishment.' She thrust the loaded pram toward him. 'Help yourself.'

She took her place on the lawn chair again, watching as he poured coffee into two china beakers. 'Sugar and cream, ma'am?' He looked inquiringly at her.

'You have nice manners.' She settled the ratty fur elegantly round her shoulders as though it were luxurious sables. 'I've taken coffee black all my life, thank you, and I'm not about to change now. Though of course the doctors say I should. Bah, what do they know, silly old fools. I always tell them if they know so much, how come they die too?'

She took a sip, seeming not to notice that it was scalding.

Theo had just burned his mouth on it. 'Pass me a bit of that baguette, young man, with some butter.'

He had never seen a sterling-silver knife before, and this one was elaborately carved on the shaft. 'It's too beautiful to use,' he said, amazed, turning it over and over in his hands.

'Remember this, young man.' She stared into his eyes. Hers were a clear transparent blue, paler than a winter sky. For a second he almost believed if he looked hard enough, he would see into her soul. He shivered, wondering if she was a witch. 'Remember,' she said again, 'that a thing of beauty is even more beautiful if it has a use.'

Theo thought about that for a minute. Maybe she was right.

'Isn't it about time you introduced yourself?'

She was sitting up, drinking the coffee, perky as a sparrow now, with a touch of pink in her cheeks as the drink warmed her.

Theo put down the hunk of baguette smothered in butter. It was the best thing he had tasted in almost a year, and he was reluctant to leave it even for a second. But he remembered his manners, and that this lady was responsible for his breakfast and his current good fortune. 'Ah'm Theodore Rogan, ma'am. Youngest son of Farrar Rogan, deceased, of Hainsville township, East Tennessee.'

'Never heard of it. But then, I can't think many have. Hainsville doesn't exactly sound like a metropolis.'

'That it ain't, ma'am,' Theo agreed.

'Well then, I am Dorothea Jefferson Duval, kin to the famous president on my mother's side of the family. And to the Creole Duvals on my father's side.'

'Is that so, ma'am, Mrs Duval.' Theo was polite but he was itching to get back to his breakfast.

'*Mademoiselle*,' she corrected him sharply. 'That is *Mademoiselle Jefferson Duval.* Remember that, Theo Rogan.'

'Oh, ah will ma'am, Mam'zelle Jefferson Duval,' he agreed hastily.

'Finish your breakfast,' she instructed, taking a sip of her coffee again. 'And then we shall talk.'

I slept in the conservatory every night after that, Ed remembered. *And every morning, Mam'zelle Jefferson Duval would show up with the old pram with the bread and butter and hot coffee. I stopped asking her how she got it, and where she spent her time, and where she slept at night. She never talked about herself over our shared breakfast, but she did ask a lot of questions. I was more surprised than she, when I found myself telling her about Mitch and the murder of my family. About how ashamed I was that I had not tried to save them. And how much I had wanted to kill my brother.*

Holding the tumbler, newly replenished with bourbon in both her small, blue-veined hands, Mam'zelle Dorothea took another sip. Her pale, penetrating eyes met Camelia's. 'So I asked, why didn't you kill him? And do you know what he replied? *"Then ah would have had blood on my hands too,"* he said. *"My ma would not have wanted that."*

'I told him it was a rational answer, and then I asked him, "And what exactly do you propose to do with the life that was spared you?"'

Her hand holding the empty glass shook as she placed it carefully back on the stained antique table. 'I want to become someone,' he told me. 'A real person.' And I thought to myself, *And I am the one who can help you do just that.*

She leaned back against the cushion, her skull-like face fading into the shadows until it seemed she was almost not there. *A ghost from Ed's past,* Mel thought.

'I'm tired,' Mam'zelle Dorothea murmured. 'Tomorrow is another day. Come back and see me then ...'

She was already sleeping when they crept out of the room, leaving her with the scent of gardenias and the tinkling fountain, and her dreams of a once glorious past.

Camelia closed the heavy door soundlessly behind him. You learned the ropes quickly in a place like this, he thought.

As they strode down the steps to the car, Camelia stole a quick glance at Mel. She had not uttered a word during Mam'zelle's story, never interrupted, never shed a tear. But he could see the tension in the stiffness of her back, in her tightly curled fists, the stern line of her mouth.

He slid an arm around her shoulder. 'You gonna cry, or what?'

She turned to look at him, then she shook her head. A weary smile curved her lips. 'Poor Ed,' she whispered. 'That poor boy. How did he ever survive?'

'He wouldn't have. Not without Mam'zelle Dorothea.'

'Thanks be to God, and to her,' Mel said softly. But like Mam'zelle's, her heart ached for the boy who had become the man she loved.

Chapter Thirty-eight

Back in the rented convertible, Mel was doing the driving while Camelia sat back with his eyes closed.

'Remember, I'm a cop,' he said. 'I could cite you for doing double the speed limit.'

Mel slammed her foot on the brake. Dropping back to a modest fifty, she flashed him that wide smile. 'Sorry, Detective. Somehow I figured I was with a friend.'

Their eyes met. 'You know you are.'

She nodded, looking quickly away, but she was smiling.

Camelia stared straight ahead through the windshield. It was the closest he could come to telling her he was in love with her. It was ridiculous, he knew. And they surely looked ridiculous, the odd couple – her so tall and blonde, him shorter and dark. The tough Sicilian cop and the daffy Southern belle from California. He sighed. She was such a touchy-feely woman; she linked his arm when they walked down the street; held his hand at the dinner table as he talked to her; lay her head on his shoulder when she was tired and he was driving them home.

And he envied a dying man because she loved him.

'Thanks for the Tylenol Flu,' Mel said. 'I'm feeling better.'

'Was it the pills, or Mam'zelle Dorothea's story that made you feel good?' She threw him a smile and he added, 'Okay, okay, do I say I'm sorry now? For suspecting that Ed might be Mitch?'

'You do. Unless you still want to see which way the cards will fall,' she quoted him, mischievously.

'So, I apologize. But let me remind you, we still do not have the full picture on Ed Vincent, aka Theo Rogan.'

'We do not. But as Mam'zelle Dorothea said, tomorrow is another day.'

They were driving north now, through countryside, on a narrow road Mel knew only too well. Strange, she thought, how much shorter the drive seemed than on that long, fateful night, when the wind had tossed trees around like matchsticks and the ocean had flung its roaring power over the land.

She braked as they came to the bridge, letting the engine idle as she stared once again at the place where she had thought she would die. The bridge had been repaired now, and the sea glittered below it, a benign silver blue. She felt Camelia's hand on her shoulder, turned and met his eyes.

'It's over now, Mel,' he said, gently. 'There's no need to fear this place again.'

But inwardly she was still quaking. It wasn't until she got to the other side and her breath came out in a great whoosh, that she realized she had been holding it in. She drove on, up the rough lane, through the trees to the beach house. She switched off the engine, put the car into park and they sat, silently contemplating Ed's private retreat, basking in the mild sunshine.

'Kinda nice,' Camelia said, finally. He got out and walked up the steps onto the porch. 'Yeah, nice,' he said approvingly. He was mentally upgrading his image of Ed Vincent-the-big-shot-rich-man-developer. This place was low-key comfortable, more like a fishing cabin than a palace at the Hamptons, which is what he might have expected.

Mel loped up the steps. She stood next to him, peering through the windows. She grabbed his arm. 'This is it. This is the room where the body was. And the safe is over there behind the painting, the landscape of a log cabin in the forest.'

'Ed's cabin,' Camelia guessed, and Mel realized it was

probably true. Ed had not forgotten his old home, and where he came from, even after all these years and all his success.

'Let's go inside,' she said.

Camelia guessed she wanted to put her fears at rest by facing them. 'I'm a cop,' he said. 'I don't break into other folks' houses. At least, not without a warrant.'

'Well, I'm the owner's lover. And I can break into his house anytime I want.' She grinned. 'Besides, it wouldn't be the first time.'

'Do you have a key?'

She shook her head and he sighed as he walked back along the porch and checked the door. The lock was ancient, even a child could have jimmied it. It took him about five seconds with a gold Visa Card.

'My, oh, my, honey.' Mel watched admiringly. 'Anybody would think you did this for a living.'

He flung open the door and they stood on the threshold, peeking in like a couple of petty thieves, afraid of being caught.

'It's not nice to invade somebody's house like this,' Camelia said, uneasily. But Mel was already walking past him into the lofty room that overlooked the ocean. He saw her pause outside the door on the right, saw her square her shoulders, take a deep breath before she flung it open.

Sunlight flooded the room she had seen only for a few terrible seconds before the lights wents out. There was the place where the dead man had sprawled across the carpet in the vivid pool of blood and an ugly yellow spatter of brains and flesh and bloodstained dollar bills. Now there was just an immaculate antique Oriental rug in a blurred pattern of blues and reds. The book-lined walls were free of dust, and the only sign of neglect was the wilting scarlet begonia on the windowledge.

Mel's heart slowed down and she took a cautious step inside the library. Then another, and another. *It was okay*, she told herself, *everything was okay, there was no need to be afraid any-*

more. This was Ed's room; these were his books; his desk stood under the window; the pens he used were stored in that small seashell-studded box. How sweet, she thought vaguely, that he had that little seashell box, when he could have the best desk set from Dunhill or Marc Cross. But that was Ed.

She heard Camelia behind her, and she pointed out the place where the body had lain, showed him where the wall safe was.

Camelia took it all in, but there was nothing for him to learn here. The beach house had been cleaned thoroughly, and also gone over by the local police, as well as Ed's PI. His interest was academic at this point.

He took her hand, walked out of the library and closed the door firmly behind them. 'Just look at that view.' He headed for the row of tall french windows, opened one up and led her outside.

They took off their jackets, and Camelia loosened the silver necktie and rolled up his shirtsleeves. They stood for a few minutes, just breathing in gusts of the fresh ocean breeze, lifting their faces to the sun. 'Like day-trippers at Jones Beach,' he said.

The Grand Banks 38 Europa was moored at the private dock to the right of the house, with a flight of wooden steps leading down to it. Camelia was a boat man, though he had never owned one, and he thought this was a very fine toy for a man to possess. For the second time that day, he envied Ed Vincent.

He walked down the steps to the deep mooring, stepped onto the immaculate teak deck. No fiberglass here; this was a proper craft, old but beautifully restored. The varnish was perfect, though the kelly-green canvas bridge cover had been ripped to shreds in the hurricane. He took a peek at the new engine, complete with Walker Airseps and a silencing package. It was powerful. He thought it probably cruised at a top of fourteen knots.

Mel jumped down beside him. She walked slowly along the deck, ran her hand along the teak rail, which somehow she just

knew Ed had polished himself. There was a single stateroom forward, with a tapered island bed and an oversized hanging locker. In the tiny, narrow galley was an electric cooktop, a microwave and a Gruernet refrigeration box with a teak cover.

This was a man's boat, no fuss, no frills, no decor, and immaculate as an operating theater. She edged up to the bow and leaned her arms on the rail, staring into the green depths. Her mind was back in New York, in that hospital room with the uniformed cop outside, guarding a dying man. Tears slid uncontrollably down her face, plopping into the still water, and she rested her head on the rail, letting the emotion wash over her.

After a while, Camelia found her there. He stood awkwardly to one side. The sobs shook her slender body, and but for the life of him, he could not find the right words of comfort.

'There's nothing to say that hasn't already been said, Mel,' he told her finally. 'Nothing to do that isn't already being done.'

She nodded. 'I know.' Her voice was muffled and he went to stand next to her at the rail. He wanted to hold her, just the way he had that first day he had met her. Only now he knew her, and the ache for her was different.

Something caught his eye. Something drifting, pulling on the anchor chain. He leaned over the rail, peering at the shape, just visible under the shifting water.

He searched around for a grappling iron, found one in the locker, hurried back. He leaned over the side, maneuvering until he hooked it. He was sweating, it was a dead weight, he couldn't lift it. Somehow it had hooked onto the anchor chain.

He let go of it. 'Mel, honey,' he said and, God bless her, she lifted her head and gave him a watery smile.

'I told you that "honey" thing was catching,' she said with a hiccup.

'Baby,' he changed it firmly, 'why don't you go and take a nice little siesta, on one of those comfy loungers back at the house?'

Her eyes opened wide. 'Why?'

He sighed, but he guessed he would have to tell her some time. 'I think we may have found something of interest on the boat. I'm gonna call the local Sheriff, have him come out here.'

She hung over the rail. 'I don't see anything.'

'Something's caught on the anchor chain. I need help to get it up.'

Her eyes rounded with alarm. 'You don't think . . . ?'

'I don't know what I think. Meantime, go and make yourself a cup of tea or whatever Southern belles do when they are not wanted around.'

'Camomile tea,' she said, mopping her red eyes with a tired-looking Kleenex. He offered her his handkerchief.

'Déjà vu all over again.' Still sniffing, she managed a grin, remembering when she had guessed he was married because of the clean handkerchief he always carried. 'But don't think you're getting rid of me so easily, Detective Camelia. I'm staying right here until we find out what's in the water.'

'You might not like it,' he warned.

'I'll take my chances.'

Mel walked back along the deck. She took a seat in the shade, while Camelia called the local cops. He came back, sat next to her. 'They'll be here in ten,' he said, and they sat silently, looking out at the ocean. Waiting.

Chapter Thirty-nine

The Sheriff's Department was efficient. They brought a diver with them, plus enormous grappling irons, steel cutters and a couple of burly Deputies. They shook hands, said they were glad to meet them and got to work.

Banished to the terrace, Mel watched the diver slip over the side, then disappear under the water. In no time at all, he popped back up again.

'Its some kind of cooler,' she heard him say. 'Except somebody went to the trouble of wrapping a load of heavy chain around it. Fucker weighs a ton.'

The Sheriff handed him the steel cutters and he dived back down again. Mel waited expectantly for him to emerge, but this time he took forever. She could see Camelia pacing the deck, hands behind his back, looking as out of place in this seascape as a dandelion in Times Square. The wind ruffled his sleek dark hair and she smiled. Camelia was a hunk, though he probably didn't even know it. But she'd bet Claudia did. And Claudia, she thought, was a very lucky woman.

Finally the diver surfaced, struggling with a couple of lengths of heavy, rusted chain. The burly officers leaned over, grabbed them from him, then with the grappling irons, maneuvered the box to the surface.

Camelia was on his knees, getting his immaculate dark gray

pants wet, even though he knew the sea water would ruin them, helping manhandle the still weighty box over the bow onto the deck.

The men stood looking at it. A blue plastic cooler, stained with rust and sealed with waterproof yellow electrical tape.

They ripped off the tape and eased off the lid.

'God,' Mel heard Camelia gasp, and everyone took a quick step back, hands over their noses.

'For Chrissakes, put the lid back on,' the Sheriff choked, getting on the phone and immediately summoning the coroner's wagon.

'Yeah, it's a body alright,' Mel heard him say. 'But whose, or even what, is hard to say. At this stage, it could be a dead dog for all we can tell.'

Camelia made his way back up the wooden steps toward Mel. She reached out for him. 'This isn't real,' she whispered, horrified. 'This doesn't happen to nice women like me. This is a nightmare and it's getting worse.'

Camelia slid his arms round her. He could feel the softness of her against his chest, feel the tremors that shook her body, smell her faint floral perfume. 'There'll be an autopsy,' he said, 'it's impossible to know, at this moment, who it is, but I'll bet it was the body in the library.'

'Hooray for Agatha Christie,' she muttered in his ear, 'now all we have to do is find that darned butler.'

He let go of her, reluctantly. 'Let's get out of here,' he said, handing her her leather jacket. 'I'm a man in need of fresher air than this, as well as a stiff drink.'

She linked her arm through his as they hurried back to the car. This time he drove. At the single-lane bridge they encountered the arriving coroner's wagon as well as a squad car with the police photographer, and they waited for them to cross before continuing.

'They'll need to talk to you later,' Camelia told her and she nodded.

'Just as long as they don't think I did it,' she added wearily.

Unlike Hainsville, there was a reality to Charleston. It was a piece of history: gracious, elegant, genteel. And the Omni at Charleston Place was a rather grand hotel, lording it over historic downtown, with marble floors and glittering chandeliers. It had a pretty good bar, too, which was, Camelia thought, where they seemed to be spending a lot of time together these days.

'You gonna end up like Mam'zelle Dorothea?' he asked with a grin, as Mel hooked herself onto a stool and ordered up a Cosmopolitan – with Grey Goose vodka from France, please, if they had it. And, of course, they did.

'I doubt Mam'zelle Dorothea ever had an afternoon like this to drive her to the drink. My guess is she got there all by her tiny little self.' Mel swirled the sliver of lime into the pretty pink cocktail. 'She's obviously a lady. She lived in one of these grand mansions, before she blew all the money on booze.'

'Happens to the best,' he said, sipping the single malt that was almost exactly the color of her eyes. And why the hell couldn't he forget that? He took a gulp and ordered another, promising himself to switch to clear, colorless vodka tomorrow. Today, though, he had seen enough to turn any strong man's stomach, and the whisky warmed his vitals in a very positive way. He stole a glance at Mel out of the corner of his eye.

'You doin' anything special tonight, lady?'

She turned to him, thinking about it. He held his breath. Looking into her eyes was like watching a slot machine in Vegas, waiting for those matching cherries.

'Well,' she said slowly, 'I was thinking of just soaking in a tub, then maybe a bowl of grits . . .'

His face dropped and she laughed. 'Just kidding. Nope, I am a woman alone tonight. Whaddya have in mind?'

'Dinner? No greasy spoon, though. Somewheres nice, suitable for a Southern lady.'

She laughed again, that pleasing tinkling sound that he was beginning to associate with Southern women. 'You must be mixing me up with Mam'zelle Dorothea,' she said, 'she's the Southern lady.'

'Yeah, and she's not about to let you forget it. See the way she dealt with Rhianna Fairland? Like the countess with the peon.'

'I suspect our Mam'zelle is a toughie with a heart of gold,' Mel said, then added, 'She had to be something special for Ed to love her.'

'He picks all the best women,' Camelia said softly. Then to cover his embarrassment, he ordered another drink. 'More for you?'

She shook her head, slid off the barstool. 'Maybe I'll just go take that long soak in the tub. Make myself presentable for you.'

He took her in: the white stretchy T-shirt, short black skirt, the old leather jacket slung over her shoulders . . . he would have taken her any which way. 'You look just fine to me,' he said longingly, and heard her laugh as she strode, chin up, blonde bangs bouncing, out of the bar.

It wasn't easy to get a reservation at 82 Queen, but Camelia had heard it was the best, so he pulled a bit of rank and the concierge came through. He had been waiting in the hotel lobby for half an hour now, anxious not to be late, eager for every moment of this night. He didn't know what to anticipate, he surely wasn't planning anything. He would just let things take their natural course.

Mel erupted from the elevator, late and, as always, in a hurry. As she strode toward him across the marble lobby, Camelia swore that every man's head turned to watch her. She moved, molten as

hot maple syrup, confident and unaware of the sensation she was causing in the black-stretchy-bandage dress and towering heels. She was an out-of-this-world experience, a golden girl; he had never known anyone like her; never seen anyone like her. He got to his feet, shaking his head.

'You look stunning.' He took her hand and lifted it to his lips.

'Why, Detective Camelia, thank you.' She laughed. 'It must be this dress,' she said, running her hands over the curves and tugging at the hem.

He shifted his eyes hastily from her long, bare, sunkissed legs. Jesus, he was getting to be a romantic in his old age, thinking of legs as sunkissed. And him a forty-six-year-old married man with four kids. And on top of it, he was a cop and she was ... He had forgotten exactly what Melba was in relation to this case, except she was here to help him find out about Ed Vincent's past. But the one thing he did know for sure, she was head over heels for Vincent.

He straightened his tie, smoothed back his hair in that familiar gesture she found so movie-star and which made her giggle, then offered her his arm. Still laughing, she linked herself to him, and they wafted together onto the street and into a cab. Camelia could have sworn he was walking on air.

82 Queen was mobbed; people milled in the entry, sipping drinks and waiting for tables, and there was a buzz of conversation and laughter. But Camelia and Mel were shown immediately onto the charming red-brick courtyard, and seated at a candlelit table under a trellis of wisteria and roses.

'Ed would love this,' Mel said, half to herself as she looked around.

'He probably knows it well.' Camelia took the menu offered by the waiter. 'After all, it's his home town.'

'His *adopted* home town. And thank the Lord for that,' Mel added.

He didn't ask what she wanted to drink, but instead ordered

a bottle of champagne. But he did consult her on what she liked. She chose the Perrier Jouet Fleur de Champagne Rosé, because she loved the pink color as much as the taste.

'Champagne is so . . . celebratory, I guess is the right word,' she said, giving him that ear-to-ear again. 'And this is Riley's favorite.'

'*Riley* has a favorite champagne? At seven years old?'

She laughed. 'Sure, she does. I always give her a taste. That way, I figure curiosity won't kill her later, at puberty when the pressure's on. All she gets is a taste, nothing more. She's rather keen on caviare, too. Beluga by choice, though Sevruga is acceptable.' Mel laughed again. 'That was Ed. I could never afford caviare. And anyhow,' she added, remembering what champagne cost, 'we're splitting this bill, Marco Camelia. You can't afford champagne on a cop's salary.'

'And you can't afford champagne driving a moving van.'

They laughed together, and once again she reached over and took his hand. 'Y'know what? I really like you,' she said. 'I mean, I hated you at first. I thought that you thought you were Al Pacino in a cop movie and I was the blonde suspect who you just knew had done the dirty deed.'

'Oh?' He grinned. 'And what do you think now?'

'I think . . .' She contemplated him, taking in his jutting cheekbones, his firm jaw, the severe lines of his mouth, and ending up at his eyes. Deep, dark, soft brown eyes that were gazing into hers with a slightly bemused expression. 'I think that you are my hero,' she whispered. 'You are the man who is going to find Ed's shooter. I owe you an enormous debt of gratitude, Marco Camelia.'

He shook his head. 'Not yet, you don't, Zelda – Melba Merrydew. I haven't found him yet. Besides,' he shrugged, 'I'm only a cop doing his job. I'm nobody's hero.'

'Oh, yes, you are,' she said. And she got up, walked round the table and planted a kiss full on his mouth.

It was, Camelia decided shakily, more potent than the bottle

of champagne. 'Jesus, what d'ya have to go and do that for?' He put a hand to his lips, stunned. 'You were all over me, like kudzu.'

She plonked back down in the chair opposite, laughing. 'Because, my dear Marco, I love you. I love you for being an honest man, for being a dedicated man, for being a tender-hearted man. And for being my friend.'

The waiter poured the champagne and Camelia picked up his glass. 'I'll drink to that,' he said, shaken. But there was no way he could tell her what he felt about her.

'Friends.' Mel lifted her glass, touched his and they drank. She sighed, happily, secure in the knowledge that Ed, though still in a coma, seemed to be holding his own. 'No better, no worse,' was what the doctor had told her.

'And here's to Ed,' Camelia said, and again they clinked glasses. 'To his speedy recovery. And,' he added, 'may all your dreams come true.'

Mel's eyes filmed with tears that she would not allow to spill over. 'Thank you,' she said simply. And then she went ahead and ordered she-crab soup laced with sherry, and barbecued shrimp, and grits dappled with Cheddar cheese and scallions. She persuaded him to try the oysters stuffed with crab, and the grilled Georgia lamb chops served with a golden pear chutney.

'So I can taste yours too,' she added hungrily. Then, 'Oh, bother,' she remembered, 'I can't eat in this dress.'

'I thought it expanded.' He eyed her curves doubtful-ly.

'Well, maybe it does.' She beamed at him again. 'Gosh-darn it, I'm surely gonna give it a try.'

He hadn't realized she was a foodie. All he had ever seen her eat – and that reluctantly – was bacon and eggs and bagels. But when it came to real food, this girl could tuck it away. He grinned at her enthusiasm as she ooh'd and ahh'd her way through the soup, stealing a couple of his oysters, just to taste, and rolling her eyes to heaven.

'I thought you lived on power bars and Diet Coke.' He was laughing at her, but she didn't seem to mind.

'So I do. But not when somebody else is doing the cooking. And this, Camelia my man, is *good* cooking.' She glanced up. 'So, tell me more about yourself.'

'All I can tell you is, my story is not nearly as romantic as Ed's.'

She shuddered. 'His sounded like a version of hell, to me.'

'It was, but it's the stuff of romance novels. Poor guy makes good against all odds. I never thought it really worked out like that in real life. My grandfather wasn't so lucky. He came to the US from Sicily, got a job in a hat factory – everyone wore hats in those days. He shared a room with another Sicilian, saved what he could. Then his roommate said he had a family emergency. My grandfather lent him all he had. Every cent. He never saw his fellow countryman again. And he never trusted another Sicilian.

'It took a few years, but eventually he was able to send for my grandmother. They lived in a one-room apartment in a tenement on the Lower East Side. She worked too, helped out in the local store, cleaned other folks' houses, looked after other folks' kids ... did what she could. Until she got a baby of her own. A boy. My father, Ottavio Camelia.' He paused as she speared a barbecued shrimp, then offered it to him.

'Go on, try it,' she urged, holding out the fork dripping with Cheddar and sauce, 'you'll never have another one as good as this.'

He took the fork, tasted. The faint tang of her lipstick overlaid the shrimp and held onto the memory of it.

'More,' she urged. 'Tell me more. About your father.'

He shrugged. 'Not much to tell. He was a studious kid, finished high school but, like a lot of others, there was no chance of college, he had to get out there and earn some money. He held down a dozen jobs over the years. Then he became a cop. He married a beautiful Italian girl, Carmela.' He grinned.

'Who then had to live with the unfortunate name of Carmela Camelia for the rest of her days. They had three kids, myself and two daughters. Bought a little house in the Bronx, managed to raise us, put us through school, pay for a couple of fancy Italian weddings.' He shrugged again. 'I joined the force.'

'Like father, like son,' she added, eyes shining with interest.

He nodded. 'Then I met Claudia . . .'

'A Puerto Rican beauty.'

He nodded again, smiling. 'I agree with that description. And you know the rest.'

'No, I don't.' He looked at her, surprised. 'I still don't know what your dreams are,' she added softly.

He took the bottle from the ice bucket, refilled their glasses. 'I'm not sure what my dreams are. But I suspect that, like most folks, somewhere along the way they got buried in the reality of life.'

'Like mine.' He looked questioningly at her. 'I always wanted to be a ballerina,' she explained. 'I was the clumsy little kid at the ballet-class concert, the lanky fairy in the pink net tutu and droopy tights and a wand with a star on top. Always pointing the wrong toe and towering over the other kids.' She sighed. 'I felt like the giant at the top of the beanstalk. And I just kept on growing until there wasn't a male ballet dancer who could have lifted me.' She gave him that wide smile, and took a sip. 'Love this champagne,' she said, dreamily. 'You think we should get a bottle for Mam'zelle Dorothea, as a treat?'

'Think she'd prefer it to Southern Comfort?'

'Maybe not, but it would be a sort of thank-you. Perhaps we could take her some little French pastries, have a tea party.'

'Without the tea.'

She laughed. 'Somehow, I don't see Mam'zelle Dorothea as a tea drinker.' She polished off the final bit of pear chutney on his plate and added with a satisfied sigh, 'Is this heaven, or what?'

He was just about to agree with her, when his cellphone rang.

She made a little face. 'Reality calls,' she complained, watching, apprehensive, as he answered. He said yes and no, and see you at eleven-thirty. Then he rang off. She gazed expectantly at him.

'The Sheriff. The autopsy is tonight. He asked if I wanted to be there.'

She took a large swallow of the champagne, trying not to think about the contents of the blue cooler dredged from the ocean. 'I'm not sure I can manage dessert.' Her voice sounded suddenly small.

'I'm sorry. It's not good dinner-table talk. And hardly the way to end a perfect evening.'

'Was it perfect, Marco?' She reached for his hand again and this time he gripped hers tightly.

Was it the champagne talking, he wondered, as he said, 'For me, it was. The most perfect evening I can remember.'

Mel took a deep breath, knowing she was on dangerous ground. 'Then your memory must be extremely short, Detective,' she said, summoning up a smile. 'Perhaps you should take Claudia out more often, buy her champagne.'

'Perhaps,' he agreed. Regretfully, Mel thought. 'Except Claudia prefers a good red wine to champagne. A hearty Chianti Riserva from Antinori is what I always get her for birthdays and such.'

'I'm glad.' She squeezed his hand and slid hers away. 'I needed to know you appreciate her.'

Their gaze locked. 'I do. Believe me, Melba Merrydew, I do.'

She was glad he hadn't slipped up and called her Zelda again. Marco Camelia was a nice man, a good man. A very attractive man. But his heart should belong to another, and so should hers.

'Friends,' she said again, as he waved to the waiter for the check.

'Always,' he said simply.

And somehow, she knew he meant it. Loyalty was yet another facet of his character, hidden, along with the tenderness, beneath that tough Sicilian-cop façade.

Chapter Forty

An autopsy was not exactly the event Camelia would have chosen to attend after a memorable meal with his more than memorable companion, but he was here to do a job.

He dropped her off at the hotel. She kissed him goodnight in the lobby under the envious gaze of the other male guests and staff, then loped to the elevator with a tiny wave of one hand, smiling, friendly-style, at anyone she passed.

Staring after her, Camelia shook his head. He would treasure the memory of the way she looked forever.

The Pathology Department was all white tile and steel, with the smell of formaldehyde overlaying the odor of decay. A bank of refrigerated steel drawers held the remains of those waiting to be autopsied, or to be claimed by next of kin. As he waited, a sheeted, toe-tagged body was wheeled past him en route to its final mortal humiliation of having its innards inspected to ascertain the cause of death.

He knew from experience that pathologists were not the gentle craftsmen and artists surgeons were. Here, bodies were sawn roughly open, their organs removed and weighed, and dropped into steel dishes; even the contents of their stomachs were inspected and accounted for. Gaping wounds were prodded and poked, and when the job was finished, the bodies were sewn up again with big darning stitches, not those neat little OR

jobs. Back in one piece, the body resembled nothing more than Frankenstein's monster, ready to rise up and claim fame on the silver screen.

Except in this case, there was no body to saw open and dissect. All they had was a sickening heap of stinking, rotted flesh and a pile of bones.

Somewhere in all that, the pathologist found teeth that could be matched against dental records for identification. And hair to be tested for DNA. And the fact that this was a male of the human species. Plus five slugs from what looked to be from a .40mm semi-automatic.

Camelia regretted the crab-stuffed oysters. His stomach churned but he forced himself to stay his ground. As a member of the Yankee NYPD, he couldn't let his team down in front of the Confederates. 'I don't know how the hell y'do it,' he marveled, when the job was done and the nauseating remains carefully sealed in a steel container.

'To be truthful, sometimes nor do I,' the gray-haired medico answered. 'Years of experience, I guess. But I don't mind admitting how many times I lost my cookies, when I was a rookie.' He grinned as he removed his scrubs then washed his hands. 'Come on, let's have a cup of good strong coffee and I'll tell you what we've got.

It was two-thirty a.m., and the hot coffee felt good in Camelia's ice-bound stomach. The pathologist told him that this was undoubtedly a male, that he had been dead when he was placed in the cooler. That five shots at close range had been what killed him and, he would guess, had blown the top of his head off. Probably a .40mm.

The same as the bullets in Ed Vincent, Camelia noted.

From the hair and skin texture, the pathologist guessed the man was Latino. And he knew he had been shot from behind.

'How the hell can y'tell all that from . . .' Camelia couldn't even begin to describe the slimy, rotting mess in the cooler.

'That's my job,' he said, coolly. 'And now, I have another

one to tackle before I can get some rest. So if you'll excuse me.'

As he shook the pathologist's cold hand, Camelia smelled the faint odor of formaldehyde and disinfectant that still hung around him. He didn't bother to finish his coffee. He was out of there and back at the hotel and on the phone to the department in a flash. Pathology always disturbed him and he felt thankful just to be alive.

He passed on the information to his colleagues, told them that the body in the cooler and how it got there was a double mystery; that they would get the DNA results in about six weeks; heard the usual grumble, and added that he guessed they could assume it was the Hispanic-looking guy Melba Merrydew had seen, dead, in Ed Vincent's beach house.

Then he sat down and wrote up a complete report on the day's events, except for the conversation with Mam'zelle Dorothea, which as yet he chose to keep to himself. There was more to come in that story, and he wasn't about to divulge any secrets until he knew where it was heading.

The hotel bed was firm, the blankets warm, and he was asleep as soon as his head touched the pillow. Which, since it was already five in the morning, didn't mean much, because he had to be up again at seven-thirty, ready for whatever the next day might bring. And for another day in the company of Miss Melba.

Chapter Forty-one

The next morning, at eleven, they found Mam'zelle Dorothea propped upright by the big leopardskin cushion, pale eyes alive with interest, waiting for them.

Bending to kiss her, Mel caught the sweet scent of face powder and was touched that the old lady had primped for them, like the Southern belle she might once have been. But Mam'zelle flinched away from her embrace.

'Bah, kissing is so commonplace these days.' She dismissed her with a wave of her scrawny blue-veined hand. 'A meaningless guesture between people who scarcely know one another, let alone care.'

'Oh, but I do care, Mam'zelle.' Unfazed, Mel took her seat on the footstool, smiling at her. From the faint hint of a blush on Dorothea's thin cheeks, she suspected she was touched by the kiss but didn't care to admit it.

'I assume, since you say you are in love with Ed, that you know his condition this morning?'

'Of course I do. I speak with the doctors several times a day. And night,' she added, remembering those three-in-the-morning blues, alone in the hotel room, when she had felt for sure something was terribly wrong and had called, sweating and half-mad, terrified of what she might hear. Ed was restless, they had told her, but his condition remained the same.

Mel thought it was as though his body had slipped into neutral gear, engine idling. Waiting. But for what?

'I wish I could tell you better news,' she said quietly, 'but Ed is still in a coma, still on the ventilator. There is brain activity, though, and that makes the doctors hopeful.'

'He always had a good brain,' Dorothea agreed. 'I could tell even then, when he was just a boy, and uneducated, that there was a spark in him. I suppose a psychiatrist might say I transferred my own ambitions and longings onto him, but they were wrong. I was the one taking from him. I took pleasure in showing him another world, in teaching him about life and how to live it.' She laughed, that witch's cackle that made Mel jump. 'And that boy absorbed everything like a sea sponge,' Dorothea added, remembering.

'But the truth was,' she said, 'he didn't know what he was going to do with his life. He had been living hand-to-mouth that summer, starving in the winter. Odds were he would not have made it through; he might have been dead by spring.

'That night, he returned to the conservatory. I had rummaged through the closets, found him some clothing, warm blankets for his rough bed. I had opened a can of beef stew and heated it through, along with some rice and bread.' Her eyes had a faraway look and she smiled, remembering the look on his face when he tasted it, as though he had already died and gone to heaven.

'Over those bleak winter days, we got to know each other a little better. I remember laughing when he asked about my hopes for the future. There is no future for me, Theo, I told him. There is only today. He looked at me and he knew I was right. I was what I was. A woman in her late sixties who was way too fond of the bottle.

'One day I asked if he would care to see the house, but I saw he was afraid. It's alright, I told him, they know me here. I promise they won't think you're going to steal the family silver.

'Ahh, my home.' Dorothea's sigh was as fluttery as a spring breeze. 'The Jefferson House was famous, y'know, once upon a time. Of course my daddy wanted to rename it Duval House, but Mama told him the Duvals were only *nouveau riche*, and of course the Jeffersons had been there forever, so the house remained as it was.

'But by now it was like the garden: a wreck. There was no money left, y'see, to keep up the place, and what bit there was I spent on drink. I was a true Southern Rebel,' Dorothea added, with an impish smirk. 'Always did things my own way, even when I knew it wasn't right. Hot damn, there wouldn't have been enough money to set the place to rights anyways. Not nearly enough. And besides, there was only me left to care.'

She fished behind her under the cushion, tugged out the bottle of Southern Comfort and reached for the glass.

'Mam'zelle, please.' Camelia was on his feet. 'Allow me.' He took the bottle and poured her a stiff shot. 'A Yankee with nice manners,' she said. 'I didn't know such a thing existed.' She gave him an amused glance.

'A Sicilian Yankee, ma'am,' Camelia corrected her, 'and my grandfather believed in the old way of doing things. Honesty, courtesy and respect for your elders.'

'Did he now.' She thought about that as she took a good slug of the liquor. 'I only wish my Southern parents had done the same for me,' she added with that wicked little grin.

'Well, anyhow, the house was like the garden, and myself. A wreck. We walked together through those once-elegant rooms, stuffed with all that dark, old furniture, full of woodworm by now, and the fraying Oriental rugs and the foggy mirrors, and the silk curtains so brittle with age, they crumbled at a touch. We stood in the library and Theo stared at all those books. Thousands of them there were, and all covered, like the rest of the house, with a few decades' worth of dust. "All that knowledge," he said in an awed voice.'

Mam'zelle sighed and took another sip of the bourbon. 'I

saw such a look of yearning on his face, and knew he was as thirsty for learning as I was for the booze.

'And he was a gentleman, too. Never even mentioned the empty bourbon bottles stashed every place. Drink, I told him. That's what ladies do when they get old and are alone.

'I took him into the kitchen. I can see him now, heading toward that fire in the grate like a homing pigeon, holding out his hands to the warmth, and sniffing the fresh coffee brewing on the stove. Then it dawned on him. 'This is your place, ain't it,' he said.

'I told him the home had been in the Jefferson family for more than a couple of hundred years. Not the Duvals. They were just upstart Creoles. From Louisiana, y'know,' she added, as though it made a great difference, which Mel, the Southerner, knew it did to Dorothea.

'Trading with France had made the Duvals rich, but it never gave them any class.' Mam'zelle gave a disparaging sniff. 'Still, Mama fell for those dark good looks and that Frenchified New Orleans accent. She insisted on marrying Monsieur Paul Duval, even though her father was set against it and threatened to cut her out of his will. But of course the Duvals had more money than the Jeffersons by then, so the threat was an empty one. She married him anyway, and I was the result.

'There were no siblings to hamper my being spoiled rotten. A little princess, I was. And my parents thought I was too good to marry. They wanted me all to themselves, and I was happy to oblige.

'Until they died and left me, the spinster Mademoiselle Jefferson Duval, all alone in her mansion. With only bourbon to warm her heart and her bed, instead of a man.'

Camelia watched as Mel bent to kiss Dorothea's hand. He caught the glitter of tears on her cheek and knew she was touched by the old woman's loneliness.

'You must be tired.' Mel wiped away the tear with her hand and managed a sniffly little smile. 'Look, Mam'zelle Dorothea,

we've brought you some pastries, from the French bakery in town. And a bottle of champagne. To celebrate our meeting.'

'Champagne?' Dorothea looked mystified.

Suddenly, apprehensive, Mel thought maybe Camelia had been right, and she should have bought the Southern Comfort instead. But she needn't have worried. Dorothea's face lifted and then she laughed, the tinkling Southern gentlewoman-style laugh this time.

'Champagne and French pastries. How *delightful*,' she said, once again the belle of Jefferson House. 'Well, we certainly can't drink this out of toothmugs, I shall ring for the proper glasses. And plates too.' She inspected the box of tiny jewel-like pastries. 'I remember this patisserie. My mother used to shop there,' she said, pleased. And Mel flashed Camelia a smile, glad they had hit the right spot for Mam'zelle.

'We drank champagne at my coming-out ball,' Dorothea reminisced. 'So delicious. And I remember, it went straight to my head. Of course, I did not partake of alcohol in those days,' she added primly. 'Save for a glass of wine with dinner, Father being French and all. My, how Ed would enjoy this,' she added, nibbling on a creamy little fruit tart. 'He always did have a sweet tooth.'

That was news to Mel, but she guessed time and a lot of growing-up had taken care of that little vice.

'I gave him a room in the house, of course,' Mam'zelle went on. 'And I began to get rid of that mountain-man accent, taught him to speak properly. And Ed helped out. He cleaned up the place, threw away all those bottles, got rid of the dust, washed the floors, cleaned the windows, polished the furniture. He was like my valet, my butler, only there was no mistress-servant relationship between us.

'We were both outcasts from society, y'see,' she added with a wistful little smile. 'I was drinking myself to death, with nothing to live for. And he was starving to death, with no one to live for. You could say we saved each other. And

we looked out for each other. And we enjoyed each other's company.

'We went for walks to The Battery. I took him shopping for food, we even dined, occasionally, in a café. I was not ashamed of my shabby young hick from the mountains, and he was not ashamed of his eccentric, alcoholic mentor. Ours was a relationship of equals. It was based on mutual need, a shared loneliness and rejection.

'So you can see,' Dorothea added softly, 'that it was inevitable that we came to care for one another. And when I found out his true age, I insisted he enroll in high school. And that, my dears,' she added with a tired, fluttery little sigh, 'is when life began to change for Theo Rogan.

'It was not easy for Theo, being laughed at at school. Laughed at for his accent, as well as laughed at for me, his weird "grandmother." That's what Theo told everyone I was. "His grandmother." What else could he say? That he was a vagrant and I an alcoholic who had given him shelter? He felt he owed it to me to make sure I had respect.'

She sighed again, remembering how tough it had been for him. 'He fought his way through that school, but he left with a diploma and a scholarship to Duke. It was,' she added, smiling, 'the first success of his life. The first time he had ever felt proud of himself.

'Theo Rogan is no name for a winner, I told him. It's the name of a loser, a part of your past. It's time you left all that behind.

'I decided on Edward, because it was a good, solid, princely name. And Jefferson, of course. I told him, a man could do no better than to have the name of a great president, and besides, it was my name and my gift to him. And then we needed a fine last name, one with no white-trashiness about it. One befitting a winner. I think 'Vincent' should do it, I said.

'So I took care of things legally, and Theo Rogan became

Edward Jefferson Vincent. Ed Vincent, A Duke University freshman.'

Chapter Forty-two

Zelda, Zelda, you've left me ... I always wondered if you would go away — just the way you came, almost in a puff of smoke, leaving me bereft, and forever wondering ... Why? My golden girl, my Georgia peaches and cream, my honey ... Where are you ... God, how I'm missing you ... Maybe I've died ... That's what this is ... and now you can't reach me. But I know you, how determined you are. You would find me even beyond the grave. Oh, my lord, I never thought to hear myself use that phrase ... especially when the grave will be mine ...

It's dark in here, so dark all the time ... Perhaps I'm already there, already buried ...

An icy sweat bristled on his skin and the hovering nurse picked up his hand, anxiously testing his pulse, checking his heart rate, his blood pressure, the myriad blinks on the machines, the inflowing and outflowing liquids in the surgical tubes and catheters.

No doubt there is brain activity, she said to herself.

Then I'm not dead, Ed thought, relieved. Not yet. There's still time. Still time to tell her I love her, that I want her, that I can't live without her. I can't get down on one knee right now, but please marry me, Zelda ... I need to hear your voice so bad, my darling ... hear you say ... Yes ...

Somewhere a phone trilled. He heard the soft squish of the nurse's rubber-soled shoes, the crisp rustle of her cotton skirt, the murmur of her voice. Then she was coming back again.

'I don't think I should be doing this,' she said, sounding hesitant, 'but that young woman of yours is very persuasive ... and what the heck, I guess it can't do you any harm.'

She was holding something cold against his ear ... a telephone ... and he heard Zelda's voice.

'Ed, I'm here in Charleston, honey. I haven't left you, so don't you worry. And you know what, honey? I know all about you now, more than I ever knew before, and my heart goes out to you. Mam'zelle Dorothea is wonderful. She sends her love to you. She told us the whole story, of how she helped you. And Ed.' Her voice choked and she paused for a moment to calm herself. 'I just want to tell you how proud I am of you. And how much I love you. Oh, honey, *do* you hear me? Somehow, I have to believe you can. I can't allow myself to think that you are not there. Wait for me, Ed. I'll be back with you ... tomorrow ... and remember, I love you. I'll always love you ...'

The nurse took the telephone away – his lifeline to Zelda, and a tear slid down Ed's now cavernous cheek.

'*Oh, my God,*' the nurse said in a slow, stunned voice. 'Oh, my God. He *heard* her. He *recognized* her.'

Ed heard the soft squish of her shoes again, only this time she was running. He heard the excitement in her voice as she summoned the doctor.

Thank you, God, he said to himself, and another tear slid from under his closed lids. *And thank you, Zelda. I am still alive. And I promise I'll wait for you, honey. At least until tomorrow ...*

He was dreaming he was back in Charleston, but with Zelda and with Mam'zelle Dorothea. Only they were all young again, or in Mam'zelle's case, younger ... Of course, Zelda had not figured in that scenario in the past, but she was here now, hovering in his dream. His guardian angel.

He did see his brother again.

He was a junior at Duke, there on that hard-won scholarship that

paid only his tuition. If he wanted to eat and a place to live, he had to work for it.

'Nothing in life comes free,' he had said, heady with anticipation when he received the letter of acceptance. For a hillbilly kid from the Great Smokies, where ambition raised its head no higher than owning your own acre and growing enough to feed your family, he was a success. Or anyhow, on the way to success.

It had not been easy. But somehow he guessed his life wasn't meant to take a smooth path.

He had worked in the fields all that summer, earning enough to buy a couple of pairs of jeans, a few T-shirts, a sweater and a warm jacket and a pair of new boots for his freshman winter at college. He had twenty-five dollars left over to get him through until he found a couple of jobs in Durham, when, hopefully, he would make enough to pay his rent and food. He was on cloud nine until the time came to say goodbye.

Mam'zelle Dorothea handed him a sealed envelope. Suddenly he did not want to leave her.

'Take this and then go, you silly boy,' she said, kissing him hastily on the cheek, something she never did. They never showed their affection for each other; it was just some unspoken rule. They were friends, co-conspirators in this game of life, beating the odds when they could. They both lived by the skin of their teeth. He by circumstance, she by choice. They never knew whether they would end up winning. Or losing.

On the bus heading for Durham, he opened the envelope. Inside was four hundred dollars. More money than he had ever seen in his life. He knew she must have sold something valuable to give him this, and he was suddenly worried for her. About how she would manage, on her own again, without him there to make sure she got to bed when she passed out from the drink. And to see that she kept warm, and ate something every now and again. He almost stopped the bus and got right off there

and then, and walked back home to her. But he knew she would only send him off again.

He was in his junior year when he got the news that Dorothea had been found, unconscious and alone. Locked up in the beautiful old house.

She had been there for a couple of days before they found her, and then only because a workman coming to cut off the electricity had not been able to gain entry, and had alerted the police. She was in hospital and not expected to live. He should come at once, the family lawyer told him, if he wanted to see her alive.

Distraught, Ed walked through the campus to the magnificent Duke Chapel. Its bell tower soared twenty-one stories high, and its Gothic stone grandeur and arcing stained-glass windows offered a sense of peace, as he knelt and prayed for Mademoiselle Dorothea Jefferson Duval's life. Except for his mother, she was the only woman he had ever loved. He could not envision life without her. The future looked bleak.

He was walking back along Chapel Drive when he saw his brother. The shock rooted him to the spot for a minute. Mitch was with a group of men, all wearing suits and ties and carrying briefcases. He looked prosperous and kind of official, swaggering as he always did. He looked mean-eyed too, as he always had, even though there was a smile on his face. He was backslapping the other guys, full of friendly *bonhomie*, and Ed knew, with that old instinct, that he was up to no good. Mitch had always acted nice when he wanted something. Except for that night when he murdered his family.

Suddenly afraid, he slipped into the shadows beside the chapel. *Now is the time*, a voice inside him was saying. *You could follow him, kill him . . . avenge your mother and father and your brothers and sisters.*

But how could he? He had not seen Mitch put the torch

to their cabin, he still did not know for sure. *Except, in his heart, he knew.*

He could not do it. Shame welled up in him once again. He slunk away, keeping to the shadows, so no one would see his pain.

The magnolias were in bloom when he returned to Charleston the next day. All pink and white, like a young girl's first bouquet. And the gardens were lush with lilies, their sweet green smell blending with the salty ocean air. He would never forget it. He thrust all memories of Mitch to some deep, dark corner of his mind and went to see Mam'zelle.

Mam'zelle, when I saw you, in that narrow white hospital bed, you looked so small and fragile I wondered how you could possibly survive. There was so little meat on your tiny sparrow bones, and you looked so cold, and so alone. I chafed your hands, talked to you, told you how much I loved you, just the way Zelda does with me now. I said, don't leave me, Mam'zelle Dorothea. I'm selfish. I need you to care about me. I need you to come home to. I need you to be proud of me, so I know I have to make something of myself. To be a success. For you. My grandmother.

He sat with her for a long while. Then, summoned by a phone call, he went to see the family attorney, Bernard Hawthorne.

The man looked even older and more decrepit than Dorothea. He had been Mam'zelle's father's attorney, but Ed would not have been surprised to learn he had also been her grandfather's. The old firm certainly had. They had boxes and boxes of dusty red files, marked Jefferson, and Jefferson/Duval, and old Bernard Hawthorne told him they worked for loyalty to the family now, and not for money, since Mam'zelle had none.

'All she has left,' he told Ed, 'is that grand old house. And

whatever remains that she hasn't already sold. Oh, and the ramshackle beach property, up the coast a ways. But that's worthless too, or so I'm told.'

He consulted the note in front of him and Ed recognized Dorothea's large, sprawling writing from the weekly letter she sent to him.

'Besides, Mam'zelle has already deeded the beach property to you.' Hawthorne glanced at Ed over the top of his half-glasses. 'It's my duty to inform you that as the new owner, from now on you will be responsible for all property taxes, plus the upkeep, should you wish to retain it. Though as I already said, I doubt that it has much value at this time, other than the land. And since it's out of the way, and not a popular area for weekenders, it's unlikely it would sell.' He shrugged, his withered voice trailing off as he closed the file.

'Mam'zelle also appointed you executor of her estate. She gave you power of attorney, so you now find yourself in the position of deciding what to do about Jefferson House, as well as taking care of the old lady.'

Ed was silent.

'I know it's difficult,' Hawthorne said. 'You are still a student and you have no income. I'm sorry about this, Mr Vincent, but it was Mam'zelle's wish. Although I have no doubt she expected to die first and not leave you stuck with worrying about her welfare.'

Stuck? Ed thought. *Stuck?* Why, he welcomed the opportunity to take care of his mentor. *But how?*

'I suggest we put the contents of the house up for auction, and place the house itself on the market, though there's not much demand for these historic old properties right now. You would have to pour money into them, and young people don't want to be bothered with woodworm and dry rot and antique plumbing. They want all the modern conveniences.' Hawthorne sighed again, regretfully. 'I hope one day things will change, but . . .' His voice trailed off again and he sat back, seemingly lost in thought.

Ed thanked him, said he would of course take care of Mam'zelle, and asked him to put the house and its contents up for sale, with the exception of the few favorite things he knew Mam'zelle would not want to part with.

He went back to the hospital and held Mam'zelle's hand for several hours, talking to her every now and again, promising her a bottle of Southern Comfort when she awoke, as well as a walk along The Battery in the sunshine, and telling her about the magnolias in bloom and the scent of the lilies. Then he hitched his way out to Hazards Point to inspect his property.

The gabled Victorian beach house was as old and ramshackle as the mansion, though not nearly as grand. Everything about it was crumbling: the timbers, the deck, the roof. Every window was cracked, and what was once the driveway was now a mass of broken stones and tall weeds. But the view from the bluff was astounding; an endless vista of tranquil blue ocean all the way to the even bluer horizon. Little shanty-steps led to a tumbledown wooden pier with a deepwater mooring, where once upon a time Mam'zelle's father had kept a smart sailing yacht.

Ed walked around his property feeling like a king. Thanks to his friend, he had a home. Dorothea had not forgotten him, and now he would not forget her. It was his turn to be the caretaker.

Chapter Forty-three

Mam'zelle reached for the bottle and Camelia hastened to do the honors. He couldn't imagine how a little thing like her put away so much liquor, and he figured by now she must have a zinc-lined stomach.

'To my sorrow, I did not die when I wished.' Mam'zelle sipped the bourbon thoughtfully. 'It was not my intention to become a burden on my young friend. I had meant for him to inherit it all, or at least, whatever was left. And now, he inherited me, instead.' She sighed, but a smile lurked in those winter-pale eyes.

'Because of me, and for urgent financial reasons, Ed was forced to take a sabbatical from college. By the time I finally got out of that hospital, he had fixed up the old beach house. He personally hauled all my old favorite bits of furniture there.' She ran a hand lovingly across the little antique table, with its white ring-marks where her glass had stood for so many years. 'He created a new home for me. Of course, I couldn't tell him that I was a city-dweller, that I hated living at the beach and that without the old familiar streets of Charleston, without my secret nooks and crannies, without my favorite liquor stores, without my old home – I was lost.

'"Hot damn,' I told myself, 'hold your sharp tongue for once, woman. He has sacrificed college for you, worked his

fingers to the bone for you, cared for you. And what other man in your miserable life ever did that? Not even your Creole daddy who loved you to pieces. But not like this. Oh, no, he never loved like this."

She held out her glass for a refill and again, Camelia obliged.

'You should know,' she said, with a hard look at Mel, 'that when Ed Vincent gives his heart, he gives all of it. And forever.'

Mel nodded. She knew alright.

Dorothea sipped the bourbon. 'Ed did see his brother again,' she said. 'Quite by chance, at the university, the same day he heard that I was in hospital and near death's door. I'm not sure which event shocked him more. He told me about it, later. Said as far as he could see, Mitch Rogan hadn't changed one bit, only now he looked successful. He never mentioned his brother to me again, after that day.'

Mel's eyes met Camelia's; they were both thinking the same thing. That Mitch Rogan was Ed's assassin.

'They told me the big old Jefferson house was worthless, though eventually somebody bought it – too cheaply, but what could I do? It stayed exactly the way it was, dilapidated and tumbling down, for many years. I heard recently it had been sold again and restored, and looks just like in the old days, but I have no desire to see it. It's part of the past, and when Ed rescued me, just the way I had rescued him, I decided to join him in his philosophy. I became a woman who lived for today. Unlike me, the past was dead and gone.'

'But *you* are still with us.' Impulsively, Mel got up and hugged her, but Dorothea gave her an impatient little shove.

'Hot damn, gal, don't go doing things like that. I almost spilled my drink.'

She glowered at her for a second, before continuing. 'Ed took that sabbatical from school. He found employment where he could, sometimes working as many as three jobs at once. He

was a handyman, a construction worker, gardener, field-hand. Anything he could get. It made me doubly sad, because I knew he was right back where he came from. He promised me he would go back to college next year … and the next year … and the year after that …

'Then we were told he would have to forfeit the beach house in lieu of unpaid property taxes. I knew an antiquarian bookdealer, and I sent Ed into town with what remained of the old books. We raised just enough to pay the taxes and to buy an ancient truck. Ed drove around Charleston, canvassing the residents to see if they wanted him to haul away their garbage, offering them a cheap rate. A bargain. He picked up those garbage cans himself and tipped them into the truck. Then he drove to the dump and shoveled the stinking garbage out.'

Dorothea's eyes met Mel's. 'My heart was breaking for him,' she said simply. 'I had thought to make a better life for him. And now he was reduced to this. But Ed had no false pride. He did whatever was needed to keep our little home together. It was not a good life, but he was his own master.

'The next year he was able to buy a second truck, and he hired a young man to help him. Over five years, those trucks grew into a fleet of fifty, and soon he had the monopoly on the garbage collection in all the new developments, as well as in the old town, and all across North Carolina. But he was like a well-kept secret. For work, he used the name Theo Rogan. I thought it was because he didn't want to sully his grand new name – especially the Jefferson part – with the taint of a garbage collector.

'I worried about him, because all he thought of was work. He saw no one socially, except for the occasional girl he met in a bar, or out walking on The Battery. But women liked him, you know. Always did. He was a good-looking young man. And he liked women. But he never brought anyone home, and he never fell in love. He was too busy.

'When he was twenty-eight, he received an offer for his

garbage company, which was now the largest in the Southern States. The money was fair, though not generous, but Ed suspected the consortium offering the deal was linked to the Mob, and if he refused, they might just take it over anyway. By force, if necessary.

'So, he accepted the offer. And with his first real money in his pocket, he moved me and all my favorite bits and pieces to the splendour of Fairlands. He closed up the beach house, leaving only the few old sticks of furniture, the picture of the log cabin and suchlike. And then he headed north. "To seek his fortune." And my, how he succeeded,' she added with a little smile.

'He told me that as soon as he saw Manhattan's towers floating along the skyline as he crossed the Triborough Bridge, somehow, he knew he had come home. This was where he was meant to be.'

Chapter Forty-four

Camelia checked them out of the Omni in Charleston, and they caught a late-afternoon flight back to New York, via Atlanta.

Mel lay back in her seat, looking drained and saying nothing, and after glancing at her, Camelia kept his own gaze straight ahead. She was lost in her thoughts, no doubt mulling over her lover's life history. Was Ed a different man from the one she thought she knew? Perhaps, but Camelia knew it wouldn't change her love for him.

Atlanta airport seemed extra busy, and the New York flight was delayed. They took a seat at the bar and ordered up a couple of beers.

'Of course Mitch did it,' Mel said, just as Camelia's phone rang. He excused himself to answer it.

Mel glanced round the airport. She could remember coming here as a child, but then it was not this huge grandiose edifice. Like everywhere else, the Southern world of her childhood had expanded and turned into a monster.

She sighed and turned her attention to Camelia. He had finished his phone call. A wry smile lifted his stern mouth.

'We got the dossier on Mitch Rogan. Like good-old-boy Sheriff Duxbury said, he was quite a guy. He did steal from Michael Haines. Served time for it, too, when they finally caught him. But he was soon back in business. And with money in

his pockets. Then Haines died ... on a vacation trip to the Cayman Islands. *And* under suspicious circumstances. But again, nothing was ever proven. The rumor was that Mitch Rogan had something to do with that, too. He had plenty more brushes with the law after that: fraud; property scams; drug deals; suspicion of murder. His rap sheet reads like a eulogy to the criminal mind. You name it, Mitch Rogan did it.'

'I told you so.' Mel shot him a triumphant look. 'Mitch wanted to kill Ed because Ed knew he had killed his family.'

Camelia gave her a pitying look. 'Mitch Rogan died ten years ago,' he said, 'in a boating accident in the Bahamas. He was on a fishing trip. No one even cared enough about the bastard to bring him home. He's buried out there.'

To Mel, the flight back to New York seemed interminable, and the ride from JFK to the hospital even longer. Depression dragged her down into the abyss. She had thought they had found the killer. And now – nothing. The trip to Hainsville and Charleston had proven fruitless. They were back to square one.

Not quite, though. At least now she knew Ed's life story, and that was something she would treasure forever. *And it may be all you'll ever have,* a little voice somewhere inside her said ominously. Nervous, she willed the driver to go faster, faster ...

Filled with a terrible urgency, she shot out of the car almost before it stopped, racing up the hospital steps and through the automatic doors that barely had time to register she was there before they opened.

Camelia watched her go. She had forgotten he even existed. He sighed, but he knew that was the way it should be. He got on the phone and called home.

'I'll be there in a couple of hours, honey,' he told Claudia, and heard her laugh at the unexpected endearment.

'You've been in the South too long,' she told him. 'Since when did y'ever call me honey? It was always *"tesoro"* between us.'

'And it still is. *Tesoro,*' he added softly.

But he thought she was right. He had been in the South too long. Mel Merrydew had grown on him. Like kudzu. He remembered her kiss with a tired grin as he headed back to the precinct house, the place Claudia called the Permanent Detective's Second Home.

Mel's heart was in her mouth as she ran down the endless shiny corridor ... *She should never have left him, she might be too late ...*

Officer Brotski was pacing the hallway, head down, hands behind his back, exactly like Camelia. Hearing her footsteps, he was instantly alert.

'Oh, it's you,' he said by way of greeting. 'Back again.'

'How're you, Officer Brotski,' she cried, ever polite, as she headed for the door.

'Hey, miss, the doc's in there. You can't go in ...'

But it was too late. She was already 'in.'

Art Jacobs was standing by Ed's bedside, a sad expression on his face as he watched over his old friend. He glanced up as Melba shot through the door. He took in her mop of blonde hair, the huge, anguished eyes, the long legs and short skirt, and the special aura that was all her own.

'How are you, Zelda?' he said, holding out his hand.

She clung onto it like he was saving her own life and not Ed's.

'Is he alright? Oh, please, tell me he's still okay ...'

'He's still the same, if that's what you mean.'

She sank onto a corner of the bed, gazing at Ed, still inert, still with all those tubes and the ventilator. 'Oh, thank the Lord you didn't die on me,' she whispered.

The monitor blipped as Ed's heart suddenly lifted a notch or two, and Dr Jacobs glanced at it, astonished. There was no doubt he knew this woman was here.

You're back ... you're back with me, baby ... Why did you go there?

Why go to Hainsville? I locked that part of my life away somewhere and threw away the key ... It hurts, even now ... And I have that permanent faultline in my heart that reminds me that I still want to kill my brother ... I know it's wrong, I don't need Ma to tell me that it's a sin ... but that hatred may never go away ... I never saw Mitch again, you know. Never, after that time at Duke ... and thank God for that, or he would have been dead, and for sure I would be the one in Rikers ...

Mel leaned close to him, whispering in his ear. *Like a blind man, he would have recognized her anywhere just by her scent, it was inlaid in his senses forever ...*

'Mam'zelle Dorothea sends you her love. She loves you so much, Ed. She told me all about you, about how hard you worked. How she looked after you, then you took care of her. I'm so proud of you, my honey. So very proud.'

He felt the wetness of her tears on his cheek, and even had he been able to, he would not have brushed them away. He was happy she was crying. It meant that she cared ... that she loved him ... *Zelda, Zelda ...*

'I'm going to have to leave you again, Ed,' she was saying, and the thought of it made him tremble inside.

'It's Riley. I have to go to her. It's been eight days now, Ed, since you were ...' She couldn't bring herself to say 'shot;' after all, he might not realize that he had been shot, it might scare him ...

Riley. That cute, sweet little girl, born of Zelda's lovely body ... he had so wanted another one, a matching set. His baby this time, too, though Riley would always be his first daughter ... He almost laughed at himself then. Look at him, making plans for kids when he couldn't even open his eyes, let alone play the father role ...

'I'll fly out, just for one night, honey,' she was sayng, and her grip on his hand tightened. 'Just one more night. But Riley needs to see her mom. She needs to hear about you firsthand, not just on the telephone. Who knows, I might even bring her back with me,' she added, inspired.

Of course you must go. He was suddenly tired, so desperately

tired ... he was drifting away ... sinking into that black hole without even the glimmer of a light at the end ...

Mel felt Art Jacobs's hand on her shoulder. 'Better let him rest now, Zelda,' he said, helping her to her feet.

She glanced up at the 'Zelda,' but this was Ed's friend. It was alright, she knew that now.

Art helped her to her feet. 'I'm afraid I overheard your conversation,' he said with an apologetic smile. 'Don't worry, I'll keep an eye on him while you're gone.'

'You promise he'll still be here when I get back?'

Her eyes had that urgent look again. He nodded. 'I promise to do the best I can,' he said.

And Mel knew that, after all, he could do no more than that.

Chapter Forty-five

Riley and Harriet were waiting for Mel at LAX, and their joy at seeing her positively shone from them, like the sunshine of the LA day.

Riley leaped into her arms, burrowing into her shoulder like a squirrel, smothering her neck, her face, any part of her she could reach, in kisses.

Oh, God, did her kid *feel* good, her string-bean legs, just like her own, wrapped tightly around her. And did her kid *smell* good: of freshly washed hair and a clean cotton T-shirt dried in the sun in the backyard, and of McDonald's fries. And did she *taste* good. 'Sweet as ice cream,' Mel assured her, returning the sloppy kisses vehemently.

'You smell of airplanes and you taste of old coffee,' Riley complained happily, and Mel laughed as she slid her back onto the ground. Holding onto Riley with one hand, she flung her free arm around Harriet, who was even less complimentary, but still glad to see her.

'You look like hell,' Harriet said, bluntly.

'Thanks a lot, friend.' Mel grinned happily back at her. 'It's nothing compared to the way I feel.'

'Mom, how's Ed? Did he say he would come on our Sundays yet?'

'Ed is doing okay, honey. I spoke with the doctor, and he

promised me Ed will be fine while I'm here with you. I'm sure Ed understood your message, and, soon as he's better, he'll become a permanent member of our Sunday schedule.'

'What about me?' Harriet complained, hefting Mel's old duffle and setting off for the parking lot. 'What am I supposed to do on Sundays? All alone?'

'Oh, Harr!' Riley's big brown eyes, so like her mother's, looked suddenly stricken. She hadn't meant to hurt Harriet's feelings. 'You can come too, if you really want to.'

'That's okay, kid. I can take it. After a week of looking after you, you can be sure I'll be glad of those Sundays off. *Alone,*' she said with a grin. 'Just kidding, Riley,' she added, in case of any misunderstanding.

Harriet drove the old Volvo wagon and Mel snuggled in the back seat with Riley, their arms around each other, kisses being given and taken, promises of special treats being made, even an ice cream before supper, if she wanted. Did she want? Riley gave Harriet the important directions to the nearest Baskin Robbins, whose locations she knew by heart. Then, licking their cones – pistachio for Mel, coffee for Harriet and vanilla-chocolate swirl lavished with sprinkles for Riley, they drove home.

Mel stared round her small, shabby house as though seeing it for the first time. It looked exactly the same. The same scarred wooden floors, the same funky mixed bag of furniture, the same old upright piano with the ivory missing from two keys and the bass pedal that stuck at Riley's most important bits of music practice. The enormous sofa bought at a house sale that was more suitable for a mansion than a cottage, with its bronze velvet draped now with creamy chenille throws; the kitchen painted cheerful Mediterranean blue and yellow; the gauzy curtains billowing from the upstairs windows in the sea breeze; the porch with its usual clutter of childish things; and the hammock piled with squashed cushions.

Lola pranced toward them on her hind legs. 'Just like a circus

dog,' Riley said proudly, as Lola yelped and nipped ankles and generally caused mayhem.

In no time at all a bottle of wine was opened, food was being cooked and they were all talking at once. Mel was bringing them up to date on the investigation; Harriet was bringing her up to date on *Moving On* business; and Riley was interrupting at every possible opportunity with her own important stories of school, and especially of Jason Mason, who was, she said, scornfully, still shadowing her, 'like some two-bit private eye.'

Mel's astonished eyes met Harriet's, then they both looked at Riley. 'Wherever did you learn that expression?' Mel demanded.

'On the Internet. You wouldn't believe some of the stuff on there.'

'I'll bet,' Mel said, grimly. 'Okay, so its supervision time again, little girl.'

'I'm no little girl, I'm the tallest in my class.'

Mel sighed with feeling. 'I know it, hon. It's known as the Jack-and-the-Beanstalk syndrome.'

Riley giggled as she took a seat at the old pine table. Then Lola jumped into her lap, and for once Mel didn't tell her to get down. Tonight was special, and, of course, Lola was counted in too.

Happiness, Mel thought, looking around at her home, and her small family, was where the heart was. Except that chunk of her heart that was still back in Manhattan. In that hospital. With Ed.

Chapter Forty-six

A hundred miles south of LA, Gus Aramanov was still in his office at the San Diego marina.

He was a yacht broker, and his wife thought he was surely good at his job because his family lacked for nothing. But there again, Lila wasn't certain exactly how much Gus earned, because he never talked finances with her. Just told her to get whatever she and the two kids needed and to quit worrying.

They had been married for seven years and owned a nice four-bed, three-and-a-half-bath home on a pretty suburban street in San Diego, with white wall-to-wall carpet, a big-screen TV in the den, and her Lincoln Navigator and his Mercedes E350 in the three-car garage next to the kids' bikes. Her closet was crammed with Nordstrom's and Macy's best; she had help in the house; and her kids attended expensive preschools. Lila was not asking any questions.

Gus Aramanov was more than twenty years older than his fluffy blonde wife. Whenever they were alone together in bed – without one of the children tucked up with them, that is – he would whisper in her ear that she was his 'little toy-girl.' And Lila called him her 'big teddy bear.' Gus was six-six and power-built like a construction worker – thick neck, muscular shoulders and long arms. He had dark hair and a jowly face, and habitually wore dark glasses that hid the fact that his

brown eyes had a kindly expression. 'A teddy' was exactly what he was.

Still in the office, Gus switched on the voicemail and retrieved the single message. It was short and to the point. And he knew only too well who was calling.

'*You fucked up twice now,*' Mario de Soto said. '*Either he's dead by next week or you are.*'

Gus felt a sudden stab in his chest. His eyes bugged. He struggled to his feet, clutching the back of his chair, thumping his chest with his fist. He was a man in acute pain.

It had been late in the evening a few months ago when Gus Aramanov, aka George Artenski, had received the first telephone call about the Ed Vincent job. He could have lived without it. The weekend was coming up and he had promised to take the kids to Sea World. But business was business. He'd told Lila to pack a bag; he would be leaving first thing in the morning.

'Oh, but you promised,' was on the tip of Lila's tongue, but she had clamped her mouth tight shut. She knew better than to grumble.

The next morning, early, he had kissed Lila goodbye, driven his Merc to the airport and caught the first flight out to New York. From there, using a different name and identification, he had taken a flight to Charleston. He carried only the small overnight case packed by Lila, and a briefcase.

In Charleston, he rented a Ford Taurus and checked into the Marriott, using the name Edgar Forrest and giving his home address as Key Biscayne, Florida.

'I'm expecting a parcel,' he told the reception clerk. 'It should be here by now.'

The clerk handed him the parcel, which he signed for, then went to his room.

Turning on the TV, he caught the local weather forecast. The rain that had plagued the area all day had been upgraded to

a tropical storm, with the further possibility of being upgraded to hurricane Julio. He glanced anxiously at his watch. He'd better get going.

Opening the parcel, he carefully unwrapped the Smith and Wesson Sigma .40 semi-automatic and fitted the suppressor. He strapped a Bianchi Ranger pocketed elastic belly band around his waist, then placed the pistol in the pocket in a front crossdraw position, just to the side of the navel. He patted it approvingly before buttoning his shirt over it. It was his favorite weapon for a small job like this one, and the body-belt position gave him a rapid draw.

Leaving the TV on, he hung the 'Do Not Disturb' sign on the doorknob.

Windshield wipers slashing, he drove the Taurus carefully through the heavy rain. It would make him late, and he cursed himself for not checking the weather earlier. It was almost nine-thirty when he crossed the narrow bridge linking the spit of land to the mainland.

Through the drumming of the rain on the car roof, he could hear the roar of the surf. He thought wistfully of his boys and the cancelled trip to Sea World. Taking a black plastic rain poncho from the briefcase, he slipped it on, then pulled on a pair of black latex gloves.

Cursing the downpour, he climbed from the car and ran clumsily toward the house. In the shelter of the front porch he took stock of his position, wondering if Ed Vincent were home yet. He knew the type of security system in the house. He doubted it was on, even though there was an emergency generator. He was a professional, and it took him less than a minute to pick the simple lock.

Inside, the house was in darkness. He stood for a moment, getting his bearings. There was a staircase facing him at the end of the hall. A big room overlooked the ocean. He had been told that the kitchen quarters were to the front left. That meant the library was on the far right.

His sneakered feet made no sound as he crossed the polished hardwood floor. He had eyes like a cat, could see in the dark, sense an object in front of him by some of kind of personal radar. At the library door he stopped to listen. A faint clicking sound came from within. Gus smiled. He knew that sound: a lock's tumblers.

Under his gentle push the door opened without so much as a squeak. A man was standing in front of an open wall safe. Gus doubted he even heard the five shots he pumped into his back; his legs just crumpled and he concertinaed to the floor. 'Like a puppet with the strings cut,' Gus thought, amused.

He walked over and took a good look at him. The top of his head was blown away and his brains were congealed messily on his face. Even so, Gus could see that his wide-open, blankly staring eyes were brown, that his skin was olive, and that he had a mustache and black hair. The man was Latino, probably Cuban.

Fat crystal beads of sweat broke out suddenly along Gus's receding hairline and dripped slowly down into his eyes.

He had killed the wrong man.

Chapter Forty-seven

Gus thought it was just his rotten luck this guy had chosen tonight to rob the house. Now he would have to wait for Ed Vincent to return. He had to complete the job he had been assigned. Scooping up the stacks of hundred-dollar bills lying on the rug, some of them spattered with blood, he stuffed them in his jacket pockets. Why waste an opportunity to make a little extra – after all, now he was going to have to do extra work. No chance of getting back to Lila and the kids tomorrow as he had promised, he thought regretfully.

And then the doorbell rang.

Gus slid deeper into the space under the stairwell, the Sigma .40 cocked and ready. He hoped this wasn't the Sheriff, or a rescue squad come to check on the house.

'Hello?'

It was a woman.

'Is anyone there?'

He could hear her movements by the door, caught her outline, a black silhouette against the blacker night. Then the light went on, blinding him.

He flattened himelf against the wall, held his breath. The silly bitch was wandering around like she owned the place, eating jellybeans for Chrissakes ... next thing, she'd be in the library – this was not a good scene ... he'd better get out of here.

The front door slammed behind him, caught by the wind. He stopped short, staring at the massive silver truck parked outside. He read the name on the side. MOVING ON. What the hell was she doing, driving a moving truck? Was Ed Vincent moving out? Tonight?

The wind threw itself at him like a prize wrestler, and he was breathless as well as soaked when he reached the rented Taurus. Jeez, what a night. What the hell was he doin' here, anyways?

Cursing, he turned on the ignition. There was a choking sound, then nothing. He tried again. The car was dead. There went his quick getaway. How the fuck was he gonna get out of here?

The stupid Cuban had ruined his night. It should all have been so easy. And now there was the woman to worry about. And what the hell had happened to Ed Vincent, anyways?

His hand rested on the Sigma, tucked into the bellyband. This was getting complicated. He guessed he would have to kill the woman too. Later, he could dump both bodies in the ocean. With these waves, they would be dragged miles out to sea, maybe never found.

But that meant he would have to wait out the storm before he could get away. *And his car wouldn't start.*

He suddenly realized that the only vehicle that could possibly make it across that bridge now was the big moving van.

He went back into the house. Clicked off the lights.

He grabbed the woman on the first scream, but she was fighting him. And she was strong, like a live electric wire, jumping all over the place. Big as he was, it was tough to hold her. She got away from him, but he moved quicker. He was in the truck first. And then he had her.

Or he thought he had, until she drove the goddamn truck right into that tree.

Gus thought his own end had come, but it was the woman

who had caught the full force of it. She lay across the seat, blood streaming from her head, still as death. And he was a man who had seen death enough times to recognize it.

Chapter Forty-eight

Somehow, he had made it back to the hotel. His bedraggled, rain-soaked appearance drew no comment; after all, it was a hurricane and he surely didn't stand out in the crowd.

Later, he had caught the news report, seen them remove her body using the jaws of life.

He had stared, fascinated, at the scene unfolding on the hotel room TV screen, wondering how the hell he had managed to get out unscathed from the mangled cab, with the tree still on top of it. *And then they had said she was still alive.*

Stunned, he'd watched the ambulance rush her off to hospital, where, they said later, she had been treated for a fractured skull and concussion. *'Lucky,'* the news reporter said, *'lucky she wasn't dead in such a terrible crash, when the big old tree crushed the cab.'*

Huh. They didn't know how lucky. That tough bitch must have nine lives. Nine? Gus hoped it was only three, and that the third time the luck would be with him. He sighed again. Right now, the odds were definitely not in his favor.

He had been clever enough to wait it out, back there in the hotel room. Late the following night when the hurricane had finally blown itself out, he had rented a sport utility and driven back to the beach house.

His heart had pounded and his palms were sweaty as he

approached that bridge. The thought of attempting to cross it again was not good, but this time the bridge, though eroded and broken, was above water.

The cleanup had not been easy, either. He'd brought scrub brushes, cloths, stain remover. There was a lot of blood, but fortunately the dark Oriental rug didn't show it too bad.

He'd cleaned up the mess, put the Cuban's body in the big cooler he had bought. Then he had taken out the Europa, weighted the cooler with chains, pushed it overboard and thrown the Sigma in after it. He had watched it sink beneath the swell. It had been rough out there, but he was okay, he knew his way around a boat and got it safely back to the wooden jetty.

Finally, he'd hitched the rented Taurus to the sport utility and towed it back to the airport. He had left no traces, no clues. That beach house was as clean as a brand-new Mercedes when he left it.

So far, though, the woman had not said anything to the cops. He knew that from the newscasts, as well as from the North Carolina newspapers he had ordered from the big newsstand in San Diego. He was hoping the concussion had blanked out her memory. Still, it was a risk he did not care to walk around with. That woman could identify him.

He had summoned up the national telephone directory on his computer and searched listings in Charleston and Raleigh and the other main cities in North Carolina for the name on the truck, 'Moving On.' He had done the same with the neighboring states of Virginia, Georgia, Tennessee and Alabama. And nothing.

Gus slumped back into his chair and took a swallow from the half-empty Smirnoff bottle. It had been ten days since he had finally shot Ed Vincent as he stepped out of his Cessna at La Guardia. He'd pumped four bullets into the bastard. Anyone else would have been good and dead. Even the doctors were saying they didn't know how he was hanging on.

If Vincent did not expire soon, he would be forced to go

to that hospital and take him out. And that would be risky. *Real* risky. Besides, he was worried about the woman in the truck, though, thank God, Mario de Soto didn't know about her. Nor about the dead Cuban. And of course he didn't know about the money from the safe. He groaned, his head in his hands. He'd give it back in a heartbeat, if he could just get rid of this problem.

The woman should have died in the accident. Ed Vincent should have died outside the hangar at La Guardia. It would have been perfect, everything would have been clean. Now he had two people to kill. He was under pressure. And he was worried.

Goddammit, he had to find her.

Chapter Forty-nine

On the other coast, in Miami, Mario de Soto pressed the End Call button on his Nokia. He was a big, bulky man, eighty or so pounds overweight, clean-shaven, with narrow eyes and dark hair streaked with gray. He was scowling as he stared out of the window of his study in the pink stucco, Italianate mansion overlooking the ocean. Had he been interested, from where he stood he could have seen the spacious green lawns surrounding the house, and the tall rows of queen palms that delineated the property's boundaries, as well as the blue-green Atlantic Ocean stretching to the even bluer horizon. But Mario wasn't looking. He had other things on his mind.

He had made a deal. One of the conditions of his participation in that deal – the elimination of Ed Vincent – had to be completed by a certain date. He had given his word. Now his promise had been broken, and he was deeply angry.

It was not difficult to hire a hitman. The trick was the quality. Gus Aramanov, aka George Artenski, was quality. He was the best. Except this time he had failed, and now time was running out. If Ed Vincent was not dead soon, something would have to be done about it.

Alberto Ricci had just been on the phone to Mario, speaking softly as he always did, telling him he had better take care of it. He didn't say 'or else,' but Mario got the drift. If he didn't, the deal was off. These things passed on down the chain: Ricci's promise to his investors; his promise to Ricci; and the hitman's promise to him. Anything could go wrong. And it had. Thanks first to a goddamn hurricane, and second to Aramanov's shaky hand.

He dialed the hitman's business number on the West Coast again, pacing the cool marble floor, listening to it ring. There was no reply. There had been no reply for two days now. Angry, he dialed his home number.

'Aramanov residence.' Gus's wife Lila's voice sang out loudly over the phone. Her housekeeper was gone for the day, but she liked to answer as though it were the maid, just so people would know she had one.

'I'm looking for Gus.' Mario's voice was impatient, rough.

'Try his office, out at the marina.' Lila sounded surprised. Gus never gave his home number to business acquaintances.

'I've tried him there. Been trying him for two days now.'

'Oh. Can I give him a message? Get him to call you?' Lila was uncertain now. There was something intimidating about the way the caller spoke. He wasn't shouting, but there was something in his tone that frightened her.

'You tell him to call Mario. *Right away*, Mrs Aramanov.'

Mario ended the call and went back to the window. He saw the view this time, but his take on it was different. He did not see the hot-red and bright-purple bougainvillaea climbing the pink stucco wall; instead he saw the electric fence and the wiring that ran along the top of it. He didn't see the sun sparkling like molten gold on the blue-green ocean; instead he saw the massive iron gates and the guard house and the two armed men with Uzi submachine guns at the ready. He didn't see the cool, dark blue infinity of the swimming pool and the immaculate red clay tennis courts; he saw infrared video cameras and motion detectors in the bushes, and attack-trained Dobermanns patrolling his property. Mario de Soto saw a jail.

Sure, the Miami mansion was different from the jails he'd

done time in; at least here he had his own chef. But lately he had lost his appetite and mostly ate just grilled vegetables, with the occasional piece of fish. He didn't drink anymore either, not since the heart attack that had almost finished him off three years ago — except for milk, always accompanied by a pack of Oreos. He never could resist them, and it wasn't just a hangover from his childhood. He had never gotten to eat Oreos then.

He had a chauffeur and a black Mercedes SL900, as well as the red Ferrari and a deep blue Bentley Brooklands Trophy Edition. But he rarely went out anymore.

He had a girlfriend, blonde, attractive, bejewelled and scented. She wore Versace and sexy lingerie. But he wasn't able to get it up anymore.

Mario had lost his appetite not only for food, but for life. Until Alberto Ricci had paid him a visit a few weeks ago.

Alberto was in the property business, via a Cayman Islands company known as Monster Development. He was in a high-stakes bidding war for airspace on Fifth Avenue, and had come up against tough competition. Ed Vincent.

Mario had made his own first fortune in property. He had also served his first jail term for defrauding investors in that same property deal, but had still come out a winner after just a couple of years — and with a well-hidden offshore bank account. He'd done time for other things too, that he didn't care to have talked about. And there were plenty of people who would like to see him dead.

But Alberto Ricci was squeaky-clean, and he intended to keep it that way: no fraud; no SEC scams; no murders ... at least none of the above that could be traced back to him. Ricci was a society gentleman, and his new young wife enjoyed that. He used other people to do his dirty work and take the rap for him. This time was no different.

De Soto had struck a deal with Ricci. He would get to be a twenty-percent partner in the Fifth Avenue property at a reduced financial stake. In return for getting rid of the competition.

It was the thought of the 'competition' that had brought him most pleasure, though. He had laughed himself sick over it. His nemesis had fallen into his hands quite by chance. Ed Vincent was the one man on this planet who had the knowledge to put him away forever – if only he had known him. But Vincent certainly did not know Mario de Soto.

He strode restlessly out of the big house and stood for a minute, hands behind his back, dark sunglasses hiding his narrow eyes, looking round at the property his fertile criminal mind had bought him. The men patrolling the grounds with the leashed Dobermanns saluted him, and in an instant, his assistant was at his side.

Mario ignored them all, striding down the steps across the lawn to the back of the house and the helipad.

The assistant was alarmed. Mario had not been anywhere in weeks; he wasn't well. He hurried after him. 'Mr de Soto, where are you going, sir?'

Still ignoring him, Mario climbed into the Bell helicopter. He strapped himself in and put on the headset. The assistant backed away quickly as the rotor blades begin to whirl. Then Mario was up and away, heading for the Bahamas.

As he looked down on his vast oceanfront property, he thought how little pleasure it gave him. And how much pleasure the Monster deal would give him. That is, when he had completed his part of the bargain.

Chapter Fifty

Lila Aramanov could not figure out why her husband was so obsessed with the news these days. He even ate in front of the TV, alone in the family room, dismissing the kids with a harsh 'go away and play, why can't you, haven't I bought you enough toys for Chrissakes?'

Lila hovered by the door, waching him switching channels, jumpy as a Halloween cat. She could swear he caught every newscast. Sighing, she decided this was her moment to tackle him on the subject, find out what was wrong, get him to share his feelings with her.

Gus was sitting in his usual chair in front of the sixty-inch TV set. A ham and Swiss on a Kaiser roll, piled high with tomato and onion – despite Lila's refined comments about what the onion did to his breath – lay discarded on a plate on the floor. She noticed he had taken only a couple of bites. And next to the plate stood a line of empty Bud cans that had now been replaced with Smirnoff vodka, which he was drinking from the bottle. Things were definitely not good.

She came up behind him, wound her arms around him, nuzzling his big neck. 'What's happened to my big teddy bear?' she whined. 'He's gone away from his little toy-girl, left her all alone and lonely.'

Gus switched from NBC to Headline News. 'Aw, for

ELIZABETH ADLER

Chrissakes, leave me alone, why don't ya,' was his surly
reply.

Lila flung away from him as though she had been stung.
'So what the hell's the matter with you?' She ran her french-
manicured fingers distractedly through her stiffly sprayed bright
blonde hair, for once not caring that it stuck up ridiculously
instead of in its usual careful fluffed-out mop. 'Y'know what,
Gus Aramanov? You're just not the same guy you used to be.'

Gus didn't even turn from the TV to look at her. 'Thanks
for sharing that with me. *Sweetheart,*' he added, maliciously.

'So what's with the nerves? The depression? The bad
temper? You even vent on the kids.' Her eyes filled with
tears, remembering the way things used to be. 'Poor innocent
babies,' she sobbed.

'Lila, just give it a rest, why don't ya.' Gus leaned forward,
suddenly intent as the newscaster mentioned Ed Vincent . . .

*Mr Vincent is still in a coma. It has been over a week now, and doctors
report no improvement in his condition. Meanwhile the perpetrator . . .*

'Y'don't even listen to me anymore,' Lila yelled, frantic.

'Shuddup, Lila . . .' He turned up the volume . . .

*. . . or perpetrators, are still at large. The police say the investigation is
proceeding as normal.*

'Bastard,' Lila screamed. She flounced out and up the white-
carpeted stairs. In their pink master bedroom, she grabbed her
night things, snatched up her favorite pillow and headed for the
guest room. The miserable bastard could sleep alone tonight.
Forever, for all she cared.

The guest room door slammed forcefully, rattling windows,
but Gus did not even notice. He was frantic. De Soto was not a
man to pussyfoot around. And his message had been blunt and
to the point.

Chapter Fifty-one

Harriet Simons had just dropped Mel off at LAX, en route once more for New York and Ed. Now, she was on the 405 heading north.

It was tough, she thought, juggling three jobs at once, but she was coping. First and foremost came Riley, though sometimes Harriet felt that clever little Riley was looking after her instead of the other way round. It was a pleasure, not a job, but it was also time-consuming. Who knew how mothers got through the days, she marveled as she maneuvered the big silver truck through the surging morning traffic.

She was on the way to her second job, packing up a condo in Marina del Rey prior to moving the stuff the following day to Santa Monica. An easy job, as jobs went, and as long as her helpers showed up on time. You could never tell, these days, because, as Melba's mom would have said, 'the help just isn't the same as it used to be in the old days.'

She grinned, thinking of Mel's mom, and the fact that Mel did not recognize that she was exactly like her. Harebrained, yet solid as a rock in her beliefs and in her friendships. Intelligent. Devoted. Scatty. And Southern.

Harriet's third task of the day was an audition at noon in West Hollywood, which was a hell of a trek from the marina and would cost her a few hours of real work time. She didn't know why she bothered. She hadn't nailed an acting job in two years, not even a commercial. Not even one where they covered you in a clownsuit so nobody knew who you were, and disguised your voice as a squawk so nobody even knew that you could act. Perhaps it really was time she *Moved On*. Acknowledged that house-moving was what she did, and forget she was ever an aspiring actress. She thought that whoever invented that word 'aspiring' was a genius — it covered almost the entire population of Hollywood. And she would bet on that.

She sighed as she contemplated her future. No man on the horizon, or at least none that she cared sufficiently for to place in the 'permanent' category. Anyhow, come to think of it, she kind of liked her life. She and Mel had a good thing going, though of course if Mel married Ed, she would become a rich man's wife and probably live in New York and leave her with the *Moving On* business. Shoot. She wasn't sure she could cope alone.

Of course you can, you idiot, she told herself, impatiently flipping back her red hair. 'What the hell are you doing now, if not coping and running the business alone?' *Besides, what if Ed dies?*

Her heart sank at the thought. Mel would be devastated. Defeated. Bereft. And so would Riley, who had come to think of Ed as part of her family. Of course, Riley knew nothing about Ed's wealth and his business, only that he was a nice man who made her laugh and who, even she could see, loved her mom.

Harriet groaned as the freeway ground to a halt. Par for the course; this happened every day on the 405. Shoot, now she would be the late one. She sank back with a sigh, fingers drumming impatiently on the wheel. Nothing was moving, and the idiot behind her was honking as though she could just shift over and let him zoom ahead. *Road rage*, she thought, angrily. *The fool.* The left lane inched forward, then began to move. She groaned; just her luck, she was in the wrong lane again.

Gus Aramanov bulled his white Merc into the left lane, ignoring the honking horns and squealing of brakes in back of him. He scowled as he slid slowly forward; it would take him forever to get to Marina del Rey, but at least this lane was moving. He accelerated to pass the large silver truck on his right, glanced at it, and saw MOVING ON inscribed in lipstick-red script on the side.

Gus almost rear-ended the car in front. He stamped on the brakes, ignoring the blasting horns, slowing down, until the truck came alongside again. He stared up into the cab to see if she was driving, but it was a skinny red-haired woman who gave him a drop-dead look as she caught his eye. He fell back, let her get ahead of him. As he thought, the phone number was on the back of the truck. He memorized it. It was a 310 area code. *The woman was right here in LA. She had been here all the time.*

He was grinning as he followed the truck down the marina exit. He was suddenly a man with one of the weights off his shoulders.

He watched as the *Moving On* truck edged into a parking spot immediately in front of an apartment building. The red-haired woman got out, opened up the back of the truck in readiness, then hurried into the building.

He parked opposite, then took out his Ericsson and dialed the *Moving On* number. A computer voice informed him no one was there, and suggested he leave a message, press 1 for Mel Merrydew and 2 for Harriet Simons. They would be sure to get right back to him and wished him a great day.

Cute, he thought, ringing off. Mel Merrydew and Harriet Simons. He wondered which one was his prey.

Directory Inquiries gave him Mel Merrydew's home number and address. He got back on the freeway, exited at Santa Monica and found Ascot Street. Again, he parked on the opposite side of the street, staring at number 139, taking in the shabby craftsman bungalow with its wide front porch and overhanging gables. There was a hammock with a pile of kid's soft toys in it, teddies and such, just like his own kids'.

He stored that information for future reference, then drove

back to the yacht basin at Marina del Rey. He dealt with the necessary business, then headed south to San Diego, and home. First, he would take care of the woman. Then he'd figure out how to take care of Ed Vincent. One more time.

Lila was pleased when Gus arrived home with little gifts for the children. He presented her with a bouquet of roses and a gruff apology.

'Business problems,' he explained.

Back in the pink master bedroom again, she was surprised how amorous he was that night. It was like old times. She had her teddy bear back again.

Chapter Fifty-two

As Mel's United flight was landing at JFK, Camelia was on Virgin Atlantic, en route to London.

He was leaning back in the red seat, eating a chocolate-covered ice-cream bar and watching an old Sharon Stone movie on his personal video screen. Again she reminded him uncannily of Mel. He heaved a deep sigh as he took the final bite of ice cream. He thought both women were equally remote.

Reality was that they had finally tracked down the owners of the Fifth Avenue property, an Arab consortium who were saying nothing, except, via a spokesman, that they did not want to be involved. They were deliberately out of the country and difficult to reach, but this morning, Scotland Yard had advised that one of the group owned a house in London, and that he was currently in residence. And Camelia had gotten the first flight to Heathrow.

Early-morning London was gray, with a kind of damp mist that the English termed a sprinkle, but which Camelia thought was more of a chilling rain. He shivered, waiting for a taxi; it got to his very bones and he wondered how the Brits put up with it, day after day, year after year. Did they ever get spring, summer, a nice sunny day? He suspected maybe only in the movies. He definitely was not connecting with real life today.

He checked into a vast, impersonal hotel near the Strand,

dumped his hastily packed bag on the bed, called his cohort, Inspector Macpherson, at Scotland Yard and arranged to be there, 'Like right now.'

The traffic was snarled and it took him ten minutes longer than he had anticipated, and he was angry with himself for keeping Macpherson waiting.

When he finally entered the red-brick portals of the hallowed British institution known as Scotland Yard, he couldn't help but think of Sherlock Holmes, but the reality was as modern and slick as Virgin Atlantic. And Inspector Macpherson was a lofty guy with a ruddy complexion, a beard and a booming voice that carried down the hallway as he called out a greeting.

Unlike his own department, there were no teetering piles of old files here, no stagnant cups of coffee and stale Krispy Kremes. Camelia took a seat and was offered hot coffee in a proper mug, and a shortbread biscuit from Macpherson's own private stash.

'I'm a Scot,' Macpherson said with a loud laugh. 'Can't get through the day without a nice bit of shortbread. Not as good as mother used to make, I'll admit, but good enough. Besides,' he added, 'I'm addicted to the sugar.'

Camelia accepted the biscuit and listened while Macpherson explained what the deal was. One of the principals in the Arab consortium, Khalid al Sharif, had arrived in London two days ago. His house was guarded, but Macpherson had obtained a warrant and the man would have to answer questions in connection with his property dealings.

He was Saudi, the eldest son, oil rich and a bit of a mystery. Unlike many of his mega-rich contemporaries, Khalid kept out of the gambling clubs and the nightclubs, and whatever his preference and pleasures were, he kept them private. 'They say he's obsessed with business,' Macpherson told him. 'To him the true gamble is coming out the winner in a big deal. Like this one. Hence the possible double-dealing, playing one potential buyer off against another.'

'I know that scene.' Camelia remembered being outbid on the purchase of his house in Queens by a guy who just kept upping the ante another thou and then another thou, until finally Camelia had called enough. It was just the same with Khalid Sharif, only the stakes were higher. Business was business, he guessed.

A colleague drove the unmarked black Vauxhall through the maze of central London traffic. Bedazzled, Camelia closed his eyes; he thought he would never get used to driving on the left, plus a sleepless night and jet lag had tamped down his brain cells. He had never felt less ready for an interrogation in his career. Especially one with a difficult, temperamental and very rich suspect.

The house, on posh Bishop's Avenue, in the smart sub-urb of Hampstead, was very grand. It took ten minutes of back-and-forth with the two burly bodyguards, complete with snarling German Shepherds, with the guards on the intercom to the house and Camelia puffing urgently on a Winston and Macpherson becoming steelier and steelier in a very polite British way, before they were finally admitted.

The marble front hall soared forty feet, supported at intervals by fluted onyx columns, all the way up to an enamelled blue dome, laced with sparkling stars.

A male servant in a white robe held at the waist by a blue-tasseled sash showed them into the main salon.

Khalid al Sharif was seated by the window, alone on the gold silk banquette than ran the entire length and breadth of the room, piled high with jewel-toned cushions. Small crystal tables, placed here and there in front of it, held silver and gold dishes containing fresh dates, assorted nuts and sugared almonds. The domed ceiling was again painted blue with a tiny window at its apex; rich Oriental rugs covered the marble floor, and a vase of perfect Casablanca lilies on an immense circular table cast their sweet, intoxicating scent into the room.

It was a movie set, Camelia thought, stunned. The Sultan's

palace via Cleopatra. He had never known that people lived like this, even rich people. But this was really rich. This was *staggering* rich.

'Mind-boggling,' Macpherson muttered as they waited for Sharif to greet them.

Sharif did not get up. Nor did he offer them refreshment. 'I did not invite you gentlemen here,' he said, picking a stem of fresh dates from the silver dish in front of him. 'And I cannot think what it is you need to question me about. But you can rest assured my Ambassador will make a serious complaint to the Prime Minister.' He plucked a date from the stem and bit into it, staring balefully at them with big brown eyes.

He was a handsome guy, Camelia thought. In his late forties, a lean bronze face, a mustache, dark hair partially hidden under the red and white headcloth. He could see he was fit, too, under that white robe he wore. His feet were bare and Camelia noted that his toenails wore a sheen of clear-gloss nail polish.

Al Sharif spat the date pit into his hand and deposited it in a bowl. He plucked another date from the stem, saying nothing.

Camelia glanced at Macpherson and Macpherson nodded, giving him the lead.

'Mr Sharif, sir, there is no need for alarm, and I apologize if you thought so.' Camelia was sweating with the effort of diplomacy. He was more used to scraping bodies off the streets after a shoot-up; he didn't know this sophisticated man-of-the-world crap. 'We simply need an answer to one question.'

Sharif's brows rose and he spat out another date pit.

'The question is,' Camelia filled in the long silence, 'who else is in the bidding war on the Fifth Avenue airspace, besides Ed Vincent?'

Sharif did not look at him when finally he spoke. 'I was, of course, sorry to learn of Mr Vincent's unfortunate . . . incident. However, I find it hard to believe it could have anything to do with the potential sale of my property.'

He had an impeccable British accent, upper-class to the limit. Educated at Harrow, Macpherson had told Camelia earlier, in the little bio he had given him.

'Sir,' Macpherson took over. 'I'm afraid I have to ask you to answer Detective Camelia's question.'

Sharif shot him a glance. 'And if I do not?'

'Then I shall have to take you in for questioning.' Macpherson flashed the warrant. 'Sir,' he added, carefully polite. 'And of course, I am aware of how unseemly that would be for you.'

Sharif tossed another date into his mouth. He chewed thoughtfully, then spat out the pit. 'There were several potential buyers,' he said, apparently recognizing that the odds were against him and rejecting the gamble. 'One of those men put an offer on the table that was initially not acceptable. Ed Vincent bid higher. His offer was accepted, though only provisionally, subject to contract and to the proper details being negotiated by my lawyers. Then the first buyer came back with a larger bid, subject, as before, to anonymity.'

Camelia had put his hands behind his back, head bowed in his usual stance before he commenced pacing. Pacing was a natural outlet for him; it enabled him to think, gave his mind breathing space. He said, 'And you accepted that anonymous bid?'

'I was waiting for Mr Vincent's retaliatory bid, though he had sworn that he would not make one. He said that because we had shaken hands on it, he had a deal.'

Sharif glanced away from Macpherson's glowering face.

Camelia had lost all patience now; he wanted to tell him to quit futzing around and tell them the truth. 'So who *was* the other buyer, Mr Sharif?' he said, and there was something in his voice, a low, menacing, even tone about it that had Sharif looking apprehensively at him.

'His name is Alberto Ricci,' he said reluctantly, knowing he now had no choice.

'Ahhh ... *Ricci.*' Camelia was surprised.

'Thank you very much, sir, for your cooperation,' Macpherson said.

And then they were out of there, hurrying thankfully down the steps, keeping a wary eye on the leashed German Shepherds as they climbed into the car and drove back down leafy Bishop's Avenue.

Camelia mopped his forehead with his white handkerchief. 'I'd rather have root-canal than deal with guys like that. It's just not my scene.'

'You know Ricci?'

Camelia nodded. 'Only by reputation. He's as much a philanthropist as Ed Vincent, known as a decent guy with his money and in his lifestyle. And, as far as I know, he's clean.'

'Then you don't think he's your killer?'

Camelia shook his head. 'My bet is, it's a whole lot trickier than just that.'

He said goodbye to Macpherson, phoned in a report, and, too hyped to fall asleep, took a taxi to Soho. He ate a decent Margarita pizza at a place called the Pizza Express on Wardour Street, then he wandered into Ronnie Scott's and listened to an hour or so of jazz, sipping whisky and smoking Winstons, until his head felt so fogged he couldn't hear the music anymore. So he hailed a taxi, picked up his still unpacked bag, checked out of the hotel and headed to Heathrow. He drank maybe ten cups of coffee and was on the first flight out to New York. He slept like a babe all the way.

Chapter Fifty-three

Ed heard her come in, he knew the special sound of her heels on the hard vinyl floor, the movement of her skirt against her legs ... Her scent was in his nostrils again, in his head, in his heart ... Or what was left of his heart by now. It felt as though it were on a downward slope, each beat slower than the last, each breath tougher than the last ... each thought more effort than the last. It would be so much easier to stop this fight, just to let go and slide effortlessly into oblivion ... into a Never Never Land where there was no more jagged pain; no more disturbing dreams that were half dream, half reality; no life. NO ZELDA.

It was unthinkable, life without her ... Unbearable, that he might never hold her again ... Unimaginable, that he might never hear her call him 'honey' one more time ...

'Honey,' she said, and her soft voice was like a caress. 'I'm here with you, and this time I'm not leaving. You've got me for good, Ed Vincent, like it or not.'

Oh, I like it, I like it alright ... He would have smiled if he could, but all he could manage was the next breath the machine gave him.

'Riley sends her best love, and she's looking forward to our Sundays together again. I don't know whether it's you or the Beluga, but this kid is anxious to go to dinner with you. You may have started something bigger than you thought.'

I can't wait. Can't wait to hear Riley laugh again, that hearty, rollicking little-girl laugh that comes from her gut ... She can have an ounce of Beluga all to herself, even though I guess it'll make her sick ... I just love that kid ...

'And Harriet sends love, too,' Mel said. 'She's coping with *Moving On*, in my absence.'

He could hear the grin in her voice, and wanted to smile too ...

'Although of course, she has to admit it's not quite the same without me ...'

I'll bet ...

'And I love her to pieces too,' Mel added, thankfully. 'She's just the best friend, taking care of Riley and Lola – who, I know, would send you a great big ankle-nip if she could only get at you ...'

Oh, that darn little dog ... I guessed I'm just gonna have to live with it – Lola is a big part of Riley's life ... that is, if I can only get my own act together and live ...

'I'm going to be quiet now,' Mel said softly. 'Let you rest, gain some strength back. Just know I love you, Ed Vincent, that's all.'

She was kissing him, oh so gently, on the lips. Or whatever part of his mouth she could get to, with all the tubes and the ventilator and all ... It was a happy thought to drift out to oblivion on, to a peaceful place, out there in the blackness ...

Once again, Camelia was waiting to interview a man. This time it was Alberto Ricci, and the location was a sumptuous townhouse on East 64th, with Bonnards and Picassos on the silk-paneled walls and swagged brocade draperies at the tall windows. Pacing impatiently back and forth, Camelia surveyed the priceless antiques and thought the place cost more than he would ever make in his lifetime. Yet, as Ricci came smiling toward him, hand outstretched, he did not envy this man one bit.

Inquiries had revealed nothing: Ricci was as clean as a whistle. No record, no black marks against him. Yet there was something in his eyes, an emptiness that belied the warmth of his smile, and the firmness of his handshake, his friendly slap on the back and his apologetic words.

'Of course I know Ed,' Ricci admitted now. 'Though not intimately. We often met at the same functions. You know what a generous contributor to charity Vincent was. *Is*,' he corrected himself hastily. 'Like myself, he believes in helping others.'

I'll bet you do, Camelia thought, glancing around at the plush surroundings.

'I just didn't realize that my property dealings had anything to do with Ed's misfortune. Even now, I still can't believe this involved the deal. Jesus, Detective, do you think I wouldn't have given up bidding for the property in an instant, if I'd thought there was any trouble?'

No, Camelia thought as he walked slowly back down East 64th, hands thrust in the pockets of his dark suit. I don't think that, Mr Ricci. I think you know something I don't know.

Mel glanced up as Camelia entered the hospital room. He looked the way she felt. Exhausted.

She got to her feet to embrace him, then held him at arm's length, inspecting him.

'You look terrible,' she said.

He grinned. 'Makes two of us. How about a cup of coffee?'

She glanced at Ed. The green lines on the monitor blipped calmly, endlessly. *Infinitely*, she prayed.

It wasn't Brotski on duty outside the door, but a new uniform, a replica of the skinny kid in an oversized cop outfit and a shiny new badge. He got smartly to his feet as Detective Camelia emerged, and Mel thought, tenderly, the poor young man looked bored. She guessed he had expected more excitement from police work than just long hours outside a closed hospital room door.

She linked her arm companionably with Camelia's as they stepped out of the hospital and headed for the usual deli.

'Where have you been?' she asked, sitting at the tiny plastic table opposite him. 'I missed you.'

'Oh, yeah, like the chicken-pox you missed me.'

'It's true, though.' She took a sip of coffee, and smiled at him. 'Anyhow, I kind of enjoyed chicken-pox. It meant I didn't have to go to school.'

'School? That means you were a very late chicken-poxer. My kids had their fix in kindergarten.'

'I was always a little retarded, I guess.' She laughed and took his hand. 'Really, though, Camelia, I missed you. It seems ages since Charleston and Mam'zelle Dorothea.'

'It does. And since you asked, I was in London,' he said, ordering two toasted bagels and cream cheese.

'That explains it.'

'Explains what?'

'Your unhealthy pallor. All that gray, rainy weather. And that hint of a British accent I'm hearing.'

'Bullshit,' he said with a grin.

'Okay, so what were you doing in London, besides losing weight and not sleeping?'

She was astute, he had to give her that. She noticed every darn thing, even that he had been awake for more than forty-eight hours now. 'I was on the trail of our shooter.'

Her eyes grew round, but she said nothing, waiting. He told her about Scotland Yard and Khalid al Sharif, and about Alberto Ricci, while they munched on the bagels that were not toasted well enough for his liking, but he was too spent to argue with the waiter.

'Ricci,' she said, thoughtfully. 'I've read about him. Very rich, always at charity events with a glamorous wife in designer dresses. Quite the man about town.'

'Yeah, but the question is, how did he get there? His business dealings seem above board, but they still don't seem to account for that lifestyle. I mean, a Picasso costs. And so does a Bonnard.'

Mel's eyebrows rose interestedly. 'You recognized a Bonnard.'

He saw she was impressed, and he grinned. 'Like, y'mean, any old slouch can recognize a Picasso, but how about that Bonnard, huh?'

Mel blushed and he enjoyed the process. 'Sorry. I didn't mean it quite like that.'

'Sure you did. But that's okay.' He shrugged. 'I'm just a Sicilian cop, what do I know? Except I happen to love art. I take my kids to the Met and MOMA every chance I get. Which isn't as often as I might like.'

'I saw my daughter yesterday,' she told him, wistfully. 'God, how I miss her.'

'Funny, isn't it, how those scrappy, yelling little babies grow into kids, and then into real people. And how they grow into your heart.'

'Like kudzu,' she agreed, remembering. It was such a relief to see him, to be with him, the stress simply lifted from her aching shoulders. Like the aftermath of a great massage, Camelia simply made her feel good. Maybe too good, she thought guiltily.

Oh, God, Camelia was thinking, as he walked her back to the hospital. Am I glad to be back here. With her. It's like coming home.

Chapter Fifty-four

Gus Aramanov cruised slowly down Ascot Street in the silver Camaro, again rented using a fake driver's license. Light shone from the downstairs windows of number 139, and he glanced at the dashboard clock. Almost eight. Surely the kid would be in bed by now. His own certainly would be, Lila made sure of that. She was a good mother, no doubt about it, and his boys were good boys. Like any father, he was proud of them.

It was unfortunate that the child would be in the house when he 'took out' the mother. The idea disturbed him; he liked children. But he had no choice, he couldn't shoot the woman at work, too many people around. So it would have to be in the home.

He parked the rental car in a strip-mall lot two blocks away, then walked briskly back to number 139. This was a residential street and there was no one about. There rarely was, in LA, and besides, he had already staked it out and knew the movements of the neighbors; knew when the quiet time was, with everybody in front of the TV, or out for the evening. Eight was the best time. Only the thought of the girl nagged at him, and he hoped again that she was already in bed.

The one street light was at the very end, and leafy trees cast a welcome extra shadow as he walked, unhurriedly, just in case anyone was watching, to number 139. He paused on the porch to pull on the black ski-mask, then tried the door. It was unlocked. Of course, he thought. She was exactly the kind of woman who would leave her doors unlocked.

He stepped directly into the living room. It was lit by a couple of fringed lamps and was empty. From upstairs came the blare of a TV. A wide, shallow flight of stairs was on the far right, and from the room to the left came the familiar smell of Chinese takeout. The kitchen, he guessed.

Gus palmed the Sigma .40, fitted with a silencer; this would be easy, it would be over in seconds . . .

He listened for sounds of life. Nothing. Except . . . wait, what was that? He strained his ears, heard a faint scratching sound. Then a deep, heartfelt sigh.

Riley was sitting at the kitchen table, doing her homework, which tonight consisted of writing an essay on the merits of dogs versus cats. It was tough; she was so definitely a dog person because of Lola, who was, of course, dog perfection, and therefore she was having a hard time being totally fair to cats, whom she liked a lot, but who, in her view, couldn't compete with dogs. She shoved her hands through her bronze curls, glaring despairingly at the single paragraph she had written.

Dogs are better because cats don't go for walks with you, and they don't play catch at the beach, and they don't like chicken chow mein, and Lola likes all three. And I like Lola because she is my dog, even though she bites. Just little bites though, and I know she really doesn't mean it, it's just her way of saying hello. Mom says she should learn better manners, but somehow, she just never does.

She was wondering if she had spelled chow mein right, when she heard the footsteps. She glanced up, expecting to see Harriet, who was upstairs watching TV, with Lola asleep on the bed next to her. Harriet had said she was beat tonight, after a long day moving stuff, and Riley was running late with the homework, due to a TV progam Harriet had allowed her to stay up and watch, plus the takeout Chinese, which was one of her favorites.

When she saw Gus, her eyes bugged and her mouth dropped into an 'O' of surprise.

Gus stared, shocked, back at her. Then she reacted.

'Harriet,' she screamed, 'Harriet, there's a man here . . .'

Gus heard Harriet's feet pounding down the stairs, and the yap of a dog. He stepped quickly behind the kitchen door, the Sigma cocked. He hated to do it in front of the kid, but he had no choice.

Harriet burst into the kitchen, preceded by Lola, and Riley just stared at her, frozen with shock. But not Lola. The dog sniffed him out, took a running jump and got him in the thigh.

Gus flung the dog off him and backed up. The gun wavered for a second and, instinctively, Harriet grabbed Riley. She thrust the child behind her, edging toward the door. Her heart was in her throat, and her eyes bugged with terror. All she knew was she had to get out, run to the neighbors, call 911.

The dog still had its teeth in Gus's leg and he slammed the gun on its head and, with a whimper, it fell back.

Riley dashed from behind Harriet and flung herself onto the floor next to the inert dog. 'You've killed her,' she screamed at Gus. 'That's my dog, mister, and God will surely punish you for this.'

Sweat rolled down Gus's neck. He was out of his league. This wasn't the way he had planned it. But then, he had never had to deal with a kid and a dog before, or at least nothing more than attack Dobermanns.

He pointed the gun at Harriet. Riley's horrified eyes followed. 'Ohh, no . . . ooo,' she screamed. And then she tackled him like a Green Bay Packer fullback, taking him by surprise and bringing him down.

Gus kicked her away. He was dripping with sweat. This

was turning into a farce. He hadn't even seen the woman he was meant to kill.

Harriet leaped at him. She wrestled for the gun, he gave her a chopping blow to the neck, and she dropped to the floor.

'Oh, no, *oh, nooo,*' the kid was yelling, 'Nooo, Harriet . . .'

Gus got to his feet. He backed to the door, the gun pointed at the child. 'One move, kid, and you're both dead,' he said. His accent was thicker than usual, because he was disturbed. This was all wrong. He was a professional hitman, one of the best in the business. Or at least he was, until this Ed Vincent debacle. What the fuck was he doing, waving a gun at a kid?

'Stay right where you are,' he warned Riley. 'I'll be in the next room. You move, and I'll kill you both. Got that?'

Her mouth trembled, but she nodded. She kept on watching him, big-eyed as he backed out the door.

Then he was racing down the street to the car, gunning the engine. And he was gone, looping onto the Santa Monica freeway, heading to the 405 and Marina del Rey, praying the kid did as she was told until he had time to get away.

For a minute, Riley stayed frozen in place. She was too terrified even to breathe loudly in case he heard her. She stared anxiously at the unconscious Harriet, and at Lola sprawled next to her, bleeding from the head. She could bear it no longer. Let him shoot her, she had to get help . . .

Scrambling to her feet, she reached for the phone and dialed 911.

Chapter Fifty-five

Camelia was in his 'office,' meaning the small space allotted him at the precinct house, swivel chair tilted, feet propped on his desk, lightly starched white shirtsleeves rolled, a Winston dangling from his lips.

He was trying to break the habit; God knows it wasn't good for him, but every now and again when things were getting on top of him, like now for instance, he succumbed. He guessed he was as much an addict as the next man, and he took a final guilty puff before stubbing it out in the scarred green metal ashtray that must have been around for thirty years and by now, he guessed, probably qualified as a genuine antique.

He shoved aside the brimming wire in-tray, and began one more time to look through the reports on the Ed Vincent case. They were now more than two weeks into the investigation, and apart from the Ricci tie-in to the property deal, they were getting nowhere.

Ed's past history had offered nothing, except a clue to the man himself. To his strength of character, and perhaps to the reasons why he was so charitable, and took it upon himself to help young people in need.

Absentmindedly, Camelia tapped another cigarette from the pack. He put it to his lips, then remembered. He flung it away, disgusted with himself. He had the strength of will of a flea. He couldn't even cure his addiction to cigarettes, so how could he expect to cure his addiction to Melba Merrydew?

The phone rang and he reached for it. 'How're y'doing', he said to the detective from the LAPD, wondering what was up. He sat up, though, when he heard what had happened.

He glanced at the computer. 'The information's coming through now,' he replied tersely. 'I'll be back to you in five.'

He stared intently at the report on the machine, detailing the attack against Mel's daughter, and her friend and business partner. Harriet Simons was in USC Medical Center suffering from concussion. Riley Merrydew was in protective custody. And the dog, Lola, was in the veterinary hospital.

His heart sank to the pit of his stomach. *The hitman had been looking for Mel.*

The child had given what description she could: a big man, really big, wearing a black woolen mask. And he had a funny accent.

LAPD thought it might be George Artenski, and Camelia had no doubt they were right. His leaden heart ached as he thought again about how the hell was he gonna tell Mel.

He adjusted his shirtsleeves and put on his coat. This wasn't something you could just tell a woman over the phone. He had to go back to the hospital and face her.

First, though, he got back on the phone, told the detective he believed the perp was George Artenski, and said that he was releasing a photofit identity picture of the suspect, to be run immediately on national TV.

The hunt was on.

Rick Estevez was sharing the bedside vigil with Mel this morning. He had brought a copy of the *Wall Street Journal* and was reading the latest stock deals out loud, hoping to stimulate Ed's silent brain.

Mel was stroking Ed's arm. Her eyes had not wavered from his face, but she glanced up as Camelia entered.

She shot him that ear-to-ear smile and his heart seemed to drop even lower. 'I need to speak to you.' He beckoned her out into the corridor.

She hurried after him. 'Something's wrong.' She searched his face anxiously. 'What is it? What's happened?'

'There's been an incident.'

She stared at him, not understanding. 'What does that mean?'

'Harriet was attacked at the house. We believe it was the hitman.'

Her hand flew to her mouth, and she stared at him, horrified.

'She's okay, and Riley's okay. It's concussion with Harriet, and apart from bruises, Riley wasn't hurt.'

Mel looked about to faint, and Camelia put his arm around her and lowered her into the chair outside the door where the uniform usually sat. It occurred to him that the duty officer was not there, and he glanced impatiently up and down the corridor. He guessed the officer had gone to the bathroom, but he shouldn't have left without getting the relief guy up from downstairs. He would remember to reprimand him about that.

Estevez emerged from Ed's room. He stared surprised at them; he could see something was wrong.

'Where is she?' Mel clutched at Camelia's hand. *'Where's Riley?'*

'Don't worry, she's safe. She's in protective custody.'

'You mean she's in a *police station?*' Mel's voice was a panicked squeak. 'Harriet's in hospital and my daughter's in jail. Oh, my God . . . my poor baby . . .'

Estevez's eyes met Camelia's. 'What happened?'

Camelia told him while Mel just sat there, staring blankly into space. She had put her child in danger. And her friend. She had almost lost them. What was she doing in this nightmare?

What terrible thing had Ed done, that someone wanted him dead so badly they were willing to kill children? She felt her faith beginning to waiver. Nothing was more important than Riley. The child of her body, her blood. Riley *was* her life. She was almost catatonic with shock, and Camelia was about to call the doctor when Estevez bent over her.

'Melba, you need to be with your child and your friend. You need to go now, right away. I will have the company jet ready and waiting for you at the airport. The limo will take you there. Are you ready to leave now?'

Mel's blank eyes connected with his. She came to life again. 'Yes,' she whispered.

'Good. I will arrange it immediately.' As Estevez strode off down the shiny corridor, Mel looked up at Camelia.

'Come with me,' she said.

Chapter Fifty-six

The flight to California on the Gulfstream IV passed like a bad dream. Mel might have been on the worst commuter flight for all the notice she gave her luxurious surroundings. Strapped into a gray leather seat, she barely noted the passing of time, except to complain of its length. *She needed to be there now. Five minutes ago. She should never have left.*

Guilt lurked behind her eyes, clouding her vision. It was her the hitman had wanted. If she had been there, he would have shot her, left the others alone. This was somehow all her fault. How could she ever have exposed Riley to such danger?

Camelia knew what she was thinking, but he said nothing. What could he do? Tell a mother she was wrong, that no matter what, the gunman would have come after her? And that maybe he still would?

There was no doubt George Artenski was losing his touch, though. He had turned out to be the world's most inept hitman. Camelia was still wondering why, when the phone rang, and he had his answer.

George Artenski had been traced. Aka Gus Aramanov, he lived with his wife, Lila, in San Diego. And he was the father of two young children.

So it was the child who stayed Aramanov's hand, Camelia thought. Gus had broken the unbreakable rule by which men like him plied their trade. He had allowed emotion to interfere with the job. He thanked God for the corner of mercy that had been left in Aramanov's black soul.

Camelia glanced at Mel. Her eyes were closed and she appeared to be sleeping, but he knew she was not. Her mind, like his, was churning, going over and over the same scenario, searching for answers. Or loopholes.

He grinned, remembering the story about W.C. Fields, the famous comic actor and well-known atheist. Fields had been told he was dying, and a friend came by to visit. He found him reading the Bible. 'What on earth are you doing?' the friend asked, stunned. *Looking for loopholes,* Fields replied.

The story had always struck Camelia as funny, and he wondered if that was what Artenski-Aramanov was doing now. Looking for loopholes, a way out of the mess he had created. He did not wish him luck.

A limo was waiting when they landed at the tiny Santa Monica airport, and they drove immediately to the safe house where Riley was being cared for by social workers.

She flung herself into her mother's arms, but there was no gappy smile this time. 'Oh, Mommy,' she gasped, 'he was so awful. He hit Harriet and he almost killed Lola, and he kicked me . . .'

'I know, I know, honey.' Mel stroked her daughter's curls back from her teary face. 'It's okay now, though. I'm here.'

The power of a mother's love, Camelia thought, remembering Claudia and his own brood. Of how she had cared for them, protected them, on those long days and nights when he was working twenty-four/seven on a case, leaving all the responsibility to her. What would the world be without a mother's love? he wondered. He guessed it would produce men like Gus Aramanov.

Riley went with them in the limo to the USC Medical Center. Harriet was sitting up, looking alert, though with a bandage taped to her head.

'Glamorous, huh?' she said, by way of greeting. 'I can always get a job as an extra on *ER*. The one they wheel in on the gurney on the verge of expiring. At least I look the part.'

'Oh, stop it, Harr,' Mel smiled through her tears. 'This was no joke. You were in terrible danger. And all because of me.'

'True,' Harriet agreed, equably. 'I'll probably have to call Johnny Cochran and sue you.'

They hugged each other, and Riley climbed onto the bed next to her.

'You saved our lives, kiddo,' Harriet said proudly. 'Tackled that big bag of lard like a football pro. Couldn't have done it better myself.' She saw Camelia outside the door, head down, hands behind his back, pacing, immaculate in steel gray from head to toe. His brow was furrowed, his black hair sleeked back, and he looked somehow familiar.

'You've brought the Mafia with you,' she said loudly. 'Or else he's from central casting.'

Mel's laugh rang out and Camelia glanced up. Thank God, there was laughter again.

Mel waved him into the room. 'Detective Marco Camelia, this is my friend, Harriet.'

As he shook Harriet's hand, he thought, surprised, how petite she was. Somehow, her being in a moving business, he had expected a strapping woman, capable of lifting and carrying. She didn't look as though she could lift a cup of coffee. He knew he was wrong, though, when he felt her grip, and he guessed it was a question of mind over matter.

'You look pretty good, considering,' he said, smiling.

'So do you, considering you've had to put up with Mel these last few weeks.'

Mel liked it that they grinned at each other; she could tell they were on the same wavelength. She liked her friends to like each other. Meanwhile, she wasn't about to let Harriet or Riley out of her sight.

'When are they letting you out of here?' she demanded. 'I've got a private jet waiting at Santa Monica airport to take us all to New York.'

Riley's eyes popped. 'Wow, a private jet. She had rarely traveled on a regular flight, and that only in coach. 'And *New York!* She had never been there. Suddenly the world seemed a pretty good place again.

'*A private jet?*' Harriet repeated.

Mel nodded. 'A Gulfstream IV.'

'I'm out of here,' Harriet said with a huge grin. They picked Lola up from the vet en route to the airport. Like Harriet, the dog's head was bandaged and she wore one of those big circular plastic collars that made her look like a mutt from an Elizabethan painting. They didn't even bother going back to the house, and instead, Mel promised them both a trip to Bloomingdales for new clothes. They simply piled into the Gulfstream and were off.

Safe again, Mel thought. For the moment.

Chapter Fifty-seven

Estevez was waiting for them at the airport in New York. 'Since Ed cannot do so, I must take responsibility,' he told Camelia. 'I have arranged for them all to stay at Ed's penthouse. There are two armed bodyguards, day and night. They will accompany them whenever they go out.'

But when they arrived at Vincent Towers Fifth, Estevez declined to go into Ed's home. Ed had never invited him there, and he felt it would be an intrusion on his privacy to enter now. He said goodbye, and promised to telephone and check on them later to see if they needed anything.

'All the expenses will be paid for by Vincent Properties,' he told Mel. 'Please take care of whatever they need, and see that the little girl has a good time. She has earned it.'

The two guards were waiting, tall young men in conservative dark suits and ties, with broad shoulders and alert eyes. Riley was very impressed. 'Just wait till I tell the kids at school,' she marveled. And then she almost flipped when she saw the penthouse.

Watching her running from room to room, window to window, Mel thanked the Lord her daughter was still with her. Then she sent out for pizza, arranged Harriet comfortably on the rather lumpy old sofa, planted Riley in front of the TV, and left in a hurry to check on Ed.

There and back to LA in a day, she marvelled. Oh, the power of big money. *And much good it's doing you, Ed,* she thought with that familiar pang at the heart.

She held Camelia's hand for comfort on the ride to the hospital.

Chapter Fifty-eight

Mario de Soto stood in front of the bank of TV screens in his media room. Each screen was tuned to a different channel, and Gus Aramanov's face appeared on every one. Mario's hands were clenched into fists, his back rigid with anger.

The hitman had blown it. The police had ID'd Aramanov; his picture was in every newspaper, and all over the TV. He knew it was only a matter of time until they found him, and that Gus would plea-bargain. Aramanov would tell all, in return for his life.

He left the media room and walked through the marble hall to the front door. He leaned his bulk against the pillared portico, looking around at his beautiful and hated prison. His vision of a brave new world for himself was collapsing.

When Mario had bought his big new house in Miami, he had filled it with the best the expensive decorator could buy: expensive furniture, art, silver, books. He was an avid reader, and liked to boast that he had read every book in his library, which, of course, he had not. But then, he had always been a liar.

Mario de Soto was not the name he had been born with. Or even the only name he had used. There were several others before he had fortuitously availed himself of the name Mario de Soto, when the real Mario — whom he had invited on a fishing trip in the Bahamas — 'accidentally' drowned.

It had been easy to switch identities. Nobody there knew either of them, and he had chosen the man carefully for his purpose, knowing he was a loner. A Cuban of about his own age, build and appearance, whose family was still in Havana with no chance of getting out.

He had killed Mario de Soto, taken on his identity, buried 'Mitch Rogan' in the Bahamas, and sailed home to Miami, a new man.

No one, not even the cops, had taken much notice when he took up residence in one of Miami's most exclusive areas. He was just another Cuban of suspect background, most probably a drug dealer who had struck it rich and gotten out of the business.

Then he was seen splashing his money around on flashy cars and expensive women, and the cops began to take an interest. No one knew exactly where his money came from; no one could keep track of him, or his multiple companies and business deals. Stories began to circulate, about financial maneuvers gone wrong; a real-estate deal where Mario's two partners had suddenly disappeared. He was clever, though, and there was never anything the law could pin on him. But his enemies could. There were those who wanted Mario dead, men who wanted revenge, men who wanted their money back.

It was those men Mario was afraid of. He had turned his house into a fortress, never left it without a couple of armed bodyguards. Until now, he almost never left it at all.

That was when life had lost its flavor, and when Alberto Ricci had come along with his offer. The deal had been Mario's final chance to go legit. It would put him back in the real world as a property dealer. He saw himself becoming a socialite, like Ricci, maybe even with a classy blonde wife. Plus, it gave him the opportunity to get rid of Ed Vincent. That was the greatest bonus of all time, the one that he laughed himself sick over.

But, of course, Ricci had not put his offer in writing. It had all been done on a handshake, and with the proviso that Mario take care of his part of the deal first. So now

Ricci was free and clear, and it was Mario who was in the hot seat.

Mario looked at his guards, pretending not to watch him as he stood on his palatial front portico. He wanted to kill Ricci. But he wanted Ed dead more. Only now he was forced to take care of his baby brother himself.

Lila Aramanov sat in Gus's favorite chair in front of the sixty-inch TV set, looking at her husband's mugshot on the eleven o'clock newscast. Her blonde hair was dragged hastily back from her unmadeup face, and tears trickled slowly down her pale cheeks. Lila was destroyed. Her world had fallen apart.

The media were camped outside her door. There were TV camera crews with enormous trucks, and perky female reporters in red suits and short blonde hairdos, with the ever-present microphone ready to thrust under her nose should she even stick her head out of the door. Which she did only when the pizza delivery truck arrived. The high-school kid who delivered had loved every minute of his 'fame.' He had posed for the cameras, telling them exactly what her order was, grinning like a soap star.

Gus had simply disappeared; didn't even say anything to her, just never came home. He'd left her to find out from the TV-breaking news that she was married to a hitman, the suspect in the attempted murder of Ed Vincent, and the attacker of a woman and child in Santa Monica.

At first she couldn't believe they were talking about *her* Gus. *Her teddy bear. A guy who loved his children.* But it was true, and the good life that had been hers was hers no longer. This house, the smart cars – everything would have to go.

She walked to the window, inched back the heavy silk drape. She could see a uniformed cop standing in her front yard, and knew there was another outside the front door, and yet another in back. They were staking out her home, waiting for Gus to return. But Lila knew he never would. He had left her to face the music, alone.

She would kill Gus herself, if she could only get her hands on the lying, evil bastard.

Chapter Fifty-nine

Santa Monica airport was a well-trafficked little place, accommodating everything from single-engine Cessna Skylanes, like Ed's, to Gulfstream jets carrying rock and roll stars and media executives. Plus the hundreds of small private planes whose owners flew short hops around the state, and the charter companies with their own fleets of aircraft.

Maybe it was being so near the ocean, but it had a jolly, holiday-style atmosphere about it, with people drinking Martinis on the roof terrace of the restaurant, watching the beautiful little aircraft swoop in, red and green lights twinkling in the dusk, amid the subdued roar of powerful engines.

There was still something glamorous about jet flight, Mario de Soto thought, as his pilot landed the chartered Lear and taxied to a stop. The steps unfurled, the attendant opened the door and the pilot emerged from the cockpit to bid farewell to his only passenger.

'Enjoy the golf, Mr Farrar,' he said to Mario de Soto, who had chosen his father's name as his alias.

His Vuitton case and his golf bag were already waiting, and he wheeled them himself to the rented silver Lincoln Town Car. Nothing could disguise his bulk, but he wore a silver toupee, silver-rimmed glasses and a mustache. In a golf shirt and chinos, he was a mild-mannered, bespectacled, aging golfer, lugging his bag, on his way to play a round or two with his pals.

He got in the rental Town Car and headed for San Diego. Of course, the last place Gus would be was at his home. And with half the world looking for him, he would hardly be at his office either. But the San Diego marina was a starting place in his search. He checked into the Marriott, ate grilled pompano in the coffee shop, then went to bed. Tomorrow was another day. He hoped it would be Gus Aramanov's last.

There was a cop on guard outside Gus's yacht brokerage office the next morning, plus a couple of newshounds, hoping for a break. And more cops hovered by the slip where Gus's own sleek Hatteras was moored.

Mario knew this was not going to be easy.

He spotted a Starbucks, went in, ordered an iced mocha *latte*, and sat sipping it through a straw, thinking. His criminal mind worked the way Gus's did, and he put himself in Gus's place, pondering his next move.

He finished the iced *latte*, got back in the Lincoln and headed north on the 405, back to LA. It was late afternoon by the time he checked into the Ritz Carlton at Marina del Rey.

Chapter Sixty

Mel was with Camelia in the deli around the corner from the hospital. They were regulars by now, and the waiters knew them. They always sat at the same table, the one near the window with a view of the passing traffic, and, if they were lucky, a shaft of sunlight that Mel badly missed in her long vigils in the darkened hospital room.

'*Our* table,' she said, smiling at Camelia.

'I wish it could be somewhere grander,' he said, ruefully.

'Like the restaurant in Charleston,' she remembered.

He smiled as their eyes met. 'You and I are beginning to have a history together.'

'People will talk.'

He laughed then. 'About what? How I buy you a coffee? A bagel, with cream cheese, and extra jelly if you're lucky?'

'Don't forget the bacon and egg on a Kaiser,' she reminded him, and then they were both laughing.

She was just so used to him now, Mel told herself, watching Camelia pile sugar into his mug. He had become part of her. Somehow, now, it was hard to imagine that he would not always be there for her. They were buddies, a team, united in their efforts to help Ed. But was that all there was to it? Mel stared into her coffee, wondering.

'My bet is it won't be long now.' Camelia stirred his coffee.

'When a guy is as hot as Gus Aramanov, there's no place to hide.' He was remembering the Versace murder in Miami. 'Even Cunahan finally knew there was only one way out. He took it. Shot himself on that houseboat.'

Mel shuddered. 'Are we hoping that Aramanov does the same thing?'

'Not hoping, but I'm not sure he'll see any other route.' The toasted bagels arrived and he spread hers with a thin layer of cream cheese, just the way he knew she liked it, then handed it to her. It was an intimate gesture.

'Of course, there is *one* way out,' he added. 'He could always plea-bargain. He tells us the name of the man who put out the contract, in return for his life.'

'A life spent in prison.' Mel shuddered again at the thought.

'Couldn't happen to a nicer guy.' Camelia took a bite. 'He's a paid assassin. This wasn't the first man he'd killed.' He held up his hand at her look of alarm. 'Sorry. *Attempted* to kill.'

Their cellphones rang simultaneously, and they glanced guiltily at each other, then at the other customers, but the place was so noisy, no one noticed the irritating trill of the phones.

'Hi, Riley,' Mel said softly, her lips close to the phone. 'I'm fine, honey. You're going where? Oh, the Radio City, the Rockettes ... with Hamish?' Hamish had become Riley's own personal bodyguard, and after a couple of days together, they were firm friends. Hamish put himself out to entertain her, but his job always came first, and that meant Riley's safety. Mel was comfortable with the situation, and she said have fun and see you later.

Even with the rowdy crowd and the rattling of dishes and calling out of orders, the hiss of steam and the sizzle of the grill, it was impossible for Mel not to overhear Camelia's conversation.

He was talking to Claudia. 'Forgotten?' he said. 'How could I? Yeah, *tesoro*, a lot of years together. But you can cut that in half if you remember all the weeks I was working and was never around. Okay, then, so okay . . . Yeah. Dinner Friday night. At Nino's. And when did I not get you an anniversary gift?' He was smiling as he said goodbye.

'How many years it is?' Mel asked.

'Twenty-six. Nope. I tell a lie. Twenty-seven on Friday.'

She nodded, wondering what it felt like to be with the man you loved for that long.

'Tell me about your wedding,' she said.

'Weddings are a woman thing. Y'know, it was all flower girls and maids of honor and Claudia looking . . . beautiful.'

He suddenly remembered quite clearly the way she had looked, her cloud of dark hair pinned up with a circlet of flowers, and the long, spreading veil that had half hidden her from him as they faced each other at the altar and made their vows.

'The party was good,' he changed the subject. 'The uncles and aunts flew in from Italy and Sicily. They arrived in a big bus looking like a movie Italian family. Roberto Benigni should have filmed it. The wine flowed and the women had baked Italian cookies and the little kids ran around and got under everybody's feet. Aunt Sophia slipped on the dancefloor and waved her legs in the air, showing more than she should, and everybody laughed.'

He grinned at her. 'We had a great time. Family, y'know.'

Mel laughed, but she didn't know. She had never had a family like that. She had hoped to create one of her own, be the founding member, so to speak. But now she wasn't sure it was going to happen.

She frowned as she thought of Ed. He was not responding. He was still fed through a tube and had lost so much weight, she hardly recognized him as the big, burly man she had fallen for. This morning his hand had remained perfectly still under hers. There was no movement, no flicker of response, just the endless whirr of life-support machines and monitors, as his life ticked slowly on.

She pushed the chair back, abruptly. 'I have to get back.'

Camelia looked up at her, surprised. She had that urgent if-I'm-not-there-he-may-go-and-die look that he knew too well by now.

Mel paid the check this time, in line with their unspoken agreement that they would take turns, and Camelia walked her back to the hospital and said goodbye at the door. He had to get back, see what was doing, if anything, on the Aramanov situation.

Brotski was on duty again. Mel shook her head in disbelief as she walked toward him down that long corridor. 'Don't they even allow you to read a book?' she asked.

'I'm keeping guard, ma'am. Got to be alert at all times.'

'You're a good cop, Brotski,' she told him, and saw the color rise in his fair-skinned babyface.

'Thank you, ma'am,' he replied, with a pleased grin.

Mel took her usual seat at Ed's bedside. She lifted Ed's hand to her lips, waited for a response, an undercurrent that told her he was there. Nothing. She had lost him to the blackness. Yet the monitors bleeped on, telling her he was technically still in the land of the living.

Oh, Ed, she thought, when will this nightmare end? *How* will it end?

Chapter Sixty-one

Marina del Rey was a huge yacht basin with thousands of boats. Mario had never been much of a sailor, though he had done his share of sportfishing and could manage a boat when he needed to. Like he had with the man whose identity he had stolen after he had shoved him over the stern.

There were boats up on slips, and monster seagoing yachts in deep moorings with Panamanian and Bahamian registry; old boats and new boats; sailboats and power boats and fishing boats. You name it, you could find it at Marina del Rey. Mario guessed Californians were like Floridians – they lived on the ocean, therefore they felt they needed a boat.

He wandered the slipways, contemplating the wealth sitting out there on the murky water doing nothing, and thought how infrequently each boat was probably used. He mentally amortized the cost for each outing. It added up to a tidy sum. He figured a good-looking woman worked out cheaper than a boat: dinner, dresses, a little jewelry. A woman was a better investment, plus with some expected return for your money. In his view, a man was better off renting a boat when he needed it. Owning one was a mug's game.

He strolled into the office of a yacht broker, where he expressed interest in a power vessel, and found out that quite a few guys lived on their boats. Mario thought a man could easily hide out here. But even a killer had to eat. And, knowing Gus, he also had to drink.

He drove around the immediate neighborhood in search of the nearest food and liquor stores. Within walking distance was a mini-mall with a 7-Eleven, and next to it, a small, nondescript liquor store with iron bars on the windows. There were other stores nearby, bigger, brighter, more open. He knew Gus would avoid those.

Mario was not a patient man, but he parked his car in that mini-mall, and settled down to wait. He was in this for the long haul.

It was dark when Gus walked out of the marina and crossed the road to the liquor store to buy vodka. He had no appetite, but he needed liquor to numb his befuddled brain. He picked up four bottles of Smirnoff and half a dozen candy bars, and walked back out again. He hesitated outside the 7-Eleven, then he went in, chose a couple of chicken tacos, waited uneasily in line to pay, then hurried back.

It was ironic, Mario thought, that Aramanov's disguise was pretty much like his own: the mustache, the glasses, only instead of the silver toupee, Gus had shaved his head and was now completely bald. Somehow, it only served to emphasize his pit-bull appearance.

The Town Car slipped out of the lot, idling, just keeping Gus in sight, but staying far enough back so he didn't notice. Mario had had a lot of experience at this game; he was an expert. At the marina, he parked and followed Aramanov on foot.

Gus let himself into the slip and climbed aboard an old, rust-stained, twenty-eight-foot Bayliner, in bad need of a paint job. It was owned by a man who no longer existed, having been carefully eliminated by Gus due to the fact that he owed money to the wrong people. Gus had kept the boat for himself, using it as a kind of floating bachelor pad when he was in LA on business. There were plenty of singles apartments at the marina, and a lively bar scene. It wasn't difficult to pick up a woman, especially when you had a Mercedes and a boat, and at night, in the dim light, the old Bayliner didn't look half as bad as it really was.

He stumbled down the few stairs into the cabin, slumped onto the stained blue canvas banquette and placed his Smirnoffs on the table in front of him. He opened the first one and took a long drink.

The vodka didn't make him feel better, only slowed his brain down a bit. He was screwed and he knew it. He had been going over the scenario and there was only one chance. Even that was risky, and meant a life in prison. The choice was not a happy one.

He pulled the wrapper off a Snickers bar and devoured it in a couple of quick bites, washing it down with more vodka. He wondered what Lila was doing, but he couldn't even bring himself to think about his children. They were no longer his. He had forfeited any right to them, he understood that. He wouldn't have felt half so bad about it, though, if he had come out of it with a stash of money and a new passport, plus a one-way ticket to Europe, or South America. But it was too late for that.

He was sitting there, contemplating his mistakes, when he heard a noise. He lifted his head, sniffing the air like the dog he so resembled, testing the wind for the presence of a stranger. The wind had gotten up, and he felt a movement under the boat. There it was again. It must be the rigging tapping against the masts outside.

He was thinking that if at least he had to kill a guy and inherit a boat, it should have been a worthy seagoing monster that could have had him out of here and en route to Fiji before the news had broken, when he heard the noise again. His eyes swiveled and he saw feet descending the four steps. There was no time to reach into the bellyband. Mario de Soto was already pointing the Kahr K9 at him.

For a moment, they stared at each other, acknowledging that they knew one another.

Then, 'Have another drink, Gus, why don't ya?' Mario said.

Gus just kept on staring at him. He knew this was the end, and that he was powerless to do anything about it. He thought of how many men he had faced, exactly like this, only then he had been the one in the power position. Now he knew how it felt when you were looking down the barrel of a gun, at the end of the world.

The Kahr followed Gus's movements as he picked up the vodka bottle, took another long swig. He offered it to Mario. 'Care to try some? It's the best.'

Mario shook his head. 'I'm an Absolut man, myself.'

Gus nodded. He took another slug.

'Might as well die happy,' Mario said, with a tight smile.

Gus felt the heft of the half-empty bottle in his hand. There was just once chance . . . once last chance.

Mario saw it coming. As the bottle arced through the air, he stepped nimbly out of the way, or as nimbly as a man of his bulk could. The vodka splashed on his pants and his narrow eyes tightened into angry slits.

'It's always been my theory that hitmen were stupid,' he said. 'Why else would they risk their lives doing other people's dirty work? Surely the rewards were not enough to compensate for the risk.'

Gus felt the comforting bulk of the Sigma in the belly-band under his shirt. It was an Hawaiian shirt, bought on some carefree island vacation with Lila, and was of the style you wore outside your pants, and therefore gave him quick access. Mario was the stupid one, getting his jollies by talking to him, making him squirm before he killed him. It was giving him time to think, to regroup. He could still win.

Mario had his own schedule, though. 'Get up.' He indicated

with the gun where Gus should stand. 'Hands over your head,' he commanded.

Gus obeyed. A cheap metal chair stood between them. They were of equal height, and he was fitter than Mario. With a sudden movement, he thrust the chair at Mario and reached for the Sigma.

But Mario was quicker. He pressed the Kahr to Gus's head, forced him to the ground. He had him where he wanted him now.

Gus was on the floor, staring up at him. Mario wasted no more time. He slammed the gun down and Gus's head snapped back.

Mario knelt beside the unconscious hitman. He hated getting his pants dirty on this filthy boat, but he had no choice. He was wearing plastic surgical gloves, and now he took Gus's Sigma out of the bellyband and placed it in the unconscious man's hand. He held that hand up to the temple and pressed Gus's finger on the trigger.

The bullet left a ragged hole in Gus's head and powder burns on Gus's hand. This time it was Gus's glazed eyes staring into nothingness, and Gus's brains leaking messily onto the floor.

Mario waited a moment, listening. Of course, the Sigma was fitted with a silencer; there had been only the merest pop, a sound too muffled to travel, even across water. Outside, the wind rattled the rigging against the masts again, shifting the boat slightly.

He got to his feet and walked back to the steps. He turned and took one last look at the man who had fucked up his life. Then he was out of there.

The rain was just starting, that strange LA rain that showed up suddenly and came down in solid sheets that sent you running to find the Ark and Noah. He remembered this was Hollywood: it was possible you might find Noah, or some other nut, ready to save you from the end of the world. But not Gus Aramanov. He was a goner.

There was no one to see Mario slipping through the shadows and the rain. No one to notice, in the torrential downpour, as he ran to the parking lot, and drove back to the hotel.

A short while later, he was standing under a hot shower, soaping away the grime of Gus Aramanov's boat. He stayed in there a long time, then he got out, wrapped a towel around himself, and called room service.

'A vodka Martini, straight up,' he said. 'And make that Absolut. Yup, with an olive. Ahh, what the hell, make it a double. And send up some fried chicken while you're at it. Yeah, with french fries.'

He was grinning as he slammed down the phone. He hadn't felt this good in years.

One down, and one to go.

Chapter Sixty-two

It was eight-thirty on Friday night. Camelia was having his anniversary dinner with Claudia at Nino's. He had brought her flowers, bold, scarlet-tipped pink roses; he had ordered the Antinori Chianti Riserva; and he had a gift for her, a diamond heart necklet. He knew that she thought all he had gotten her were the flowers, and he had the box in his pocket, ready to surprise her, later. The evening was going well.

Mel had spent a long day at the hospital, by Ed's bedside. Now, she needed to take time out with Riley. She kissed him tenderly, told him she would be back in a couple of hours, said, 'Wait for me, honey. Just don't go anywhere okay?' She kissed him again, squeezed his hand, stroked his hair.

Ed heard her leave, though somehow, now, the sound seemed more distant ... No matter how he fought against it, the blackness was claiming him more and more often ... An endless gloom where there were no dreams to sustain him ... no love to be felt ... no words of comfort ... He was alone on a sea of endless night ...

Come back, my love ... he wanted to yell after her ... I know Riley needs you, and I'm being selfish ... but I need you, Mel ... I want you ...

my body wants you, my head wants you, my heart wants you … What's that old song, 'All Of Me'? That's about where it's at between us, my love … Only now I'm so tired … its getting harder and harder to fight it … I'm losing this battle, and don't want to leave you … Only you are keeping me here, Mel … my honey …

Mario was being careful to cover his tracks, and the jet he chartered from LA was from a different company. It landed at La Guardia, the same location where Aramanov had bungled the hit on Ed.

This time Mario was traveling under the name of Michael Miller. Miller was his mother's family name – Ellin Miller Rogan, having used his father, Farrar's name on the trip to LA. He didn't know why he was drawn to using their names at this point in time, except somehow, with Ed finally about to join the rest of his murdered family, it seemed appropriate.

Mario had his foolproof alibi all set. He had already called a doctor from LA, complaining of cardiac problems. He had arranged to check in at the Manhattan hospital late that evening, ready for a complete physical the next morning, with a preliminary angiogram to check for arterial blockages, and the possibility of an angioplasty to destroy any clots they might find.

Mario knew the ropes: he had undergone both these procedures recently, and understood what to tell the cardiologist to get immediate attention.

He checked into the private room, was asked to remove his clothing and put on a hospital gown. He did as he was asked, climbed into the narrow hospital bed, submitted to his temperature being taken, as well as samples of blood. Then he told the nurse he was going to sleep and asked her not to disturb him.

'Sure,' she agreed, 'you have an early morning ahead of you, Mr Miller. Best to get some sleep while you can.'

He watched her walk out of the room, waited ten minutes, then he got up, put his clothes back on: a black shirt, black sweatpants, and a thin lightweight Adidas jacket, purchased in LA. He laced up his sneakers, adjusted his clothing, combed his hair. He opened the small bag he carried. It contained only a neatly folded white coat, the kind that doctors wore; a couple of ballpoint pens, and a clipboard holding some official-looking notes.

Zipping these items securely under his jacket, he opened the door and peered out. In the hospital, things had eased down into the night routine and the corridor was in semidarkness. At the end he could see the brighter glow of the nurses' station, and hear the murmur of voices.

The Emergency Exit sign glowed green over a door to a stairwell at the opposite end of the corridor from the nurses' station. Keeping close to the wall, he hurried toward it.

The fire-door was heavy and he had to be careful not to let it clang shut behind him. He eased it back into place, then took stock of his surroundings.

He was in a concrete stairwell lit by harsh overhead lights. A red-painted number indicated he was on level four. He knew Intensive Care was on level ten.

He put on the doctor's coat and stuck the ballpoints into the pocket. It made him look more official, as did the small clipboard with the sheaf of 'notes.'

His sneakers squeaked on the metal treads at the edges of the steps and the stairwell smelled strongly of disinfectant. He pulled a face – he hated that smell. And it was a long way up to level ten. He was out of breath, and the muscles in his thighs were burning by the time he pushed open the tenth-floor fire-door, just a crack.

He could see that the layout was the same as on the lower floor, with the nurses' station in the middle. And that there was no cop on guard. He guessed maybe by now they had given up on Ed. He smiled. Finally, he was in the right place, and at the right time.

He slid the Kahr K9 from the Alessi ankle holster. He loved that small gun, it fit into his hand like it was tailor-made, and because of its slim shape it was easy to conceal. A full eight-shot 9mm Parabellum, it used +P+ ammunition, and had a low recoil. It remined Mario of his first gun, an old Browning, with which he had killed his first man, a business competitor. Things didn't change much.

Sweating heavily, he stepped out into the long, shiny antiseptic corridor.

Chapter Sixty-three

Camelia was in the middle of his main course, osso bucco, a favorite, when his pager beeped. Heads turned, there were glares of annoyance and he coughed to cover his embarrassment. He had deliberately left the cellphone in the car so they wouldn't be disturbed, but the pager was his umbilical cord to the department. He couldn't live without it.

He apologized to his wife, got up and walked into the foyer to answer it. He was discreet and noncommittal in his replies, and when he had done, he walked back to their table and sat down again. Claudia knew what was coming: it was the story of her life.

Camelia told her that there was a break in the Ed Vincent case. He had to get back, things were happening fast. She understood, but it hurt.

'I promise you we'll celebrate all over again,' Camelia said as he paid the check. 'Next week, *tesoro.*' He had just put Claudia into a cab and watched it drive away, when he realized she had forgotten the roses.

Camelia called Mel at the hospital. She wasn't there, so he called her at the penthouse.

'What's wrong?' She got the sudden feeling he was the voice of doom, come to impart some terrible news.

'Nothing's wrong. Can you meet me at the deli, in about fifteen minutes?'

She didn't even hesitate. 'I'll be there,' she said.

They ordered coffee and a Danish. Mel was looking at him, big-eyed, waiting for him to tell her what was going on that was so urgent. She was wearing jeans and sneakers and a baggy white sweatshirt that said Lakers on it, and her short hair was shoved under a baseball cap.

She was, Camelia thought, a ray of California sunshine on a dark Manhattan night.

'Sorry to drag you out so abruptly.' He took a bite of the cheese Danish. It was soggy, obviously this morning's batch, and he put it back on the plate, disgusted. He wasn't even hungry, anyway. Just stressed.

Mel ignored the coffee. 'So, what's doing?' she asked.

'We got our hitman.'

She lifted her head, their eyes locked. She said, *'Oh-my-God. I don't believe it.'*

'You can believe it. LAPD found him, out at the marina, on his boat. Dead.'

She drew in her breath. 'Dead?'

'A single shot to the temple. Looks like suicide, but they're not sure. They're checking it out.'

'Oohhhh . . .'

It was the first time he had ever seen her speechless.

'The final irony, huh?' he said. 'The hitman blows his own brains out.'

She shuddered and covered her eyes with her hands. He suspected she might be crying and waited awkwardly, not knowing what to say.

Mel took a deep, shaky breath. 'Okay. I'm okay now. It was just a shock, y'know. The relief of knowing it's all over. Finally.'

He hated to be the one to disillusion her, but he had to say it. 'It's not all over yet, Mel. We have our hitman. But we still didn't have the guy who hired him.' He leaned his elbows on the small table, leaned close. 'He's our true killer.'

Her malt-whisky eyes widened as they stared into his. He saw the pupils expand and knew he had shocked her. Her face was so close he could have kissed her.

'Oh, *Marco,*' she said in a trembly voice. 'Ed is still in danger. I have to go to him.' And she was on her feet, grabbing her purse from the chair where she had slung it, spilling its contents.

He wasn't the first guy to get on his knees and help her pick up her stuff: the sunglasses; the spiral-pads; the pens; lipsticks; keys; old store receipts; old unpaid bills; a couple of McDonald's little giveaway toys that belonged to Riley; stray coins; an ancient wallet; and a small leather photoframe with a picture of Ed.

She clung to his arm as he walked her back to the hospital. 'I'd better get back to the department,' Camelia said, as they strode up the steps into the lobby. 'Will you be okay now? On your own?'

She nodded, but he could tell from her face she was nervous. It was as though, with the death of the hitman, she now thought Ed might be dead too.

He watched her walk to the bank of elevators, then stood on the steps, contemplating the night. Cool, misty, unseasonal. He felt in his pocket for the Winstons and his fingers touched the little velvet box. He groaned. Claudia's anniversary gift. Would she ever forgive him? He guessed so. Didn't she always?

Not that that's any excuse, he told himself, lighting up the forbidden cigarette. He glanced back through the glass doors, saw Mel, still waiting for the elevator. Her head was down, and she was staring at the floor, lost, he knew, in her own sad world.

She lifted her head as the elevator came, then stepped into it. There was something about her tonight that made him uneasy, an overwhelming sadness. He had never seen her like this; she was always so cheery, so brave about everything, but tonight, even though Gus Aramanov was dead, she seemed destroyed.

He wondered whether he was right to have reminded her that the real killer wasn't dead yet.

He paced the front steps, puffing on the Winston. Something about the whole scenario was troubling him.

Chapter Sixty-four

Ed heard the door close. He hoped it was Zelda, he missed her so. He listened for her familiar footstep, but there was only silence. Then he heard the squeak of rubber-soled shoes. A man, he thought. Probably a doctor. He could hear him breathing now. Hard, as though he had been running . . . He wanted to shout hello, who's there, but he could not . . .

He was so close. Ed could smell him . . . a musky, sandalwood odor . . . But there was something else, something puzzling. An alien scent. The smell of danger. The archetypal reaction of fight or flee sent adrenaline surging through his veins, jolting his heart to new peaks on the monitor. Dear God, they were going to get him after all . . . He felt a final thrust of energy . . . Life — like he hadn't felt it in weeks.

His eyes flew open. And he was looking at his brother . . .

Mitch did not speak. He did not smile. He simply stared back at him. Then he yanked the ventilator viciously from Ed's throat; and the drips and the catheters.

He was smiling as he did so, but now the monitor was going crazy, alarms were sounding . . . he had to get out of there.

Mel didn't know why she was so nervous. After what Camelia had just told her, she should be feeling more secure. But someone out there still wanted Ed dead. Instinct told her she had been away from him too long. Her long legs covered that shiny corridor like a star quarterback with a winning touchdown.

She stopped, puzzled. There was no uniform on guard outside Ed's room. She was still wondering where Brotski was as she flung open the door.

The first thing she noticed was the silence. There was no hum of machinery. *The machines that kept Ed alive.* She saw the unfamiliar doctor and the tubes and catheters spilling their vital liquids onto the white sheets. And the monitor, with an ominous flat green line.

'Oh, my God, no, nooo,' she screamed.

The doctor swung round, looked at her.

She saw the gun in his hand, felt her own heart tremble. A giant shudder rippled through her. *Ed was dead. This man had killed him.* Howling with rage, she launched herself at him. All six feet of her.

Mitch hadn't expected it. He sank to his knees, then staggered to his feet again, made for the door . . .

Ed's eyes were wide open. Mel scrambled up, bent over him, desperately trying to insert the ventilator into the tracheotomy opening.

'Ed, oh, Ed, honey, hold on,' she sobbed, 'it'll be alright, I promise . . .'

His eyes flicked beyond her, over her shoulder. She caught the warning in them, swung round. The killer was back.

Instinctively, Mel flung herself on top of Ed to protect him. And felt the stinging heat as the bullets entered her.

Returning from his coffee break, Brotski saw the man come running out of Ed's room. He sprinted after him, excited as a warhorse at the scene of battle. This was what police work was about. The guy was overweight, he couldn't run so good, and Brotski had his own gun drawn now.

'Stop,' he yelled again. 'Stop or I'll shoot.'

It was a mistake to give a killer like Mitch Rogan, aka Mario de Soto, fair warning. He turned and fired. In the fraction of a second it took Brotski to know he had been hit and to fade into unconsciousness, Mario was gone.

Simultaneously, Camelia stepped out of the elevator, saw Brotski and ran to him, bypassing the screaming nurse. Through Ed's open door he saw Mel, lying on the floor. Now other people, doctors, nurses, were coming running. He was thrust out of the way as the doctors placed Mel, bleeding badly, onto a gurney. He knelt by Brotski, who looked like a dead man. Camelia felt the weight of responsibility on his shoulders. *Poor young kid, poor little bastard.*

He watched for a second as they rushed them both to the elevator en route to the OR. And that part of him that belonged to Mel went with her.

Chapter Sixty-five

Sheer terror sent Mario de Soto stumbling back down those concrete emergency stairs, faster than he had ever moved. He paused for breath on the fourth floor. He had intended to return to his room, go back to bed, tell the doctor in the morning he had changed his mind, didn't want to go through with the tests, and leave. No one would have suspected him. There would have been no need; he would have been just another difficult patient, one among hundreds in that hospital. But he knew there was no chance of using that alibi now.

He continued on down to the third floor; then the second; the first. He got out at the underground parking lot, dodged through the ranks of cars toward the exit. He tucked the Kahr back into the ankle holster and straightened his clothing. He was still breathing hard as he walked out onto the street, ducking into the shadows as he heard the scream of police sirens. He could see blue lights flashing, saw officers running into the hospital, guns drawn.

Anger burned in him, volatile as jet fuel. He was exploding with rage at Gus Aramanov for bringing him down to this. A cheap killer, hunted on the streets of Manhattan. And anger at Alberto Ricci, who had offered him the promised land, and who he knew would now deny that he ever knew him. Ricci always came out the winner. But not this time.

He stepped out of the shadows and flagged down a passing cab. 'East 64th Street,' he said.

Camelia was already running down the emergency stairs, the killer's only escape route. In the parking lot, he saw the discarded white coat, heard the scream of sirens as help arrived. He crouched, gun in hand, scanning the dimly lit lot.

He had never felt like this about a case before. The need to kill this man devoured him. If Mel were dead, he didn't know how he would be able to handle it. He had death in his own heart as he summoned extra officers to the parking lot.

Chapter Sixty-six

Julianna Ricci was giving a dinner party. It was an important occasion for her, because she wanted desperately to become co-chairman of the grandest charity event of the year, in aid of developmentally challenged children. An event that would put her right up there alongside Manhattan's biggest socialites.

Julianna was tall and blonde and elegant in a long, silk-chiffon Valentino in a muted shade of celadon. With it she wore Alberto's latest gift; a necklace of emeralds and diamonds, with matching earrings.

She had just had the house redone by the latest decorator, and it looked a dream with enormous flowers displays wherever there was space for them. Her table was set with the finest Cristofle and Baccarat and Bernadaud; a butler and a houseman waited on them, and the chef had cooked for royalty.

There were twenty at the long table, with Alberto looking handsome and distinguished at the head, and Julianna at the foot. They were just eating dessert – wild strawberries flown in from the South of France over a soufflé with strawberry eau-de-vie, served with flutes of delicate pink Roederer champagne, the favorite, she knew, of her most important guest – when the butler came in and whispered something, discreetly, in her husband's ear.

* * *

Mario was waiting in Alberto Ricci's hall. He looked around at the elegant surroundings. He had thought his own Miami mansion was the ultimate in luxury and class, but this was something else. The works of art on these walls looked like museum pieces, and this furniture had the exquisite patina of expensive antiques. Even the rug was magnificent, forty feet long and of faded silk that must have come from the Ottoman Empire. He felt sick to his stomach. He'd thought he had it all. Now he knew he had nothing.

He peered through the massive bouquet of flowers on the gilded console, into the tall Venetian mirror, at his own face. He hardly recognized himself. Was this shrunken, white-faced man really Mitch Rogan?

He turned as Ricci strode angrily into the hall.

Ricci dismissed the butler with a wave of his manicured hand. 'What are you doing here?' he hissed. 'I told you never to contact me, never to come to my house.' He already had Mario by the arm, pulling him toward the front door. 'Get out, and don't come back, you stupid bastard.'

Mario turned to look at him. He jammed the sleek little Kahr into Ricci's gut. And he smiled as he squeezed the trigger.

Chapter Sixty-seven

They had found no one in the parking lot; the suspect had gotten away and an all-points was out on him. Camelia was outside the OR when his phone rang. There had been a shooting at Alberto Ricci's home.

Camelia had always known, in his gut, that Ricci was at the bottom of this property deal. No matter who he had used as hitmen, Ricci was the true killer.

Sirens screaming, he was at East 64th in minutes.

Mitch Rogan, aka Mario de Soto, straddled Ricci's body, where it lay oozing blood onto the priceless Ottoman rug. His gun was aimed at Julianna Ricci, standing on the stairs where she had attempted to flee, screaming her stupid head off.

'You're not gonna have a head in a minute if y'don't shut up,' he told her stonily. She clamped her mouth shut, but he could still hear her whimpering. Light from the immense crystal chandelier glinted off the diamonds and emeralds at her throat, and reflected in his envious eyes.

He had been a fool, a great stupid fuckin' fool. It was men like Ricci, this *dead* man, who won all the big prizes. While men like him scrambled for the smaller pickings, thinking they were such big shots. His whole fuckin' life had been a sham.

He heard the police sirens and the cries of the terrified guests, still huddled together in the dining room. He almost laughed. They surely hadn't expected this when they had donned their fancy designer outfits and pricey jewels for Ricci's dinner party.

The door burst open. That goddamn woman was screaming again. He turned to look ... saw them coming. He knew this was the end.

He put the Kahr into his mouth and pulled the trigger.

Chapter Sixty-eight

Camelia was watching the coroner do his stuff, while police officers attended to Julianna Ricci and the dinner guests in the elegant sitting room. The sound of their hysterical sobbing faded into a background buzz of noise as he stared down at the two bodies.

Both had been evil men. Greedy men, who would let nothing stop them in their race for more. More money; more possessions; more power. Now they were powerless. And more than likely facing their Maker, who, he sincerely hoped, would send them straight down the chute to hell.

Activity swarmed all around him: prints men, forensics, police photographers, detectives, uniforms. Ricci would certainly never have expected to see this in his fancy home.

Camelia wondered about his wife, how much Julianna had known about her husband's activities. She would soon find out, he was sure of that. And there went Julianna's future on the charity circuit. She'd likely be trading in the pale green Valentino and the emeralds for orange prison garb and an ID tag.

He took one last look at the bodies, and lit up a cigarette. To hell with the smoking rules, he thought wearily. Too much had gone down tonight.

*   *   *

It was several hours later. The twilit silence of the recovery room was soothing. They had removed the bullets from Mel's left arm and leg, and she was still in that hazy fog of post-operative sedation. A great lethargy consumed her, and she wondered lazily if this were how Ed felt, hovering peacefully somewhere in limbo. *Ed!* She sat bolt upright. *She had to get out of there . . .*

She was at the door, wobbling rockily, hospital gown flapping, when Camelia came in and caught her. He felt the pounding of her heart, the softness of her.

'Where d'ya think you're goin', honey,' he said, with a catch in his voice.

She giggled then. 'I told you that honey thing was contagious,' she said, sliding back into oblivion, through his arms, to the floor.

Camelia picked her up and carried her back to the bed, calling for the nurses. He waited while they checked her, grumbling that she was crazy to even get out of bed, and anyhow they didn't know how she had done it, and her only half an hour out of OR.

Camelia stood by Mel's bed, watching her pale, sleeping face. He blamed himself for what had happened. He should have been on top of things, should have come down harder on the young officers when they goofed off. Security was like an accident. All it took was one slip, one tiny mistake, and it was all over.

Brotski was still in the OR. He had taken a bullet to the chest. His career as a member of the NYPD might be over almost before it had begun.

Camelia always reverted to his Catholic roots at moments like this. He was praying for him. And for himself. The would-be sinner.

Chapter Sixty-nine

It was several hours before Mel was properly awake. She grabbed Camelia's hand, wincing as the pain shot through her. 'Tell me what happened.'

'No sudden moves,' he said as calmly as he could with his heart racing like a thoroughbred at the winning post. 'You've just had bullets removed from your left arm and thigh. I guess you were thrashing around so much, Mitch couldn't get a fix on you. Or on Ed. Anyhow, you're darn lucky to be alive.'

The question she couldn't speak was in her eyes.

'And so is Ed,' he said.

She sank back, relieved. 'Ohh, thank you God,' she murmured. 'Thank you, thank you so much.'

She sat up again, suddenly. 'How ... *alive* is he?'

'He's gonna be as good as the old Ed.' Camelia grinned. 'I was gonna say *good as new*, but I thought you'd prefer him just the way he was.'

She gave him that ear-to-ear. 'When can I see him?'

He shrugged. 'Better ask the doc. And you might want to look in on Brotski, while you're doing the rounds.'

'Brotski?'

Of course, she didn't know. He told her about Brotski, that he was doing well, and like her, would suffer no permanent damage.

'Not such a good shot, our Mitch,' Mel said with a relieved smile.

'Good enough to kill Alberto Ricci. And then himself.' Her eyes bugged with astonishment as he told her the outcome. 'So there's no need to worry anymore,' he said finally. 'You and Ed are both home free.'

Mel thought it was as though a great cloud had lifted. The worry; the stress; the fear for Ed; for Riley; for the lives of those she loved. She held onto Camelia's hand and squeezed it. 'Whatever would I have done without you?'

Camelia shrugged uncomfortably. 'Some other member of the NYPD would have taken care of you, ma'am. We are only here to serve.'

'Oh, sure. Over and above the call of duty.' She squeezed his hand again. 'Riley said to say thank you. She's going to write you a letter.'

'I'll have it framed. We don't get many letters of thanks.'

A doctor appeared in the doorway. 'You're looking better,' he said to Mel. 'We have a demand for your presence upstairs in Mr Vincent's room. Feel up to the trip?'

'Up to it?' She flung back the sheets, swung her legs over the side of the bed, grimacing with pain and laughing at the same time. 'I can't wait,' she said as they helped her into a wheelchair and wrapped her in a blanket.

Camelia watched them go. 'Oh, by the way,' he called. Mel turned. 'Tell Ed there'll be a couple of good Bonnards on the auction block before too long.'

Her laughter floated back to him.

Chapter Seventy

Ed was propped up in bed with a small mountain of pillows. There were no more tubes, no ventilator, no catheters. Just the ever-present monitor, marking his steady, even heartbeat.

It was ironic, he thought, that in trying to kill him, Mitch had succeeded in bringing him back from the dead. His brother almost qualified as Dr Frankenstein, except now Mitch was the dead one. He sighed. It had been a long, hard haul. He wasn't sure he could even remember those endless twilit dreams of the here, and the hereafter. It didn't matter anymore. Zelda was with him.

The nurse wheeled her to the side of his bed, and for a long moment they looked at each other.

She was pale under that peachy golden tan, big-eyed with emotion, unable to speak. He shook his head, marveling at her. She had jump-started his heart, blown away the cobwebs of the past weeks. And she wasn't just take-your-breath-away gorgeous. She was knock-your-socks-off beautiful, in an oddly innocent, yet sexy kind of way. He smiled as he reached for her hand.

Mel was lost in his gaze. She was so grateful to him for just living, she could have wept. Instead she dropped a kiss on his hand.

Light as gossamer, he thought, remembering their nights of love together.

'You don't look bad, for a guy who almost didn't make it,' she said tremulously.

'I made it because I needed to get back to you.' His hand gripped hers tightly and she flashed him that familiar smile.

'Flatterer.'

'You bet,' he said. 'Just prepare to hear that kind of stuff for the rest of your days.'

'I was here for you, Ed.' She was wondering if he recalled anything, or whether it was all lost in the blackness of the coma.

'I know. And thank you.'

'You're welcome.' Suddenly shy, she didn't know what to say to this newly alive person, and yet she had spilled her guts to him when he was unconscious. 'I might have to get to know you all over again.'

He laughed. 'Just think of what fun that will be.'

Their eyes locked again. Then Mel levered herself from the wheelchair and onto the edge of the bed. She swung her damaged leg up first, and the rest of her followed. She rolled over until she was lying next to him.

His arm was around her, his mouth on hers. They clung together, never wanting to let go.

When they finally came up for air, she laughed. 'Whatever will the nurses say when they find me here?' she said with that contagious giggle.

He looked at her and grinned. 'Frankly, my dear,' he said in his best Rhett voice, 'I don't give a damn.'

Chapter Seventy-one

'The truth will out,' Detective Camelia said to them, much later.

'It sure will,' Mel replied, thankfully.

'Mom always said Mitch was a changeling.' Ed's voice was still only a rough whisper. 'She knew he was no good.'

'And she was right.' Camelia stood looking down at the man in the hospital bed. He had lost a lot of weight, but he was looking better. And at least he was in the land of the living. Thanks to that plucky Georgia peach.

He glanced at Mel, who was looking at Ed. She never took her eyes off him, as though she couldn't believe he was sitting up and holding her hand and talking to her. And Ed was looking at her as though no one else existed. They were in their own magic place, a world only lovers knew.

Camelia sighed. It was as it should be. As for him, he would carry his own private torch for Melba Eloise Merrydew to the grave. No one would ever know how close he had come to telling her he loved her. Especially Claudia. He could never expect her to understand that what he felt for Mel was a one-off, a once-in-a-lifetime thing. An insurmountable emotion that had taken him by surprise — and taken him over.

It didn't affect his love for Claudia. He would die for her, just the way Mel would have for Ed. He would go home, hold her in his arms as she slept, and she would smell sweetly of Arpège as she always did. He was a lucky man.

He crossed himself hastily. *This* time, thank heaven, he was.

He bent and dropped a quick kiss on Mel's soft cheek. She smelled good. It wasn't Arpège, but it was good.

Mel stood up to her full height. She looked into his eyes and he saw that she knew. She wrapped her arms round him, crushing him to her bosom. Tears streaked down her face.

Camelia was red with embarrassment, his face pressed against her breasts. Which, come to think of it, was exactly where he wanted to be.

Mel walked out into the hallway with him to say goodbye. 'Where are you going now?' she asked, still holding his hand.

'Home, I guess.'

She gave him a sideways look. 'To Claudia,' she said. 'Your one and only.'

'My one and only,' he agreed.

She nodded. 'Thank you, Marco.'

'Thanks for what?'

'For loving me,' she said simply.

He drew a deep breath. His heart was thudding like a teenager's. He smoothed back his thick, dark hair in the gesture that made her smile. 'Ah, it's nuthin',' he said.

'Oh, yes it is.'

He waved his hand and walked away from her, down that long, shiny hospital corridor.

'Hey,' she called.

Camelia turned to look at her, one last time.

'Did anyone tell you, you look exactly like Al Pacino?' she said.

He was laughing as he left.

The elevator door slid closed behind him. He had done his

job. It was over. For a split second, Camelia wondered what might have happened if Ed Vincent had died. He shook his head. Nothing. That's what would have happened.

There's no fool like an old fool, he reminded himself with a sigh. Mel would have gone back to California, to her daughter, to her friends, to her business. Eventually, she would have found someone else, though he knew from what she had told him that it would never be the same as with Ed. And he would have gone home to Claudia and his kids, just the way he was doing now. He shrugged. Nobody knew. Nobody had been hurt. Except himself. And maybe he could even learn something from it.

Remembering Mel's story about Ed and the roses, on his way home that night he stopped by the florist and bought five dozen enormous red blooms. They smelled sweet as Arpège, and he knew Claudia would love them. And he loved her too.

He thought that maybe, after all, inside each man's heart there was room for more than one woman.

Chapter Seventy-two

Their eyes burned into each other's. The rest of the world was locked out.

Ed wanted to tell her everything he had been thinking. Everything that had gone down in his life. But then he realized he didn't need to. Zelda knew him. Knew who he really was. What he was. And she loved him. It was enough.

'Marry me, Zelda,' he said.

She sniffed back her tears. Her voice trembled as she said, 'Okay, you big oaf. As long as you promise not to keep getting shot like this. I don't think I can take it.'

'Nor can I.'

He was laughing as her lips covered his.

He had won the battle. Life was great.